REBEL

WOLFES OF MANHATTAN ONE

HELEN HARDT

REBEL

WOLFES OF MANHATTAN ONE

by
Helen Hardt

HARDT & SONS 💛

❀ Created with Vellum

For my family

When Rock Wolfe was fourteen, he tried to kill his father.

Twenty years later, someone else finished the job.

Now Rock is returning to New York for the reading of the billionaire's will. No way did Derek Wolfe leave anything to his oldest son, but according to Rock's brother, his presence is required.

Estate attorney Lacey Ward isn't looking forward to the reading. None of Derek Wolfe's children will be happy, least of all his oldest. When Rock enters the conference room, Lacey is stunned. He's a rebel—a biker all muscled and gorgeous in black leather. This won't be easy, especially since she can't stop staring at him.

Rock pays no attention to the reading. He's lost in a fantasy of bending his father's hot attorney over a desk. He's not a commitment kind of guy, though, and she screams white picket fence. Sparks fly between them, but the murder lurks in the back of their minds.

Rock knows all his family's secrets...or so he thinks. Mysteries seem to hide everywhere—mysteries that threaten not only his and Lacey's future but their lives as well.

PRAISE FOR HELEN HARDT

STEEL BROTHERS SAGA

"*Craving* is the jaw-dropping book you *need* to read!"
~ Lisa Renee Jones, *New York Times* bestselling author

"Completely raw and addictive."
~ Meredith Wild, #1 *New York Times* bestselling author

"Talon has hit my top five list...up there next to Jamie Fraser and Gideon Cross."
~ Angel Payne, *USA Today* bestselling author

"Talon is a sexy, intriguing leading man and Jade, our lady left at the altar is a sweet and relatable girl you just want to hug. Together they build a steaming hot relationship you really root for from the first chapter!"
-CD Reiss, *New York Times* bestselling author

"Talon and Jade's instant chemistry heats up the pages..."
~ RT Book Reviews

"Sorry Christian and Gideon, there's a new heartthrob for you to contend with. Meet Talon. Talon Steel."

~ **Booktopia**

"Such a beautiful torment—the waiting, the anticipation, the relief that only comes briefly before more questions arise, and the wait begins again... Check. Mate. Ms. Hardt..."

~ **Bare Naked Words**

"Made my heart stop in my chest. Helen has given us such a heartbreakingly beautiful series."

~**Tina, Bookalicious Babes**

BLOOD BOND SAGA

"An enthralling and rousing vampire tale that will leave readers waiting for the sequel."

~ **Kirkus Reviews**

"Helen gives us the dark, tormented vampire hero we all love in a sensual paranormal romance with all the feels. Be warned... The twists and turns will keep you up all night reading. I was hooked from the first sentence until the very end."

~ **J.S. Scott**, *New York Times* **bestselling author**

"A dark, intoxicating tale."

~ **Library Journal**

"Helen dives into the paranormal world of vampires and makes it her own."

~ **Tina, Bookalicious Babes**

"Throw out everything you know about vampires—except for that blood thirst we all love and lust after in these stunning heroes—and expect to be swept up in a sensual story that twists and turns in so many wonderfully jaw-dropping ways."

~ **Angel Payne, USA Today bestselling author**

WARNING

The Wolfes of Manhattan series contains adult language and scenes, including flashbacks of child physical and sexual abuse. Please take note.

1

ROCK

When I was fourteen years old, I tried to kill my father.

The stunt had cost me my freedom. I'd have gladly spent the rest of my life imprisoned as the love slave of a Greek battalion had I been successful. But to be put through hell when the bastard was still alive? So not worth it.

Military school. Not just any military school, but a private academy where millionaires sent their troubled kids to be beaten down, where the rules were that there were no rules. Where survival of the fittest was no longer reserved for the animal kingdom.

I survived.

I grew stronger living through the hell that was Buffington Academy. Secluded in the Adirondacks, the school was home to the most spoiled young men in the world...and the most troubled. After two weeks, I knew I didn't belong there, but I spent four years in that hellhole.

Those years made me wish for juvie.

But no, my parents didn't turn me in. Instead...Buffington.

I spent those years plotting my father's demise, but of course by the time I turned eighteen and released myself, I knew better. I'd learned my lesson. My father wasn't worth it. Trying to take him out had cost me four years of my life.

Even so, I dreamed of his death. It was no less than he deserved.

But when it finally happened, I was totally unprepared.

"Dad's dead," my brother Reid said into the phone when I answered.

I froze, as if ice water had replaced the blood in my veins.

"Did you hear me?"

"Yeah. Yeah. What happened?"

"We're not sure yet. But I have to ask you, bro..."

"What?"

"Were you anywhere near Dad's penthouse last night?"

"Are you fucking kidding me?"

"Someone shot him in the head in the penthouse."

I couldn't help a chuckle. Most guys might freak out hearing this kind of news. Not me. The bastard had it coming.

"They're going to get in touch with you," Reid continued.

"I'm at my cabin, Reid. And by the way, you don't sound too broken up."

"None of us are. He was a bastard. That's public knowledge."

"So why the interrogation? There're a thousand people who probably wanted him dead."

"True, but Dad sent you away when you were so young. The cops are going to think you might be getting back at him."

"Don't you think I'd have done something before now?"

"Whatever, man. Still, Riley, Roy, and I need to know. Did this in any way involve you?"

"I just told you. I'm home."

"You could have hired it out."

Seriously? I'd been a model citizen since I left Buffington—well, maybe not model in the sense of perfect, since I'd been arrested in a biker brawl once, but I hadn't started it and the charges were dropped. I'd driven after too many drinks a few times, but I hadn't gotten caught. I'd made my own money, never stole a dime. And never took one penny from that motherfucker who'd fathered me. Not that he would have given me any. I had a few biker buds who might have been able to handle a contract on a human life, but I'd have never asked.

The asshole warranted better than a paid hitman who bore him no ill will. He deserved to be taken out by someone he'd wronged, someone who could look into his cold eyes so he knew who was doing the deed.

There were a ton of us out there.

"I didn't," I told my brother. "Trust me. I had nothing to do with it. But I'm glad the asshole's dead."

"None of us are crying, like I said." Reid sighed through the phone line. "Thank God."

"Relieved, are you?"

"Of course. You're my big brother. I don't want you rotting in prison for the rest of your life."

I hadn't seen my brothers and sister in years. Reid was the only one who kept in touch with me regularly. I heard from Roy and Riley every once in a while. Roy didn't keep in touch with anyone, and Riley had her own issues.

"I won't be. I was out on a ride last night with buddies who can vouch for me. I got in around one a.m."

"They think the murder occurred around four this morning. You couldn't have gotten here by then."

"Plus the fact that I'm still in Montana right now."

"Yeah. Right. I'm not thinking straight." Reid cleared his throat. "You need to get on the next flight to New York."

"Fuck that. I'm not coming home."

"You have to. The cops want to talk to you."

"There's this little thing called a phone."

"Damn it, Rock. You need to come home."

"Burn him and be done with it. You don't need me for that."

"We haven't made any funeral arrangements yet."

"What do you need me for, then?

"The attorneys are reading Dad's will tomorrow morning."

"Why the hell should I care? You know he didn't leave me a damned penny."

"It specifies that we all have to be present. They won't read it without you there."

"You've got to be kidding me." The bastard was going to rub my nose in it from the grave. All his billions...and I'd get nothing.

Not that I cared.

Much, anyway.

"Sorry," Reid said. "But it'll be good to see you, bro. I've... missed you."

Truthfully, I'd missed him as well. He was my youngest brother, and he and I had been close once. Roy, who fell between us, was a classic introvert who'd spent most of his childhood in his room painting or reading. That left Reid to be my primary playmate, even though he was five years younger. Riley hadn't come around until I was eight and Reid was three.

"All right. I'll get a flight."

"I'm one step ahead of you. I'm emailing you your confirmation. Pack a bag. Your flight leaves out of Helena in three hours."

LACEY

The estate of Derek Paul Wolfe...

I'd drafted the last updates to his last will and testament just three weeks earlier. He'd made some changes that puzzled me, but I was an attorney. My job was to do what the client wanted as long as the law allowed it.

And the law allowed a person to bequeath whatever he wanted to whomever he wanted with whatever contingencies he wanted.

I fiddled with my hair. I was about to meet Derek Wolfe's ex-wife and children. His longtime live-in lover, ex-supermodel Fonda Burke, would probably show up as well.

I'd never met any of them, but I'd seen plenty of photos. They were all spectacular, as anyone descended from or associated with Derek Wolfe was bound to be.

He had a reputation as a wolf—no pun intended—in the boardroom and the bedroom. Not that I'd know, though he'd tried to lure me to his bed more than once. Admittedly, I'd considered it, even though he was thirty years my senior. The man was gorgeous.

His sons were even more gorgeous. At least the two younger

ones were. I'd never seen so much as a photo of his oldest son, Rock. His daughter, Riley, was quickly replacing Fonda Burke as the most successful supermodel of all time—a fact I was sure perturbed the latter more than a lot.

I needed caffeine. Actually, I needed a shot of tequila, but coffee would have to suffice. I couldn't meet the children of Derek Wolfe with alcohol on my breath.

Today I'd deliver some news that none of them could possibly be expecting.

$\sim$

I SAT at the head of the table in the conference room. I'd only been made a partner during the last year, so when my mentor, Robert Mayes, had given me the Derek Wolfe estate file, presumably at the client's request, I'd been more than a little flabbergasted, but large estates were my specialty, so I'd dived right in.

To my right sat Constance Larson Wolfe, blond and beautiful and botoxed, perfect "first wife" material. She and Derek had been divorced for the last five years, and she'd been living the high life on her spousal maintenance. She wouldn't like what was in the document I held before me, but nothing could be done about that.

Next to her was Riley Wolfe, supermodel extraordinaire, and Derek's only daughter. Dark hair and eyes, definitely a winter type, though she modeled during all the seasons. She was in demand and was fast accumulating her own fortune.

To Riley's right was Roy Wolfe, the middle brother. He was an artist—though not a starving one—by trade, living off his hefty trust fund. He had the most perfect face of all the brothers, a male version of his baby sister. His long hair was as silky and shiny as hers was, though it was pulled back in a low ponytail. He was known as somewhat of a recluse.

Next to him was Reid Wolfe, the youngest brother, who sported the signature Derek Wolfe dark hair—all of the children did—but instead of brown eyes, his were a searing blue that held a seductive look, even when he was sitting and waiting for his father's will to be read. Small wonder he was so popular with the ladies. He was a playboy of the first order, always with a new woman on his arm.

Fonda Burke sat on my left. Still a beautiful woman at forty-two with flaming orange hair and striking green eyes, she had much to look forward to. She wouldn't be happy with the reading of the will.

None of them would be.

We sat quietly, waiting for the missing person.

Rock Wolfe—the oldest child of Derek and Connie Wolfe.

The rebel.

Rock had a troubled past, though no one actually knew the facts other than his family, and I wasn't sure they even knew. Derek had made no secret of his animosity toward his firstborn son.

We sat, no one speaking. Until Reid said, "He should be here by now. His flight got in an hour and a half ago, and I told him to come straight here."

"Rock has always been on his own time schedule," Connie Wolfe said. "That's part of his charm."

Then two harsh knocks on my door. "Come in," I said, expecting my assistant, Charlie.

Instead, in strolled a man who could only be the elusive Rock Wolfe.

While his brothers' hair was sleek and combed into place, Rock's dark tresses were wavy and unruly, falling below his shoulders. His jawline was sculpted and laced with black stubble, and his nose slightly crooked, clearly had been broken at least once. His lips were full and beautiful. And his eyes... A green so clear and powerful a person could get lost in them.

I had to break my gaze away from his magnificently handsome face to notice his wardrobe. While his brothers were clad in Armani suits and ties, Rock wore Levi's that accented his ass and thighs to perfection. A black leather motorcycle jacket—over gorgeously broad shoulders—and black boots completed his ensemble.

He'd at least put on a button-down black shirt for the occasion, open at the neck, a few dark chest hairs peeking out.

"Please have a seat, Mr. Wolfe," I said, willing my voice not to crack. "Everyone else is here, so we can get started."

He glared at me. "Who the hell are you?"

"I'm Lacey Ward, your father's estate attorney."

"Lacey, huh?"

"Yes."

Charlie sat down at the opposite end of the table to take notes. She glanced at me with an "I'm sorry" look.

Rock chuckled and took the seat next to Reid. "Did your mother name you after the lingerie she was wearing the night you were conceived?"

Reid nudged him. "Jesus Christ, Rock."

My cheeks warmed. This was Derek Wolfe's son all right, clear down to the douchebag gene. *Stay professional, Lace.*

"My name isn't up for discussion right now. Since we're all here, let's get to your father's will."

"I can't fucking wait," Rock said with a touch—okay, a huge amount—of sarcasm.

I cleared my throat and began.

3

ROCK

Lacey Ward was fucking hot.

Oh, she tried to hide it in her navy-blue blazer and tight-ass high-necked blouse, her dark blond hair pulled into a high ponytail so tight that her facial muscles could barely move, and her unglossed lips pressed into a straight line, but I knew the type.

A fucking tomcat in the sack.

I could tell by her eyes. They were big, blue, and vibrant, and they looked me over as if I were a hunk of USDA prime beef tenderloin.

Yup, a tomcat.

Not that I'd ever know. Hell, not that I cared.

I was here for one reason only—so my mother and siblings could hear the contents of the shithead's will. I already knew he'd left me a fat lot of nothing.

And I didn't care one fucking bit.

Lacey Ward's voice had a rasp to it. A sexy rasp. It wouldn't be a hardship to listen to her for the next few hours. Hell, I didn't even need to listen to the words. I knew what they'd be anyway.

Rock gets nothing.

Fine with me.

"Section Five, distribution of personal property," Lacey said. "All of my mother's jewelry in my possession and in the safe deposit box at First National Bank is hereby bequeathed to my daughter Riley Doris Wolfe."

No surprise there.

"My automobiles, except for the Tesla and the Porsche, are bequeathed to my sons, Roy and Reid Wolfe, with Roy, as the older, to have the first choice. They will then choose alternately. The Porsche is bequeathed to my daughter, Riley Wolfe."

His cars. Daddy's pride and joy. He loved those damned cars more than he ever loved any person in his life, least of all me.

I stopped listening. I sat back, closed my eyes, and basked in the rhythm of Lacey's sexy voice.

Yeah, Rock. Fuck me good, baby. Pound that hard cock into me...

My groin tightened. Hell, I didn't care. Just get this day over with.

That's it, baby. Fuck me. Make me come...

Damn, she'd look good on the back of my bike, that blond hair flowing out of a helmet. Yup, I was a helmet man. No point in splattering my brains all over the place. Now that I had a life I enjoyed, I wanted to keep it that way.

I hated Manhattan. I wanted to go back to Montana, where the sky was big and blue and everything was open. New York was so closed in. And it smelled. Even in this posh Manhattan office, the stench of the streets still wafted in the air.

I looked around. My brother Roy was looking down at his lap, while Reid was ogling Lacey. Not that I blamed him. He'd probably fucked her already.

A spear of jealousy hit my gut. Why? I didn't know. So what if he'd fucked her? Reid fucked anything in a skirt.

My little sister, Riley, sat next to my mother.

Riley... The sight of her brought it all back. We weren't close, and I was sorry about that. I'd been protecting her that day, but she didn't know that, and I could never tell her.

Then of course...Mommie Dearest.

Constance Wolfe.

Bitch extraordinaire, who'd had no issue with turning a blind eye to her husband's extracurricular activities.

My gaze floated back to Lacey Ward. I closed my eyes again and sighed. This was going to be a long day.

"Section Seven, real property..."

Can I please doze off now? The villa in Tuscany, the ski chateau in Aspen, the loft in Paris. Who needed all that shit? I had my small cabin in Montana, a Harley, and a job doing construction. It kept me fit and paid well, enough to pay my mortgage, keep food in my belly, and gas in my bike. I got to spend a lot of time outdoors. Who needed anything else?

Man, that voice...

Sink that big cock into me, Rock. Yeah, just like that...

Then...

Silence.

My eyes shot open.

Five gazes, belonging to my mother, my siblings, and my father's current slut, were darting arrows straight toward me.

4

LACEY

Had Rock Wolfe heard what I said?

I'd expected a major outburst.

The outburst came, but not from Rock.

"You've got to be kidding me," Reid said, standing. "You misread that."

I cleared my throat. "I assure you I didn't."

"Dad couldn't have agreed to that," he said.

"It's outrageous," Connie Wolfe said, her perfect lips a straight line. "Nothing to me? Or my other children?" she added, most likely as an afterthought.

"You're the *ex*-wife, Connie," Fonda said, smirking, "in case you've forgotten."

"I'm the mother of Derek's children," Connie snarled back at her, "and I don't recall hearing your name being read either."

These two were about to have a mega-catfight if I didn't regain control of this meeting. Roy remained silent, but that didn't surprise me. He was known to be quiet. Riley, however, looked distant, as though she were somewhere else entirely.

I cleared my throat. "These were Mr. Wolfe's wishes. I have all the notes in my office, and I recorded all of our meetings."

"We'll just contest it," Connie said. "Reid has been Derek's right-hand man for years. None of this makes any sense."

Right. That viper wasn't concerned about Reid at all. Her gravy train had ended with Derek's death, and she was far from happy about it.

"You may certainly contest the will, Mrs. Wolfe," I said, "but you'll be wasting your time and money. Your ex-husband made his wishes very clear."

Constance Wolfe darted her gaze to her oldest son, who was staring at me wide-eyed. "Rock, don't you have anything to say about all of this?"

"Why should I?" he asked.

Connie shook her head and scoffed. "You haven't changed a bit."

"That's a good thing, from where I'm sitting," Rock said, smiling. "Why the hell is everyone staring at me?"

"Uh...because our father just mandated that you become CEO of Wolfe Enterprises," Reid said.

Rock cocked his head, one eyebrow rising. "Excuse me?"

"Christ, Rock, haven't you been listening?"

"Of course I haven't been listening. Do you think I give a rat's ass what the bastard put in his will? He only mandated that I be here so that he could rub my nose in the fact that I was getting nothing. What he didn't count on was me not giving a flying fuck."

"Rock," Roy said softly. "Dad just put the fate of our birthright in your hands."

TEN MINUTES LATER, I found myself in my office with a rabid Rock Wolfe.

"I'm out of here," he'd said, standing and heading toward the door.

Charlie had looked at me with pleading eyes, so I'd turned to the family. "I'll take care of this." Then I'd headed out the door after Rock.

Somehow I'd convinced him to follow me to my office.

"What?" He looked at me irately.

"Were you truly not listening to anything I said in there?"

"Honestly? No. I was imagining the two of us fucking."

Warmth spread to my cheeks, and my pulse thumped, despite myself. A torpedo shot between my legs.

I cleared my throat. "I'd like to keep our relationship professional, please, Mr. Wolfe."

"Sure, we can keep it professional. You asked if I was listening. I told you what I was doing instead of listening. Nothing unprofessional there."

Best to ignore him. Rock Wolfe was trouble. Trouble I didn't need in my life at the moment.

I cleared my throat again. Time to cut to the chase.

"Mr. Wolfe—"

"Rock. Mr. Wolfe was that bastard who died."

He wasn't making this easy. "All right. Rock. Your father just mandated that you move to Manhattan and take your place at the head of his company—rather, *your* company—as chief executive officer."

"What? No way. What the hell is he trying to pull? He hates me. And I don't know anything about his fucking business. I also don't give a shit."

I sighed. "Believe me, I tried to talk him out of this scheme, but he was adamant."

"*You* wrote this thing?"

"That's what he paid me to do."

"Jesus fuck." He sat down in one of the leather chairs across from my desk. "I won't do it, I tell you. I won't. I wouldn't know what I was doing anyway."

I walked around my desk and took a seat, facing him. "You really weren't listening, were you?"

He smiled. God, he was gorgeous. I hated the effect he was having on my body.

"I already told you what I was doing, Lacey Lingerie."

I seethed, despite the tickle between my legs.

"I still bet your mother was wearing lace that night. Where else would you get a name like Lacey?"

"You're one to talk, with a name like Rock."

"My mom was a fan of the old Rock Hudson and Doris Day movies. Riley's middle name is Doris."

"You do know that Rock Hudson was gay, right?"

"Yeah, I do. So what? That doesn't mean everyone named Rock is gay."

"And neither is every Lacey named after undergarments."

He smiled again, but this time he didn't push it.

I cleared my throat. "Your father has left his business interests in Wolfe Enterprises, which, as you know, is a three billion dollar corporation—"

"I haven't seen my father in twenty-some years. I don't know shit."

"All right." I sighed. "Now you know. You are heir to a three billion dollar corporation."

"You're telling me I'm as rich as Bill Gates now?"

"Hardly, but you *are* rich. Once you get into billions, does it really matter?" Indeed, any amount in the billions was incomprehensible to most, myself included.

He sat, stunned, his green eyes wide. "What the hell am I going to do with all of that?"

"It's not solely yours. He left it in equal parts to you, your brothers, and your sister."

"Good. They deserve it."

"But there was a stipulation." I stood. "Didn't you wonder why everyone was staring at you in the conference room?"

"It was obviously my devastating good looks," he said, smiling.

I couldn't fault his observation, even though he was clearly just flirting with me. If I were the type to go for a leather-clad bad boy, I'd be all over Rock Wolfe.

Fortunately, I wasn't that type.

At least that was what I kept telling myself.

"Mr. Wolfe—"

"We've been through that. My name is Rock."

"Rock." I sighed. "The stipulation I'm talking about is this. For you and your siblings to inherit the business holdings at all, you, Rock Wolfe, must move to Manhattan and take your place as CEO of the company. You need to run the company, or it will be sold to the highest bidder."

5

ROCK

Fucking bastard.

This had to be some kind of a sick joke.

"I assure you it's not," Lacey said, when I mentioned the same. "I tried to talk him out of this. I told him you had no idea how to run a billion dollar company, and that it was irresponsible to put his company in the hands of a son he'd been estranged from for so long, a son who'd never had any experience in business at all."

A son who'd tried to off him once.

But she didn't know that.

"And he didn't listen to you? What the hell kind of lawyer are you? Can't you control your clients?"

She walked around her desk and stood right in front of me, forcing me to look up at her. "It's my job to advise my clients what the law is and what is in their best interests under the law. I didn't feel this decision was in his company's best interest, and I told him so many times. However, the law allows a person to bequeath his property to whomever he chooses with whatever stipulations he chooses. I did my job, Mr. Wolfe."

There she went with the Mr. Wolfe again. She looked cutely

irate, her hands glued to her hips and her cheeks flushing a glorious pink.

"Well"—I stood, this time making her look up to *me*—"I won't do it. I don't give a flying fuck about Wolfe Enterprises."

"Do you give a flying fuck about Roy, Reid, and Riley?" she asked adamantly.

I sat back down with a plunk.

Roy, Reid, and Riley.

Of course I gave a fuck. They were my brothers and sister. I'd protected them as best I could before I'd been sent away.

"Well?" she asked again.

I closed my eyes. "Yes."

"Then you don't have a choice," Lacey said. "They lose their inheritance if you don't do as the will stipulates."

"You mean as my bastard father stipulates," I said. "He's coming after me from the grave, the son of a bitch."

She placed her hand on my shoulder. The gesture was caring, but it ignited a spark under my skin.

"He is. But if you don't do this, Rock, your siblings will suffer. They won't get their share of the business."

"They still got plenty from that will," I said. "I was lucid when I heard that Reid and Roy got all the cars, Riley all the jewels. They can still live the high life. Who got the home in Tuscany? Aspen?"

"You did."

I stood. "What the fuck?"

"You got all the real property, including the Manhattan penthouse."

"Well, that's easy enough to remedy. I'll give all the real estate to my siblings."

"You can't."

"Why the hell not?"

"It's all part of the stipulation. You take the reins at Wolfe Enterprises, or everything is sold to the highest bidder."

"What about cash on hand?"

"There isn't any. Nothing of substance, anyway. Your father died without any liquid assets. It's all tied up in real estate and business."

"You've got to be kidding me."

"I wish I were. I'm sure your siblings wish the same thing."

"I can't do this, Lacey. I just can't. I have a life, damn it. A life I love in Montana. I'm free there. Free to do as I please. Take off on my bike whenever I want."

An image appeared in my mind, of Lacey, clad in tight leather chaps and a leather halter top, climbing on the back of my bike and wrapping her arms around my waist.

Then taking off, the roar of my pipes, the wind in my face... and Lacey clinging to me.

"I understand. Really, I do."

"You don't. You sit here in your tight-ass office wearing your tight-ass suit, when you should be outdoors enjoying life."

"Mr. Wolfe, I—"

"Rock," I said. "Damn it. Call me Rock." My groin was tightening, and I couldn't stand it any longer.

I grabbed her and crushed my mouth to hers.

She kept her lips pinned shut, but I traced my tongue over the seam of them, nudging them open. "That's right, baby. Open for me." I swept my tongue into the warmth of her mouth.

She tasted minty fresh with a touch of vanilla. Delicious.

I glided my lips over hers as our tongues slid together.

I'd kissed a lot of women. Almost every weekend I took a new luscious treat to my bed.

But this kiss...

She pulled away and pushed at me.

I didn't move.

"Mr.—"

"Rock, damn it. I just had my tongue in your mouth. Call me Rock."

"Rock..." She swayed a little, steadying herself by placing her hand on the edge of her desk.

I couldn't help smiling.

"This... I'm not... This isn't...professional."

"It's not? That was a damned good kiss, baby. I'd say you could do it professionally."

Her cheeks went from rosy to crimson. Again, I smiled.

"You know what I mean."

"You're my father's lawyer. You're not mine. You and I don't have a professional relationship."

"It's not—"

I quieted her by placing two fingers over her pink, swollen lips. "You know what I'd like to do, Lacey Ward?"

She gulped.

"I'd like to lift up that blue skirt and bend you over that desk." I inched closer to her. "I bet you're already wet for me."

She squirmed, crossing her legs.

Yup. She was wet.

I inhaled. I could already smell her musky arousal. I inched forward again, until only a few centimeters separated us.

She backed up against her desk. "I don't think—"

"Don't think, baby. Now isn't the time for thinking. Where the hell would thinking get us? Just give in. Turn around." I lightly touched her arms, turning her around. Then I buried my nose in her neck and inhaled. "You smell like a fantasy."

"I'm not wearing anything." She let out a nervous chuckle. "Any perfume, I mean."

"I know. I smell *you*. I smell your arousal. You want me just as much as I want you." I grabbed the firm globes of her ass.

She let out a soft gasp.

I massaged her ass softly, pushing my hard cock into the small of her back. "You feel that? I'm hard for you, Lacey. Rock hard. Tell me what you want me to do with that fucking hard cock."

"I want..." She moaned when I slid one hand up her side and then around in front to cup one firm breast.

"Yeah? What do you want, baby?"

"You. God. Fuck me. Fuck me hard."

All I needed. I slid her skirt up. Fuck. She was wearing a garter belt and stockings. I didn't know women wore those in an office anymore. And it was fucking hot.

And a thong. A pink lacy thong.

Lacey. Maybe she wasn't named after lingerie, but she was wearing it, lace and all. Her taut luscious body had been created for it.

"I'm going to rip this off of you and shove my hard cock into that hot pussy."

She groaned.

"Tell me you want it, baby. Tell me."

"God, yes. I want it."

With one yank, the pink thong was gone. I tossed it aside. Then I slid my fingers through her slick folds. God, so wet. I pulled my fingers out of her and ran them over my tongue. Mmm, sweet and tangy. If I weren't so fucking hard, I'd bend down and bury my face between those gorgeous ass cheeks and suck on that tasty pussy.

Next time. Not this time. This time would be fast and furious and delicious.

I unbuckled my belt and unzipped my jeans, releasing my erection. I slid it between her ass cheeks, teasing her.

"Please," she sighed. "I need you."

"Since you said please." I stopped for a few seconds to roll on a condom and then thrust into her.

She let out a low moan.

Yeah, that husky voice that had made me horny when she was reading the will. That's how I wanted to hear it, moaning as I fucked her.

"Feel good, baby? You like that?"

She inhaled sharply. "God, yes."

I pulled out and slid back in balls deep. Already my nuts were tightening, crushing to my body. This wouldn't take long.

But I wanted it to. Screw fast and furious. I wanted to fuck her long and slow and deep.

I pulled out and plunged in again. God, sweet suction. I wanted to touch her clit, rub it, make her come, but I couldn't in this position.

"Play with yourself, baby," I whispered into her ear. "Make it feel good." I grabbed her hand and led it around her front and under her skirt. "I'm not going to last long. You have such a tight cunt. I want to come inside you. Fill you up."

"I can't believe I'm doing this," she said on a sigh.

"Believe it, baby. Feel me. This is real. Feel me fucking you right here in your office."

6

LACEY

I still couldn't believe it.

This wasn't me. Lacey Ward didn't do things like this. She didn't have sex in her office, certainly not with some bad boy biker rebel, the son of her deceased client.

He thrust in and out of me, and damn, I hadn't been filled so completely since... Had I ever?

He was huge, and the feeling of him inside me made me crazy. As if he were opening something that had previously been closed off to the world.

I was hardly an innocent. I'd had a few relationships in my day, even a few casual fucks.

But this...

This was something I'd never had. Might never have again. And despite myself, I was enjoying the hell out of it. I touched my clit and—

"Oh, my God!" The orgasm rolled through me like a tidal wave, and my legs wobbled like jelly.

"Yeah, that's right, baby. You come. Come for me. Come all over my hard cock. Fuck, I can feel you coming. You're amazing, baby. Fucking amazing."

Thank God he was pushing me against my desk, or I wouldn't have been able to stand. Still he pumped in and out of me, and now that my pussy had tightened up from the climax, it felt even better, as if he were tunneling through a narrow cavern that had never seen light before.

"I can't last much longer, Lacey," Rock said against my neck, kissing it. "You're so tight. I can't— Fuck!" he roared.

He pushed into me with such an urgency that I fell over onto my desk, my breasts hitting my blotter.

I breathed in and out rapidly, trying to catch my breath, sadness sweeping over me that it was over.

For it *was* over.

This would never happen again.

I didn't do things like this.

Rock touched my arms, gently pulled me up, and turned me around to face him. I couldn't meet his gaze.

He lifted my chin so I had no choice. "You're incredible."

I didn't feel incredible. A tug of war was raging inside me. Half of me wanted to slink away and hide in a cave of embarrassment. The other half of me wanted to rip the clothes off of his muscular body and start all over again.

One orgasm, and I was usually done.

I'd just had the most explosive orgasm of my life—fully clothed and in my office, no less—and I was ready to go again.

I opened my mouth to speak but then shut it abruptly. What could I say to him? Tell him that the last ten minutes had been the most exciting in my life, but it could never happen again? Ever? Tell him I was sorry for acting so unprofessionally? Yes, I had been unprofessional. Ridiculously unprofessional. But sorry?

No. I wasn't sorry. Not the least bit.

I cleared my throat and pulled my skirt down over my ass and thighs. Remarkably, my stockings and garter belt were still in place. In the corner of my eye, I could see the remains of my thong on the carpet.

"It's a shame to cover you back up," Rock said, grinning.

I cleared my throat again, trying—and failing—to think of something to say to defuse this situation. He discreetly disposed of the condom and the threads of my thong, and then re-buttoned his jeans.

It's a shame to cover you up too.

The words were lodged in my throat, unable to emerge.

I hadn't even seen him. Only felt him. And suddenly it became of the ultimate importance to me to see his dick, to lay eyes on the instrument that had given me so much pleasure.

Too bad that would never happen.

"I must be better than I thought I was," Rock said. "I seem to have rendered you incapable of speech."

If my cheeks weren't already red as a stop sign, they sure as heck were now.

"You going to say anything?"

Once more, I cleared my throat. "I think we need to set up an appointment. Your father gave me explicit instructions for your takeover of the company. Not that I understand any of them as I'm not a corporate attorney, but Reid will. We need to nail down—"

He touched my cheek ever so gently. Sparks shot through me.

"The only thing I want to nail down, Lacey, is you. I want to fucking nail you again and again."

I gulped.

"We just had sex," he said. "Really good—albeit too damned short—sex. Are you going to acknowledge that at all?"

"I have a job to do," I said. "The fact that we just had sex—"

"Not sex. *Really good* sex."

I closed my eyes and exhaled. "All right. *Really good* sex. Satisfied?"

"For now," he said with a lopsided grin. "But I want more of you, Lacey Ward. In a real bed. All clothes off. Hours and hours of dirty, nasty sex."

"I don't...do that."

"Oh, yes, you do. No one as responsive as you are doesn't have dirty, nasty sex."

Responsive? I was always responsive. At least I thought I was. Rock Wolfe had brought out a new level of responsiveness in me, though. I was still dripping wet for him. My nipples were still hard. One orgasm—my best one ever, at that—hadn't satisfied me. Had only left me wanting more.

"Mr.— I mean...Rock. We have a lot of work to do. *You* have a lot of work to do. Your father—"

"Fuck that bastard."

"Clearly, you and he weren't close, but—"

"No, we weren't close. That's putting it nicely."

"Still, the family is depending on you to do what's right here. You have to take control of the company. Reid can help you. I'll help you."

"What if I don't want your help or Reid's help? What if I want to go back to Montana and live my own damned life?" He grinned again. "In fact, you can come with me. I'm not even close to done with you yet."

What a life that could be. A life with Rock Wolfe in a secluded cabin in gorgeous Montana, riding on the back of his Harley...

Until he was done with me. Until he found someone new who struck his fancy.

Rock Wolfe would never be satisfied with just one woman. And I'd never be satisfied with a man for whom I wasn't enough.

I opened my mouth to speak, but a knock on my door interrupted me. I fidgeted with my skirt. My hair was in a ponytail, and I hoped it looked okay. I cleared my throat. "Yes?"

Charlie opened the door. "Sorry to interrupt, Lacey, but the Wolfe siblings are still here, and they want to talk to their brother."

7

ROCK

Lacey's assistant was a hot little number—a curvy little brunette with dimples and gray-blue eyes. I'd be all over her in a minute normally. Right now, though, I didn't feel so much as a spark. All I could think about was Lacey in her tight-ass suit and that delectable pussy underneath.

Her lips were red and swollen from our kisses, and I couldn't wait to have them around my cock.

Oh, yeah. That was going to happen. Later today, if I had my way.

"Fine," Lacey said. "We're done here. Rock, you need to see to your family."

Yeah, I suppose I had to deal with this. Fucking dick screwing me from the grave. I should have known.

"I know you're not happy with this situation," Lacey continued, acting like we hadn't just had a hot little fuck in her office. "But you do need to talk to them. You can use the conference room for as long as you like."

"Not unless you have a full bar in there," I said.

"It's three p.m.," she said.

"It's five o'clock somewhere. Where's the nearest place I can get a stiff bourbon?"

"There's a bar in the lobby of this building," she said.

"Great. Come on."

She shook her head. "This is between you and your brothers and sister. I have work to do."

"Yeah, you do. With us. I'm not going through with this unless you come along. Don't worry. You'll get your full hourly rate."

"I wasn't worried about that," she said. "But I have an appointment on another case—"

"You come along, or this isn't happening."

She sighed. "Fine. Charlie, could you call Jimmy Trask and reschedule our four o'clock? I have some time tomorrow morning, I think."

Charlie nodded and left.

"Let's go, then," she said, not looking me in the eye.

"None of us is happy about this, Rock." Reid downed his bourbon. "Believe me."

"Isn't there some way we can contest this?" Riley asked Lacey.

She shook her head. "Like I said before, the will is ironclad. Your father made sure of that. I tried to talk him out of this, but he was determined."

"Determined to ruin my life," I said.

"Clearly he was determined to ruin all of our lives," Reid said. "This isn't what any of us expected. We all thought *I'd* be in charge."

"Please. Take charge," I said. "I'd love nothing better."

"I would if I could," he said, "but you heard the attorney. We do it Dad's way, or it all gets sold off."

"Then let's sell it off," I said. "The four of us split the profit. Sounds good to me."

"Weren't you listening at all?" Riley said.

Hell, no. I'd been dreaming of fucking Lacey Ward. A dream I'd just made a reality...and I wanted to repeat it. Badly.

"The proceeds from the company and all the real estate go to charity," Lacey said.

"For God's sake," I said. "Which charity? The Wolfe Foundation?"

"No. Your father figured if he left it to his own foundation, the four of you would find a way around his will. It will go to The Coalition for the Homeless."

Reid led out a sarcastic laugh. "Dad hated the homeless. Thought they were all losers."

"He'd rather give losers his fortune than his own kids," I said, scoffing. "Unbelievable."

"He *is* willing to give it to his kids," Lacey said. "As long as you take your place here. Look at it this way. Your father wanted you back in the family business. Back in the family fold."

"Bullshit," I said. "That bastard never once tried to contact me after I left the state. He hated me, and he knew *I'd* hate this. He put me in the position of making or breaking every-thing for my brothers and sister. If I do what I want, my siblings lose. This was his last laugh. He didn't do it to get me back in the family fold. He did it to punish me, and I hate him for it."

"You can't hate a dead man, Rock," my brother Roy said.

Roy was usually quiet. This was only the second time I'd heard him speak since I got to town.

"Yes, I can, Roy. I'll hate him until the day I die and every day after that too."

"Turn the tables on him, then," Lacey said. "Become CEO of the company and do a better job than he ever did."

Reid laughed again, and I darted him a stink eye.

"Come on, Rock," he said. "You don't know anything about running a business."

"He's right," I said to Lacey. "I don't know anything about it, and I don't want to know."

"You're going to have to, or you're all screwed."

I didn't give a shit if I was screwed. I didn't want anything from Derek Wolfe. But my siblings deserved better. I turned to Reid. "Will you help me?"

He nodded. "Not like I have a choice."

"Great. Then I'll be the CEO in name only, and you can run the fucking business."

"No," Lacey said. "You need to be involved in day-to-day operations. It's—"

"In the fucking will. Christ." I raked my fingers through my hair. "Fine. I'll do it, but only so the three of you aren't screwed. The only one who's screwed here is me, and that's exactly how the fucker wanted it." I signaled the waitress. "Another round here."

"Count me out," Lacey said. "I have to get back up to the office."

"Hell, no. You're done for the day."

"Uh...no, I'm not."

"You want me to do this? To become CEO of my father's corporation? Then you're going to help me."

"I'm happy to help in any way I can, but I'm a trusts and estates attorney, not a corporate attorney. I don't have the knowledge or resources to help with this. The company has a full legal staff. They'll be able—"

"I want *you*."

"Rock," Reid began.

"You heard me. If that bastard is going to control me from beyond the grave, I will at least have the staff I want. You, Lacey Ward, will be my personal counsel. I'll double whatever you're making at the firm."

She reddened. "I'm not qualified—"

"You'll learn."

"Rock," Reid said again. "This isn't helping. We have a great legal staff, and I'll show you the way around the company."

"That's right. You'll be the COO, Reid. Chief operating officer. That's who really does all the work anyway, right? Did our esteemed father issue any other edicts?" I nodded to Lacey. "What about Roy and Riley? Are they mandated to be involved?"

She shook her head. "The only mandate is that you head up the company and take a day-to-day role."

"So if I do this, Roy and Riley can do whatever the fuck they want with their lives and still get their quarter share of everything?"

"That's correct," Lacey said.

"That asshole." I downed my second bourbon.

"None of us are happy about this," Riley said. "If you want... I'll stop modeling and work for the company. I'll do my share."

I eyed my baby sister. She was beautiful, a female version of Roy, who was considered the best looking of the Wolfe brothers. And she had a successful career ahead of her as a model. I couldn't take that away from her. Not after what she'd been through, what I'd tried like hell to protect her from. She hadn't seen me in over a decade, but she was willing to make a sacrifice for me. I always knew I'd done the right thing all those years ago, trying to protect her, but her selfless gesture further cemented it.

"No," I said. "You do what you want to do. There's no reason for all of us to suffer." I turned to Roy. "You too. Keep working at your art. Someone's bound to discover your talent someday."

"That's big of you, bro," Reid said.

"You sound surprised," I said. "Though you may think the worst of me for staying away all these years, I'm not a bastard like that jerk who fathered us. But I do have my condition. And that rests with Lacey."

8

LACEY

All eyes gazed at me.

I wasn't going to be Rock Wolfe's tool. We had only just met, despite the quickie in my office, and he wasn't going to drag me into this.

"You come work for our company," Rock said.

"You're nuts."

"I agree, Rock," Reid said. "Lacey's a great lawyer, but she's an estate attorney. We have no need for her at the company."

"I told you. I'm hiring her as my personal counsel. She comes along or no deal."

"You're not being fair," I said. "I only drafted the will, for God's sake. I'm not to blame here."

"You couldn't talk my father out of this hare-brained scheme," Reid said.

"You're siding with him?" I shook my head. "Your brother has lost his mind."

"I'm siding with keeping the company in the family," Reid said. "All of us get that Rock's life has been hijacked here. It's not fair to any of us."

"Yeah, well, I'm not part of the family. This has nothing to do with me."

"Not fair to *any* of us, Reid? I'm pretty sure I've cornered the market on getting shit on here." Rock stood, his green eyes full of fire. "You and I need to talk, Lacey. Now. In private."

"I don't see what we—"

"I said now." He grabbed my arm and pulled me into a stand.

I tried to ignore the sparks from his touch. "I'm not going anywhere with you."

"Hear me out," he said, and then he walked outside the bar.

I looked at Roy, Reid, and Riley. "What exactly is going on here?"

"How would we know?" Riley said, still seeming distant. "We know our brother about as well as you do. He's a stranger to us. Reid's the only one who's had any contact with him."

"Yeah, and it's been very little contact," Reid agreed.

"I'm not taking a job with your company," I said. "I don't have the qualifications."

"He's just blowing off steam," Roy said. "Talk to him. He'll see reason. He's a smart man. A little bit of a loose cannon, but he's not irrational. He's just had his whole life upended."

"Fine. Wait here." I walked out of the bar and into the lobby of the office building.

Rock was leaning against a wall near the restrooms in the lobby. He'd purposefully gone out of the way. Clearly he wanted privacy.

"What took you so long?" he said as I approached.

I ignored him. "What do you want?"

"This." He pulled me to him and smashed his mouth into mine.

I opened without thinking. We were slightly secluded, but if any of the Wolfe siblings walked out of the bar to use the bathroom—

I pulled away, breaking the kiss with a loud smack.

"What's wrong? You were kissing me back."

"This is my office building," I said.

"Yeah. And we just fucked upstairs in your office. What's a little kiss in the lobby?"

I willed my body to stop responding. Didn't work. My nipples were hard knobs poking against the lace of my bra. My bare pussy—he'd destroyed my thong earlier—pulsed between my legs. I wanted to continue that kiss, wanted so much more...

"This is where I work, Rock."

"Correction. This is where you *worked*."

"You're insane." I inched away from him, flattening my hands on the wall.

"I've always been a little crazy," he said.

"That appears to be an understatement." I cleared my throat. "I'm happy where I am with my firm. I'm a partner now, and my client base is growing. I don't want to leave. And I'm not qualif—"

"Stop saying that. You're an attorney, aren't you? You're perfectly qualified to be someone's personal counsel."

"Is it a personal counsel you want? Or a personal fuck buddy?"

"Well..." He grinned.

"I figured. Then what happens when you get tired of me? When you want a new flavor of the month? Or week?"

"What makes you think I'll get tired of you?"

I couldn't help but laugh. "Have you ever been in a relationship, Rock?"

"What's that got to do with anything? Did I *ask* you for a relationship?"

Damn. Anvil in the belly. I hardly knew the man, but those words stung me like a hornet.

"No, but—"

"No buts. This is a make it or break it situation. You come

along for the ride, or I don't do this."

"Why would you do this to me? I've never done anything to you. You're making me responsible for the well-being of your family. That's not fair."

"It's not fair that my father did it to me either."

Rock Wolfe was a jerk. An asshole. He was pulling me into this because he was pissed off and wanted to punish someone else as he'd been punished.

And still...I wanted to fuck him again. I wanted to fuck a supreme douchebag. What the hell was the matter with me?

Maybe if I honeyed up a bit, I could get him to see reason.

"No, it's not fair that this happened to you," I said gently. "None of us thinks it's fair, and we all feel for you. Really. But I have nothing to do with any of it."

"You drafted his will, Lacey."

He had me there. "That doesn't make this my fault. I have an obligation to every client who comes to me to do as they ask as long as the law allows it. I have to zealously represent every client I take on. It's part of the oath I took when I was admitted to the bar."

"Consider me a client, then. I want to be zealously represented. I already told you I'd double whatever you're making at your firm."

"I'm a partner now. I make...a lot."

"Whatever a lot is, I'll double it. You of all people know what my father's business—"

"*Your* business, Rock."

He took a step back, his eyebrows arched.

Was this just now dawning on him?

"Your business," I said a little more gently this time. "It's yours. Not your father's. It's yours, as long as you fulfill the terms of the will. Your father is no longer a part of this equation."

He closed his eyes for a few seconds and then opened them.

"I need help."

"You have Reid."

"He must hate me. This should have been his."

"He knows what kind of man your father was. So do Roy and Riley. No one is blaming you for this. They're blaming *him*."

"I'm really going to have to do this, aren't I?"

Without meaning to, I reached out and cupped his cheek. "Yes. If you want to do right by your siblings. They're innocent in all this." *And so am I.* But I didn't add that part.

I'd tried like hell to talk Derek Wolfe out of all of this, done the best I could. I'd had my mentor and the most senior attorneys at my firm try. To no avail.

The man would not be budged.

He'd created this chaos, and he was no doubt looking up—yeah, he was in hell for sure—at us now, laughing his ass off.

I hoped Rock would have the last laugh.

"Like I said in the bar," I continued. "Do this. Do this not just for your brothers and sister but for yourself. You'll be a rich man, Rock. You can use that power for good. Show your father who you really are. A good man. You have what it takes to be a great CEO."

"Are you kidding me?"

"No. I'm completely serious." And I was. "You fill a room with your presence. People will follow where you lead."

"The only problem is, I have no fucking idea where to lead them."

"You have Reid. He knows the business. He'll help you."

"And you?"

Were we back to this again? "You don't need me."

"Fine. You don't need to be my personal counsel. Stay where you are." He moved toward me, the bulge in his jeans pushing into my belly. "But if you think I don't need you, you're sadly mistaken, Lacey."

9

ROCK

I was so fucking hard. I wanted to pound her right against this wall, right in public.

What was it about her?

I'd had hotter women, more beautiful women, curvier women, thinner women.

But Lacey Ward had awakened something in me I couldn't deny. Maybe it was just the fact that my life had been stolen from me, and she was there. That's what I'd thought at first, but right now, all I wanted was to sink myself into her lush body and get lost. Forget. Forget that I wouldn't be going back to Montana. Wouldn't be going back to my life of working outdoors, riding every weekend, taking each day as it came. Living in the moment.

"I think we need to go back to the bar," Lacey said. "You need to tell them what you've decided."

I pulled back. "What if I can't do it, Lacey? What if my father was right about me?"

"Have you considered looking at this a different way?" she asked.

"What other way is there to look at it?" *Especially when all I want to look at is you, naked on my bed.*

"Your grandfather built Wolfe Enterprises from the ground up. And your father, especially, made it what it is today. Why would he want to sell it off to the highest bidder?"

"Gee, I don't know. Maybe because he's an asshole who wants to screw over his kids?"

"Okay, fair enough. But think about it, Rock. That company was his pride and joy."

"True. More so than any of his children," I said with disgust.

"Maybe it was. He had fucked-up priorities, if that's the case, but you might be right."

"Oh, I'm right. Trust me."

"Would he really want his pride and joy sold off to the highest bidder? Possibly to a rival?"

"Obviously the chance to screw me over meant more to him than his billion dollar company. Seems like classic Derek Wolfe to me."

"Seriously, Rock. You say yourself that his work meant more to him than his children. This company represents his work, what he considered the most important. He wouldn't just let it go."

"What does he care? He's dead."

"Maybe, just maybe, he did what he felt would be putting it in the best hands."

"You've got to be kidding. The bastard hated me."

"Maybe. I don't know. Or maybe he thought you were the perfect person to run his company. To run *your* company."

I thought for a moment. Actually considered her words. But, "Nice thought, but it's bullshit. Nope, he hated me so much that he put me in a position to either ruin my own life or my siblings'. Classic Derek Wolfe."

She sighed. "All right. He put you in an impossible situation as a form of punishment. Let's say you're right."

"I *am* right."

"Fine. Then rise to the challenge."

"I don't have a choice."

"You do. But you're a good man who can't turn his back on his siblings. That says a lot about you. You're one hundred times the man your father ever was."

Her words ignited a fire within me. "Do you really think so?"

"I know so."

"Damn, Lacey." I pushed her back against the wall and crushed our mouths together.

She opened at once, and I dived in, kissing her, licking her, running my tongue over her teeth, her gum line. I wanted to touch every part of her. I poured my appreciation for what she'd said into that kiss, and she responded with all the vigor I imagined.

She broke the kiss and gasped. "Not here!"

"Please," I said. "I have to have you. I'm hard as a rock, baby. I need you."

"I work here."

"Don't care."

She pushed me away. "Well, *I* do. And your brothers and sister are waiting for us in the bar."

I adjusted my jeans. Damn, I was rock hard. "All right. We'll go deal with them. And then you're coming to my hotel room."

"Rock, I—"

"I'm not taking no for an answer. You want this as much as I do. Admit it."

She closed her eyes and bit her lower lip. I touched her cheek, and her eyes popped open.

"Admit it, Lacey. Admit that you want me. That you want to be in my bed."

"I... I want to be in your bed."

I nearly creamed my pants right there. "You'll be there. Right after we finish this meeting."

I steadied her and we walked back into the bar. Reid, Roy, and Riley were still seated, talking, but went silent when Lacey and I sat back down at the table.

Silenced droned on as eyes burned into me. "I'll do it," I said. "And Lacey won't be part of the deal. Though I do want your help," I said to her.

"Of course. Whatever I can do," she said.

"Finally you're talking sense," Reid said.

"Sense? No, I'm not talking sense. I'm about ready to take a job I'm in no way qualified for. If it was Dad's desire to see his company run into the ground, he may just get his wish."

"You won't run the company into the ground," Reid said. "I won't let you."

I shook my head. "I won't let me either. The bastard may have fucked me over royally, but I won't let him fuck the rest of you over. As much as I'd like to go running back to Montana, I can't let that happen."

Riley smiled, and for a moment, she was that happy toddler I used to play with. "Thank you, Rock. That means a lot to all of us. To our mother too."

"Hey, I'm not doing any of this for Mommie Dearest."

"You're not going to make sure she continues to get an allowance?"

"Is that part of this deal?" My mother was no candidate for mother of the year. She wasn't as bad as my father. Only Hitler and Stalin had that honor. But she'd turned a blind eye to his antics the entire time we were kids. She let him beat the shit out of us, and she'd let him go into Riley's room at night. "Why do any of you care about that shrew?"

"Because she's our mother, Rock," Reid said. "She was his victim too."

Boy, was my brother short-sighted. "I don't buy that. Not at all. If we're going to talk about Connie, I'm going to need another drink." I signaled the waiter.

"He cut her off," Reid said. "Spousal maintenance ceases when the payor dies. He didn't leave Fonda anything either. They're both pissed."

"Then maybe they'll have to stop wearing designer clothing and going in for plastic surgery every other month," I said. "Cry me a river."

Roy stood, his countenance rigid. "Seriously, we're all about this? About Rock's upended life? About Mom and Fonda being broke? Don't any of you care about the real mystery here? Our father was murdered."

"Good riddance," I said.

"I have to agree with Rock," Reid said. "He was a bastard. Everyone is better off."

"You're missing the point," Roy said. "Someone killed him, and they could very well come after one of us next."

10

LACEY

"Since Dad was a paragon of society"—Rock rolled his eyes —"obviously he couldn't have had any enemies."

That got a laugh out of Reid. "Who *wasn't* Dad's enemy?"

"That's my point," Roy said. "Shouldn't we be watching our backs?"

"Dad's enemies aren't our enemies, Roy," Riley said.

"Besides," Reid said, "if we try to nail down all the people Dad screwed over in his lifetime, that list would be a mile long."

"But he was murdered. Someone hated him *that* much." From Roy.

"A lot of people hated him that much." Reid rubbed his forehead. "Including all of us."

"But someone hated him enough to murder him." Again Roy.

"Including all of us," Reid echoed again.

"My point," Roy said quietly. "They're going to come after us. We need to figure this out before they drag us in as suspects."

"Reid," Rock said, "You and I don't have time to try to track down Dad's killer. We have a company to run, and I have a hell of a lot to learn. Roy, if you want to look into it, have at it. I, for one, don't give a damn. Whoever killed the fucker did the world a service." He downed the last of his bourbon and turned to me. "Let's go."

"Go?" Reid said. "Where the hell are you going?"

"Anywhere but here."

"But—"

"I'll be in at ten on Monday morning. We can figure out the company bullshit then. For now, I have plans."

All four siblings eyed me, Rock with a lascivious gaze, the others questioning.

What could I say? I didn't owe any of them any explanation. None of their business if I was going to go to my client's—my client's son's—hotel room for wild and crazy sex. We were both consenting adults.

So why in hell did I feel like I had to say something?

"We're just going to..." Warmth crept into my cheeks.

"It's none of their business." Rock stood and held out his hand to me.

I took it and rose. "It's just some business stuff," I mumbled.

"If business means me fucking you until you can't see straight," he whispered into my ear.

I willed my legs to stay steady. "I'm...so sorry for your loss," I said to the siblings.

"You don't see any of us crying, do you?" Reid chuckled and gestured to Rock. "He's trouble, though. Watch out for him."

Trouble. How well I already knew.

Trouble I really wanted to get into.

MY LIBIDO WAS in overdrive as Rock unlocked the door to his hotel room. A spacious suite greeted me. Of course. Wolfe money.

"Reid made the reservation," Rock said, almost apologetically. "This really isn't my style."

"What *is* your style?"

"I'm a bare bones kind of guy. I don't need a lot of fluff in my life. Just a cozy place to hang my hat and rest my body, my Harley that goes like the wind, and decent food in the belly. A good bourbon now and then. That's me."

"You mean you weren't raised this way?"

He scoffed. "I was raised in a golden palace. Until I was fourteen, that is. Then everything changed."

I'd heard the rumors. Rock had been sent off to military school, though I didn't know why. Derek Wolfe never told me, and neither did any of his kids. I got the feeling no one talked about it. But if we were going to have a relationship, I needed to know.

"How did it change?"

He stalked toward me, his gaze igniting fire between my legs. "I don't want to talk about that right now."

"Then what do you—"

His lips came down on mine.

And I no longer cared why he'd been sent to military school.

I cared only about his tongue touching mine, his hard body against mine. He pushed me against the wall and ground into me, groaning into my mouth.

The kiss...so wild, raw, and untamed. Just like Rock Wolfe himself.

Rock Wolfe, a rebel who'd left everything behind. But a good man. A man who was now leaving everything behind again to save a company for his siblings.

He slid one hand down my arm and took my hand, leading it to his crotch. I cupped the huge bulge.

He broke the kiss, panting. "See what you do to me, baby? I'm so fucking hard around you. Just your voice makes me hard. That sexy rasp. You were all I could think about while you were reading my father's will. All I could think about." He pressed a light kiss to my neck. "You smell amazing, like sweet cherry wine."

I closed my eyes and let out a soft sigh. *I* smelled amazing? *He* was the one who smelled amazing. Like leather and the outdoors. Like a man. A real man who cut down trees and made stew by the fire. Who rode his Harley, speeding down country roads with me on the back, holding on to him for dear life.

My legs wobbled, but I stayed standing, Rock's body pinning me against the wall.

"I want you here. Now," he rasped against my ear, hiking up my skirt.

"Don't you want to—"

"Yeah. The bed. Later. All fucking night. But right now I'm going to lose it if I don't get inside you."

I was bare under my skirt, since he'd ruined my thong during our escapade in my office.

"I can smell you, Lacey." He inhaled, closing his eyes. "I can smell how wet you are for me."

No doubt. I was throbbing, and already my juices were clinging to my inner thighs.

The fabric of my skirt cinched around my waist, and Rock unbuckled his belt and unbuttoned his jeans. Then he lifted me in his strong arms and forced me down upon his erection.

"Ah!" I cried out. He filled me so completely. Good slow burn.

"You feel perfect around me," he groaned. "So good."

I clamped my arms around his neck as he pumped into me.

Yes, yes, yes.

No! No! No!

"No! Get off me!"

"What? What is it?" He put me down gently, his cock still hard between his legs. I was still throbbing, so close to the edge of orgasm.

"Condom. We forgot the condom. Thank God you didn't come."

"Shit," he said. "I was just so..."

"So was I. I'm clean, by the way. But you..."

"What about me?"

I cleared my throat. "I'm betting you've had a lot of women in your bed."

"I have. But what makes you think I haven't practiced safe sex with all of them?"

"Well..." I hedged. "You didn't practice safe sex just now, and for God's sake, Rock, we just met today."

He raked his fingers through his already disheveled dark hair. "Yeah. Honestly, Lacey, this isn't like me. I'm really careful. And I am clean. I get tested regularly."

"Oh, thank God," I said.

"Then the only problem is not getting you pregnant."

"I'm on the pill. No worries."

"Thank God," from him this time, his voice a low growl, his gaze melting over me like hot lava. "Go to the bedroom."

"But—"

"Go to the bedroom, damn it."

I wasn't one to submit, but something in his voice made me comply. Maybe it was the fact that I wanted him so damned much. I didn't know, and I didn't much care at the moment.

I walked toward the open doorway, shedding my clothes as I went. First my blazer. It took root on the sofa as I walked. Then my blouse, on the arm of a chair. I wiggled out of my skirt and left it in the doorway between the living area and bedroom. Clad only in my bra, garter belt, and stockings, pumps still on my feet, I reached the bed and then turned to face Rock.

He had hiked his jeans back up around his hips and was still fully clothed.

I was dying to see him naked—that incredible light-bronze body—but somehow, being all but nude in front of him while he was still fully clothed was a major turn-on.

I was his. His to use as he saw fit.

And that thrilled me to no end.

He wanted me. I saw it in his gaze, his dark eyes that smoked with fire, his slightly parted lips, his hands clenched into fists.

He wanted me as much as I wanted him.

He was still hard, his cock protruding against his boxer briefs.

I drew in a deep breath, my skin tingling all over. I slowly sat down on the bed and spread my legs, giving him a bird's eye view of my wet pussy.

My body prickled.

I wanted his mouth on me.

I hadn't yet felt his mouth on my nipples, between my legs. I wanted his lips to mark every inch of my body. Every inch of my soul.

"Is that an invitation?" he said gruffly.

I reached behind my back and unclasped my bra, letting my breasts fall gently against my chest. He widened his eyes. Only slightly, but I noticed. He liked what he saw. I discarded the bra on the floor. Then I leaned down to take off my shoes.

"No," he said. "Leave them on. Leave the stockings on. You're so fucking hot."

I sat back up straight, my legs still spread wide.

He didn't move.

I didn't move.

For what seemed like forever, he stayed still. Just looking at me.

Finally... "Uh...Rock?"

He turned his lips upward in a sexy crooked smile. "Just trying to decide which part of you I want to taste first." Then, "Oh, fuck."

He stalked toward me, pushing his jeans and boxer briefs over his hips, forced me onto my back, and plunged his hard cock into me.

11

ROCK

She gasped as I pushed into her perfect heat. God, she felt good. Every inch of her pussy sucked around me, took me in, like a perfect glove. "No condom, Lacey. I can feel every part of you. Just like before. Never a condom with you."

"Yes, yes," she sighed.

I'd wanted to suck on her sweet tits, lick that gorgeous plump pussy between her legs, touch every part of her silky body...

And I'd do that.

But right now, I needed immediate satiation. She'd stopped me before, with a good reason. I was never unsafe. Never...

But God, with her...I wanted to be inside with no barriers.

And it felt fucking great.

I drove into her again and again—her moans fueling me, my own lust fueling me—until I was damned near on the edge.

"I want you to come, baby. Come for me."

As if in reaction to my command, she exploded around me, her pussy pulsing against my cock—all it took to drive me over the edge and empty my load into her.

No barrier. Into her body.

An orgasm so complete, so satisfying... I'd never experienced anything like it.

Of course, it was because I wasn't using a condom. I wasn't used to going in bare. It had nothing to do with Lacey or how fucking hot she was.

I knew that.

But I didn't care. I savored it. Kept myself embedded in her sweet body until she'd milked every last drop out of me.

And then I still stayed there.

A few moments later, she squirmed beneath me.

I moved off of her, turning and lying face up on the king-sized bed, one arm over my forehead, breathing rapidly.

She turned to face me. "That was amazing."

"Baby? Amazing doesn't even begin to describe what just happened here."

Then her stomach growled. Her cheeks reddened. She was embarrassed, but I thought it was adorable.

"You hungry?"

"Sorry. Yeah, I guess I am. I haven't eaten since lunch, and now it's"—she checked her watch—"after six."

"I guess I should feed you, then." I sat up. "Let's see what room service has to offer."

"Really, it's okay."

"Hell, it's on my father." I stood, yanking up my boxers and jeans, and grabbed the room service menu from the desk. Then I laughed. "I guess it's on me, now. Wow." I still couldn't believe the bastard had done this. Put me in charge of his billion dollar enterprise.

I wouldn't get used to this for quite some time. I was far from happy with the situation. Just because I'd agreed to it didn't mean I'd like it.

"Hey," I said to Lacey, still holding the menu. "How long do I have to be my father's indentured servant? The terms of that will can't last forever, can they?"

"I don't believe there was any time limit mentioned in the will, which probably means as long as you're living."

"There's got to be a loophole."

"I doubt it, but I can look into it."

"Yeah, do that. Bill me. Oh, hell no. Bill the company."

She smiled. "All right."

"What kind of food do you like?"

"Anything."

"Okay. Liver and onions it is."

Her eyes widened. "There's no way this hotel serves liver and onions."

"Hey, you said anything. If I wave my father's money—God, *my* money—around and request liver and onions, I'm betting they'll find me some."

"You don't really like liver and onions, do you?"

"As a matter of fact, yes, I do. It's a good hearty meal, and it's inexpensive. I wasn't exactly living in luxury in Montana."

She reddened. "I didn't think—"

"Baby, I'm kidding. I'm not ordering liver and onions. But yeah, I do like it. I'm feeling more like a big hunk of steak right now. How about you?"

She smiled. "Steak sounds perfect."

"Rare?"

"Medium."

"Medium? You'll kill it."

"I'll try rare, then."

A woman willing to try new things. I liked that. In fact, I liked almost everything about Lacey Ward. At least the little I knew of her. I ordered the food plus a bottle of wine. "Now," I said, "what can we do in the meantime, while we're waiting for our dinner to be delivered?"

She reddened again. God, she was adorable. "I don't know."

"I know what *I'd* like to do," I said.

"What?"

I walked back to the bed and pulled her to the edge, spreading her legs. I got on my knees and gazed at her swollen pussy. "I think this will make an amazing appetizer." I dived in.

She was smooth as silk, slippery as wet grass. And the fact that I was licking my own come out of her turned me on even more. I'd never done that before—hell, never wanted to—but the fact that *I* was inside her, my very essence....

I groaned, shoving my tongue far into her heat.

She moaned above me, and a few seconds later, I felt the pull of her fingers in my hair. She tugged gently, which fueled my passion even further.

"You taste like sweet apples, baby," I said against her slick folds. "Yeah, a perfect appetizer." I moved upward to her clit and sucked it between my lips.

She jerked, arching, pushing my head into her pussy, grinding against my lips.

It was thrilling.

Never did I think I'd be fucking my father's lawyer after hearing her read his will, but this seemed perfectly natural to me. I couldn't get enough of this woman. I ate at her furiously, savoring her fragrance, her flavor, her fingers in my hair, her moans like the sweetest melody in my ears.

My cock was hard again, and I was naked, ready to plunge into her, but I couldn't tear my mouth away from her delicious pussy.

I devoured her, slid my tongue around her clit, over her folds, shoved it deep, and licked the warmth inside of her. Then I moved back to her clit and flicked it.

She ground into me harder. "I'm coming, Rock. Oh my God!"

I continued licking her as I thrust two fingers inside her,

stretching her tightness, reaching for her G-spot and rubbing ferociously. The pulsing around my fingers spurred me further, and I took her clit between my lips and sucked hard.

"God, no! Stop. No, don't stop. Oh my God!

She shattered again, gushing, her juices so sweet in my mouth.

And then a knock on the door.

She jerked at the sound, her orgasm stopping abruptly. Fuck. Our food. They were fast here, no doubt due to the Wolfe name. Too fast, actually.

"That's our dinner." I stood and walked out of the bedroom and into the living area. I got the food, scribbled a generous tip on the check, and then wheeled the table into the room.

Lacey walked out, a sheet wrapped around her like a toga.

"A shame to cover that up, baby," I said.

Her body was still flushed from her climax, and she smiled timidly. No need to be timid around me now, but I didn't say so. Instead, I smiled. "Come sit down. I'm going to feed you."

12

LACEY

Dressed in the sheet as I was, I felt like Cleopatra getting ready to have Marc Antony feed her grapes. So it would be bite-sized pieces of rare beef instead. What did I care? I'd milk this night, get everything I could out of it.

Because Rock Wolfe and I didn't have a future. Even though, right now, I was fantasizing about one. Part of me wanted a house with a white picket fence and gorgeous little kids fathered by this amazing man I barely knew.

Why was he making me think these things?

Did I want a future like that?

I'd always been the consummate career girl, married to her work. I'd been the youngest attorney ever to make partner at my firm, and only the second woman. I was what *Manhattan Magazine* called a "rising star" in the Trusts and Estates field.

I had everything in the world. I dated now and then. Had a few quick fucks now and then as well. Never had I wanted anything more. So why was I thinking about that now? Rock Wolfe was gorgeous, no doubt, but he was hardly my type.

Rock took the cover off one of the plates and sliced off a

nibble of steak. Then he swirled it in the port wine reduction puddled on the plate. He held it to my lips.

I took the bite. "Mmm." Melt in my mouth good.

"I take it that's your approval?" he said.

"So good. You have to try it."

"Don't mind if I do." He cut another piece, chewed, and swallowed. "Mmm. Excellent. But it pales in comparison to the last thing I tasted."

A warming flush crept up my body, and my nipples tightened against the soft cotton sheet. I squirmed. The last thing he'd tasted was already getting wet for him again.

How could he have such a bizarre effect on me? I wasn't some teenage girl with a high school crush on the bad boy who rode a motorcycle to school. I was a thirty-one-year-old attorney. A rising star.

Rock Wolfe was a mountain man who was being thrust into a position with a company, for which he was anything but prepared.

He'd do it. The man emanated power. He'd be a natural leader, and with his brother Reid at his side, he'd do just fine as the CEO of Wolfe Enterprises. I didn't follow the business side of the company with any regularity—I wasn't a corporate lawyer, after all—but I knew the basics because Derek Wolfe had been my client.

The company was a gold mine. They were just about to break ground on the new Wolfe Hotel and Resort in Las Vegas, which would be the biggest and glitziest hotel Vegas had to offer. It was a huge project, complete with a golf course, wild animal reserve, and of course, a casino that made every other casino in Vegas look like a convenience store.

I'd heard there were some contractual issues with the groundbreaking, but I didn't know enough to feel I could warn

Rock. Reid would do that. First thing Monday morning when Rock went into work. No need to worry him about that now.

He fed me another piece of steak. After I swallowed, I said, "Do you own any suits?"

"What? You mean like swim trunks?"

"No, silly. Suits. Coat, pants, and ties. You'll need to have them for work."

"For God's sake." He put down his steak knife. "Seriously? I have to wear a monkey suit?"

"Only for black-tie events."

"What?"

"A monkey suit is a tux, Rock."

"Oh." He reddened a little, and it was adorable.

"Don't worry. Your brother can take you shopping. The company is probably business casual most days. Most organizations are now. My firm is. But for business meetings you'll need suits, button-downs, and ties."

"I hate wearing a tie," he said. "It feels like a noose."

I laughed. "It is kind of a barbaric custom, I agree."

He scoffed. "Seems kind of appropriate that I wear a noose. This is the end of my life as I knew it, Lacey."

A swarm of sadness hit me. He was being forced to give up a life he loved. That would not be easy, and I understood more now why he'd been so reluctant to agree to it.

In the end, though, he did it for his siblings, and I admired that.

"You're doing something very admirable, Rock," I said. "Remember that."

"You know, the world doesn't really need another billion dollar corporation. What the world needs is for people to spend more time outdoors. To see the beauty of the world. Not be cooped up in some office deciding which new tower to build and desecrate the earth."

"You're an environmentalist?"

"I'm not a freak about it. No. But I appreciate the beauty of the outdoors. Why do you think I worked construction? I got to work outside. The money was decent, and it kept me in great shape." He closed his eyes.

I stared at him, my mouth watering. From the savory aroma of our feast? Ha! More likely from the man next to me. Great shape indeed.

"Have you ever been to Montana?"

"No, I haven't."

"It's beautiful. I'm not a religious man, Lacey. Never was and never will be. But when you look up into that big blue sky, you know there's something more powerful than all of us out there somewhere. The sheer beauty of it..." He opened his eyes. "That's over for me now."

"It doesn't have to be."

"You think I can just move the Wolfe headquarters to Helena or Billings?"

"Of course not. But keep your cabin. You can go there whenever you want. Executives do get time off, you know."

He shook his head. "It won't be the same."

No, it wouldn't be. I didn't bother to deny his claim. Instead, I said, "Try focusing on what you're gaining here. A lot of money, for one."

"And no free time to enjoy it."

"You'll have free time, Rock."

"Yeah, sure. But I'll go home at night to a penthouse in some high rise—"

"Your *own* high rise, Rock."

He threaded his fingers through his hair. "Would you stop saying shit like that? None of this is mine. I'll never think of it that way."

"You will when you start working there. Once you're running things, it will be yours."

"No, it won't. It'll be Reid's. Even Roy's and Riley's. Never mine."

"Of course it will. Your father left you in charge."

"Doesn't matter."

I scooted closer to him. "Let's finish dinner before it gets cold."

We ate in silence. Rock cleaned his plate, but I left over half of mine. Suddenly my appetite had gone south.

Rock looked so forlorn, almost tragic, which was a far cry from how I'd seen him before. He was so big, so strong—a man who could take on anything and come out on top.

He needed to believe that he could come out on top in this new position as well. I'd done all I could to convince him of that. Now it was time to try a new tactic.

I'd get him on top...of *me*.

13

ROCK

Lacey stood, her eyes sparkling, and slowly unwrapped the sheet from around her body, letting it fall to the floor in a white puddle.

My cock tightened. I hadn't been able to come after I'd brought her to orgasm from licking her pussy, and now all I could think about was getting inside that tight little cunt again.

Nothing on except those stockings and that garter belt. Those pumps.

I was still fully dressed.

Fuck.

I tore at my shirt until I'd tossed it on the floor.

Her eyes widened.

"You like?"

"Wow. You're amazing."

I sat down and pulled off my black biker boots, socks, and then my jeans. My cock jutted out, yearning to get inside her again.

"Take me to the bed, Rock," she said, her eyes flaming. "Take me, and then fuck me. Get on top of me and fuck me."

I wasn't used to being told what to do, but who was I to argue with her when I ached for the same thing? I picked her up and slung her over my shoulder, giving her ass a little slap. Then I walked into the bedroom and gently laid her on the bed. She looked up at me, her eyes full of lust, and she spread her legs and pulled her thighs upward, baring her swollen pussy to my view.

"Take me," she said. "Command me. Show me who's the boss."

My cock tightened even further. My God. She was giving me exactly what I needed, as if she'd looked into my mind. I needed control right now. I preferred control in the bedroom anyway, but right now, when my life was spearheading out of control, I truly needed it.

I trailed my fingers over her slick, wet folds and rubbed the moisture over her swollen clit. She closed her eyes, inhaling, moaning softly. I massaged her pussy, loving the satiny texture, her silky moans.

My cock throbbed, and a drop of liquid appeared on the head.

I needed her. Needed her lips around me. Yeah, I was going to sink into that sweet pussy, but first I was going to fuck her beautiful mouth.

I gave her clit a quick pinch, and then I hovered over her beautiful body, raking over her with my gaze. I nipped at one nipple, eliciting a gasp and then a groan. And then I climbed above her, my cock dangling against her full lips.

"Suck me, baby. Take me between those gorgeous lips."

She dropped her mouth open into a perfect O, and I entered.

She swirled her tongue over my head and around my shaft, and I nudged farther in. I so wanted to thrust in all the way, let my cock touch the back of her throat. That was the control I wanted over her. Over Lacey Ward, who was the sexiest woman

I'd ever met. I wanted to place a spider gag around those perfect lips and fuck that sexy mouth into oblivion.

And maybe one day I would.

I nudged in a little farther, millimeter by millimeter, holding back, waiting for her to complain.

But she didn't.

She let me go farther and farther...and soon I felt the back of her throat.

She gagged slightly, and I pulled back slightly. "Okay?" I asked.

She nodded, and I sighed in relief. I nudged the back of her throat again, and I damn near exploded on the spot.

But no. I was going to fuck that amazing pussy and come inside her.

I withdrew from her mouth.

She gasped and swallowed.

"Too much?" I asked.

She shook her head. "I'm fine. I want you to take what you need. If you need to fuck my mouth, I want you to do it."

"I intend to." Oh, yeah. Spider gag city soon. "But not right now. Right now I need to take you." I positioned her slender legs over my shoulders, giving me great access to her treasures. I rubbed my cock against her wet labia, teasing her, teasing myself. I closed my eyes and groaned.

"God, please, Rock."

I thrust inside her balls deep. Already I could feel the pulsating at the base of my dick. I closed my eyes, held my breath, drew on all my strength to hold on for a few more amazing minutes.

When I finally had myself in check, I pulled out and then pushed back in.

She shattered around me, her pussy contracting against my cock, and that was all it took. I pumped into her with all my might, and for the first time, I felt every pulse as my semen left my body and pumped into her.

I closed my eyes and groaned, staying embedded deep inside her, my cock still pumping.

"Damn, Lacey. Fucking goddamn."

I stayed buried in her body, relishing the feeling of completely consuming another person.

I'd wanted control.

This wasn't control.

This was consumption.

Yes, I'd consumed her.

But she had also consumed me.

Still, I didn't move, until she pushed gently at my shoulders. Then I rolled to the side and lay on my back, my eyes closed.

The soft touch of her fingers feathered over my forehead.

"Hey," she said.

I didn't respond. I couldn't. I'd just had the most earth-shattering orgasm of my life.

"Rock?"

I exhaled.

"Hey," she said again. "You okay?"

I opened my eyes. "I'm good. Better than good."

She smiled at me. God, she was beautiful. "Good. That's what I was going for. Remember this, okay?"

"What do you mean?" Not that I was ever going to forget it.

"I mean, remember this when you go into that office on Monday morning. Remember who you are. What you are. *You* are in control. You are the CEO of Wolfe Enterprises. You are Rock Wolfe."

I *was* Rock Wolfe.

I just wished she hadn't mentioned Monday morning.

14

LACEY

He looked amazing lying there, his tan skin glowing from perspiration, his dark hair sticking to his brow, his full lips parted slightly. His eyes were smoky and heavy-lidded.

"You're up for anything now, right? You know you can do this. You can be the CEO and kick ass."

He chuckled in a humorless way. "Is that what this was about? You let me fuck you so I'd feel like a big stud who could do anything?"

Had I been that transparent? "No, I just wanted—"

"Don't even go there, Lacey. If this was a manipulative fuck, we're done here." He sat up.

"No, Rock. Of course not. I wanted you. You have to know how much I wanted you." How had this gone so wrong? I'd have fucked him again no matter what. Yes, I'd wanted to show him he had control, but... Oh my God, I'd screwed this up. Majorly.

He stood and grabbed his boxers, sliding them over his gorgeous hips. Such a shame to cover his amazing body.

I stood next to him and slid my palm up his forearm to his shoulder in what I hoped was a comforting caress. "Hey, please don't get the wrong idea here. This was *not* a pity fuck. None of this was. Do you think I fall into bed with every man I meet in my conference room? This is a first for me, Rock. And look at you. You are *anything* but an object of pity."

"If there's one thing I can spot a mile away, it's a manipulative woman." He brushed my hand away. "You were trying to build me up so I'd go into work on Monday and take the bull by the horns. That way my siblings wouldn't get screwed over, and your precious bills would be paid."

Sparks of anger traveled up my spine. Yes, I'd wanted to show him he had control, but never had I pitied him. "My bills are paid by your father's estate, not you."

"Seems I'm in charge of my father's company now," he said.

"But not his estate. Reid is the executor, and he makes sure the estate pays its bills. You have nothing to do with it."

"Thank God," he said, rolling his eyes. "Then you have nothing to worry about."

"For God's sake, I wasn't worried!" I stalked to the bathroom and slammed the door shut. I looked in the mirror. My hair was in disarray, and I was flushed all over. My lips were swollen and pink from all the kissing, and my pussy... Oh my God. It was so red and engorged. I had been thoroughly used. I'd enjoyed it. The best fuck of my life.

But now I was pissed.

How dare he accuse me of a pity fuck so my bills would be paid? My first impression of Rock Wolfe had been spot on. He was an asshole of the highest order.

An asshole who was the best looking man I'd ever laid eyes on. The best kisser. A man who knew how to play every inch of my body like a concert master played his violin.

This couldn't end with both of us angry.

That wasn't what I wanted, and I hoped it wasn't what he wanted.

Was I truly just a fuck to him? I sighed. Maybe I was. I didn't do this type of thing very often—had I ever?—but he probably did. Just a fuck with a woman he wanted at the moment. His fuck *du jour*.

And now it was over.

But I wasn't ready to throw in the towel just yet. As much as Rock Wolfe was a dickhead, he had enormous potential. He was bright and intelligent, though pigheaded. He was determined, though obstinate. He had a fire and passion that could take the business world by storm.

He could make Wolfe Enterprises great.

I was sure of it.

Oh, he had a lot to learn, and some of it wouldn't be easy. But he was twice the man his father had been. His father had been twice the dick, too.

How well I knew.

I splashed some cold water on my face, drew in a deep breath, and wrapped a towel around my naked body. Time to set that stubborn man straight. I turned the knob and walked back into the bedroom.

No Rock. His clothes were all gone. He must have gone into the living area.

Nope. No Rock.

He had left.

Left me in *his* hotel room.

Dickhead.

Nothing to do now except get dressed and go home. It was Friday night, and as usual, I didn't have any plans. I'd recently ended a short relationship with a young partner in another law firm when I'd discovered him in bed with another woman. I could hardly fault him. He was nice and sweet and handsome, but we didn't really turn each other on. I'd started wondering whether I was becoming too married to my work, that it was making me frigid.

Today had gotten rid of that fear. I was far from frigid. Rock Wolfe had thawed whatever needed thawing in me.

I laughed out loud. It would serve him right if I just stayed here. This was his suite, and he'd be back eventually. Then he'd have to deal with me.

But that wasn't my style. I wasn't a chaser. I had no issue with letting a man know I was interested, but never would I push myself on anyone.

I was better than that.

I got dressed quickly and left the suite, keeping an eye out for Rock as I went. I even walked into the hotel bar, hoping to catch a glimpse of him, but no dice.

He'd gone somewhere else.

Not that I cared.

Yeah, right.

I did care, even though I didn't want to.

Rock Wolfe had gotten under my skin in a way no man ever had, but I had to accept reality. I was just a fuck to him.

And now it was over.

15

ROCK

I'd grabbed some sweats and a T-shirt and headed for the gym.

I tried several machines, but this manufactured workout couldn't compare to lifting lumber and pounding nails in the great outdoors.

Man, if there was one thing I hated, it was a manipulative woman. I'd met my share, but the true queen of manipulative women was Constance Larson Wolfe. My mother. I'd watched her manipulate my father, my brothers, even my baby sister. I winced at that one. Connie Wolfe had convinced six-year-old Riley that it was okay for her father to come to her bedroom. That it was just something daughters had to put up with. That it would be over soon. That it had happened to her, and she had turned out just fine.

Yeah, just fine. Thinking it was okay for a man to molest his six-year-old daughter was not "just fine."

I'd overheard the exchange between my mother and my weeping baby sister. "It hurts, Mommy!"

God. Remembering it made acid creep up my throat.

Whatever my father was doing to Riley, it wouldn't happen

again. I was determined. So I watched. And I waited. And the next time my bastard father sneaked into my little sister's room, I was ready, butcher knife in hand.

I'd kill the motherfucker.

But at fourteen, I wasn't as strong as my father. Not as mean, either.

I got a few stabs in, but he overpowered me.

All the time, Riley was crying in her bed. "No, Rock. Stop it! Don't hurt Daddy!"

Even after what he'd done to her, she still defended him. My bitch mother had brainwashed my beautiful little sister.

I'd ended up in military school. Sent away. No longer able to protect my precious baby sister. My mother and father didn't let me speak to my brothers before I left. I'd written Roy, telling him he needed to protect Riley, but later he told me over the phone that he never got the letter.

To this day, I didn't know if my brothers knew what had occurred. I'd detached myself from them, from my whole family. It was the only way to exist. For a while, I thought of them often, but it faded. Even Riley. I couldn't protect my sister, so I couldn't let myself think of her. Thinking of her, of what she might be going through, made me rage, and when I raged, I did things I couldn't do in military school, or I'd have gotten my ass handed to me on a platter. I went through enough during those years as it was.

I smiled slightly. Seeing Riley again had given me some hope. She had grown into a beautiful young woman with a promising career ahead of her. She'd gotten through it. She'd found her strength and she'd persevered.

I could learn from her.

I knew where my strength was. The next thing was to harness it and pour it into Wolfe Enterprises, even though the thought nauseated me.

I left the gym after an hour, not feeling like I'd worked at all. How was I going to survive without the outdoors?

I sighed, heading back up to my suite. I'd do it. I had to.

I waved the keycard in front of the lock and then opened the door, hoping Lacey was still there. I'd love another fuck, and perhaps I'd been too hard on her. Now that I thought about it, maybe she'd just been trying to help me. To convince me that I could do what I had to do.

"Lacey?" I walked in.

She wasn't in the living area. She wasn't in the bedroom. Not in the bathroom.

I was alone.

~

REID HAD TEXTED me to be at the office at nine o'clock Monday morning. I arrived at nine fifteen, wearing a clean pair of jeans and my best shirt—a white cotton button-down. No tie. I didn't own one. I stopped to tell the receptionist who I was, and she directed me to my father's—*my*—office.

Reid was already there. "You're late."

A boyish-looking man stood next to him.

"Since I'm the boss, apparently, I guess I can be late if I want."

"Dieter is here to measure you for clothing, and his time doesn't come cheap."

"Ah. Well, Dieter," I said to the man who looked like he couldn't be more than nineteen, "you'll be well compensated. As the newly minted CEO of Wolfe Enterprises, I hereby double whatever you've been getting."

"The company doesn't pay for your clothes, Rock."

"They don't? Then fuck this shit. I'm instituting a new dress code. Jeans and T-shirts."

"We're business casual on Fridays," Reid said. "And you'll be paying for your own clothes."

"With Dad's money."

"With your *share* of Dad's money," Reid corrected me. "Dieter has been tailoring my clothes for a year now. His father was Dad's tailor. He retired last year."

"Great."

"I need to get your measurements, Mr. Wolfe," Dieter said in a slight German accent. He came at me with a tape measure.

I backed up.

"It will only take a few minutes," Reid said. "Then you'll need to choose fabrics. He'll need eight suits plus two tuxedos, Dieter, about thirty cotton button-downs, and thirty ties."

"That's overdoing it," I said. "I own three pairs of jeans and a few T-shirts and flannels. Plus this shirt I'm wearing."

Reid ignored me. "Make that ten suits plus the two tuxes. A camel hair overcoat for winter. And then if you could do the foot measurements, I'll get them to our cobbler."

"Are you going to measure me for boxers too? Socks? Condoms?"

Dieter laughed...sort of. "No, sir."

Reid was right. The measuring only took a few minutes, though he came perilously close to my goods when measuring my inseam.

Once Dieter had written everything down, he brought out what appeared to be hundreds of fabric samples.

"Wool for suits." He handed me a booklet of samples.

I looked through the fabric. Some of the colors were so close I couldn't tell the difference. I handed it off to Reid. "You choose for me. I don't know what the hell I'm doing."

"Fine." He sighed. "Not like I won't be doing everything else around here anyway."

I rolled my eyes. "Look, Reid. I know you wish you were in

charge. I wish you were too. This sure as hell isn't what I expected for the rest of my life."

"I know. Dad fucked us all over."

"Give yourself a raise, then. You should be making at least what I'll be making."

"Believe me. I will be."

"What am I making, by the way?"

"Cushy eight figures, Rock. Plus options and benefits and Dad's Manhattan penthouse, as soon as it's cleaned up and the detectives are done gathering evidence. You're doing fine."

Cushy eight figures. Damn. Whether it was ten million or ninety-nine million didn't matter. I wouldn't be able to spend that much money in a dozen lifetimes. I'd made a cool fifty K in a good year of construction, and it had been more than enough to suit my modest needs.

"So what do you think?"

I jerked my head back to Reid. "About what?"

"These for your suits." He pushed several pieces of fabric into my hands.

"What are they?"

"Wool."

"They don't feel like wool." I imagined the heavy sweaters I wore in Montana during the winter.

"They are."

Dieter approached us and took the fabric Reid had chosen. "Wool is a very versatile fiber, Mr. Wolfe," he said. "It can be woven into coarse yarns or very fine silky thread, and everything in between."

"Whatever. Yeah, these are fine." Just what I needed. A lesson in textiles. Christ.

"Let's see the cotton poplins and oxfords for his shirts," Reid said.

Dieter brought over another booklet of samples.

"You a fashion expert now?" I said to Reid.

"I know how to dress myself for the business I'm in. Something you should learn. Something you *will* learn."

I eyed my youngest brother. Sharp dresser, that was for sure. I'd have taken him for a designer suit guru, not personally tailored. He was even slightly taller than I was, and I was no slouch at six-three. My little brother had grown up.

Reid chose my shirt fabric and then we went through soft silk for ties. Solids, paisleys, stripes... By the end my eyes were bugging out.

"Can you have a suit ready by tomorrow?" Reid asked.

"Sorry, sir. Next week at the earliest."

Reid pulled out his wallet and peeled off a couple of Ben Franklins. "I'll make it worth your while."

Dieter pocketed the bills. "It will be here by seven in the morning. I appreciate your business. But I'll have to send over a premade shirt and tie, plus some shoes."

"Fine," Reid said. "Thank you, Dieter."

Dieter bowed—yes, he fucking bowed!—and left.

Reid looked at his phone. "Time for our conference call. They're breaking ground in Vegas today. Go to the conference room. I need to make a quick call first."

16

LACEY

I'd spent the weekend at the office. I had no shortage of work, and it was the best way to keep my mind occupied.

Even so, my thoughts strayed to Rock Wolfe more than once.

Now, back at my office once again, I faced a morning of no appointments. Nothing to keep my thoughts from grazing over to Mr. Asshole Extraordinaire.

I wasn't falling for him. I'd known him for all of three days, had spent not more than five hours with him—though they were five pretty exciting hours. Still, I had relationships with leftovers in my refrigerator that were longer.

It had been a fuck. Several fucks, actually. Several amazing fucks.

But it was over.

Derek Wolfe, my client, was dead. Other than seeing that his estate was taken care of, I was finished with him and his family.

Saying goodbye to Derek Wolfe was no hardship. My thoughts wandered to the sixty-five-year-old dead billionaire.

Someone had shot him in the head in his Manhattan penthouse.

Derek Wolfe had no shortage of enemies, and he'd employed a highly paid security team.

Yet someone had managed to breach the unbreachable.

The police had questioned me along with everyone else who had even a slight relationship to Derek Wolfe. As far as I knew, they didn't have any leads yet, but it was still early. He'd only been dead for four days. The body had been autopsied and then cremated. None of the family seemed remotely interested in a funeral or memorial of any kind. Not that I blamed them.

And why was I ruminating on this?

Because Derek's death had brought his son into my life.

And Rock had fucked me and walked right out again.

My phone buzzed.

"Yeah?" I said to Charlie.

"Reid Wolfe for you, Lacey."

Not the Wolfe I wanted to talk to, but I took the call anyway. "Hi, Reid," I said into the phone.

"Hey, Lacey. Look. I just want to apologize."

"For what?"

"For my brother. I would have called sooner, but I didn't want to bother you over the weekend."

"Which brother?"

That got a laugh out of him. "Certainly not Roy. He hardly said a word during the reading of Dad's will. Rock had no right to make that remark about your...uh...undergarments."

I chuckled softly. After all I'd experienced with Rock, I'd nearly forgotten about his comment. "It's okay. He's far from the first of his kind I've dealt with."

"Well, don't worry. He won't be bothering you anymore. You're off limits, as far as I'm concerned, and I'm going to tell him so."

"Oh." An odd feeling swept over me.

One I didn't want.

"That's kind of you," I said to Reid.

What was more important was what I didn't say. That I didn't want to be off limits to Rock Wolfe.

No. I wanted to be back in his bed. Back in the bed of a supreme asshole, but back there nonetheless.

"No problem. I've got my work cut out for me, but I'm determined that my brother is going to make a go of this. For all our sakes."

"I think he'll do fine." And I meant it.

"Truthfully? He has a lot of potential, but there's a lot you don't know about Rock. He's volatile. And he can be downright dangerous, according to my mother."

"Dangerous? How?"

"I never could get her to elaborate, but good kids aren't sent off to military school."

I couldn't argue the point.

"If I can tamp that part of him down, he'll be fine."

Dangerous? Not Rock.

Volatile? Yes.

But dangerous?

No, Rock wasn't dangerous. He was passionate, driven, provocative.

Not dangerous.

Rock Wolfe wouldn't hurt another living soul. I was sure of it.

17

ROCK

After the conference call during which I'd uttered about four words, Reid took me around and introduced me to Carla, my secretary, and Jarrod, my executive assistant.

"Why do I need a secretary *and* an executive assistant?" I asked him.

"They both worked for Dad, and now they work for you."

"Great. I'll try to live up to his grand standard of shittiness." I rolled my eyes.

"Think what you want about Dad, but he treated his employees well. Jarrod has been with him for four years, and Carla for a whopping fifteen. She'll be retiring soon, and you can hire a brainless blonde with long legs, if you want. I don't give a rat's ass."

"Reid, come on. How the hell was I supposed to know Dad treated his people well? He treated me like shit."

"Yeah, he did. There's a lot I don't know about what went on between you two. Maybe someday you'll tell me."

"Not likely."

"Our father was a dick. Bigtime. But you had to do something."

"I didn't do shit."

"Brother, good kids don't get sent off to military school."

Yeah? And good fathers don't rape their little girls.

"Fuck you," was all I said.

I'd been a hothead. I knew that now. Instead of trying to do the bastard in myself, I should have gone to the police. But now, as an adult, I knew my father had probably had law enforcement in his back pocket.

My words seemed to jar Reid back into work mode. I tried not to hold what he'd said against him. He was my little brother, and I'd protected him as well. Though how he could live in that house and not know...

We stopped in a kitchen. "Coffee?" Reid asked.

"Man, it's not even noon yet. I feel like I've had a full day. Yeah, coffee. Black."

Reid poured us each a cup and then led me to his own corner office. He gestured to one of the cushy chairs in front of his desk. "Sit down. Let's talk."

I sat and took a sip of the hot coffee. "Not strong enough."

"That's the coffee for the staff. Jarrod will make sure your coffee is exactly how you like it."

I set the cup down on the edge of his desk. "Get him in here, then. This isn't worth drinking."

"Word of advice. Treat Carla and Jarrod with respect. They're here to make your life easier, but they won't have a lot of incentive to do that if you make theirs hell."

"Then I'll fire them and hire new flunkies."

"Christ, Rock. Turnover costs money. Carla and Jarrod are excellent employees. Why risk losing them? They're also very nice people."

"Why'd they work for Dad, then?"

"I told you. He treated his employees very well. Way better than he treated his family." My brother shoved his hand through his hair.

Reid looked troubled, and for the first time, I wondered something.

~

MY EYE THROBBED. *I'd had black eyes courtesy of my father many times, but this one felt like it had sliced into my brain. Alexandria, our nanny, gave me a raw steak. "Hold this against your eye, sweetie. It will help. I get you some aspirins."*

Alexandria was the only person in the household who showed any of us any affection, and even that wasn't a lot. A pet name or two, sometimes a kiss on the forehead when we went to bed. Never a hug. Never a smile.

My fourteenth birthday was only two days away. Aside from the throbbing in my eye, my back and my legs also hurt. Growing pains, Alexandria said. I'd shot up six inches over the summer. I was two inches taller than my mother now, and I was always starving.

Except for now.

Right now I felt like I was going to retch.

But I wouldn't. I'd hold it back as I'd learned to do. Wasn't worth it. I wouldn't do anything to show the rat bastard who was my father that his actions bothered me.

I'd stopped crying over his beatings five years ago, and three years ago, I'd perfected holding back puke.

Four more years.

In four more years, I'd be eighteen, and I'd get out of this house for good.

Alexandria returned with the aspirin, as she called it. It was actually a large dose of ibuprofen. I guess I should have been thankful for small favors. The beating before this one had been so bad that the nanny had stolen a few pills from my mother's stash. I didn't know what they were, but they'd knocked me out like someone had clocked me with a hammer.

"What you do to make your daddy so mad at you?" Alexandria handed me a glass of water so I could swallow the pills.

What had I done? Nothing. I'd put myself between him and my brother Reid. Reid was only nine, but he had a big mouth. He was resting peacefully in bed, his cute face unmarred thanks to me.

I swallowed the water and pills with a gulp. "Nothing."

"Nothing." *Alexandria shook her head.* "You always say nothing. Daddies don't beat their kids for doing nothing!"

"They do here."

She gave me a quick kiss on the forehead and then shook her head. "I'll check on you in an hour."

Unreal. Alexandria knew exactly what went on here. Though my father took care to keep most of his antics from the house staff, Alexandria's position as our nanny made it impossible to hide everything.

My father's money had a way of helping people to look the other way. Alexandria wasn't a bad person. She was a good nanny, took good care of us. She just wasn't overly affectionate, though she was more affectionate than either of our parents.

The steak was clammy against my face, but the coolness felt good on my eyelid. I switched my TV on with the remote. Watching with one eye was better than nothing.

MY FATHER HAD NEVER TOUCHED me inappropriately. Okay, a lie. My father never touched me *sexually*. He beat my ass with a coat hanger and a mop handle, to name a few. Maybe it was sexual for him. Maybe he got his rocks off beating his kid. But I was tough as nails and took as much as he dished out, never giving him the satisfaction of one single tear after I turned seven.

He'd beaten Roy and Reid too. I protected them when I could, but when I failed as a big brother, I'd heard their screams. I took them both aside after that and told them never to let the bastard see them cry.

Was it possible that what he'd done to Riley he'd also done to Roy or Reid? Not the kind of thing I could ask my brother— my brother who was wearing his custom-tailored suit and sitting in an office more exquisite than my hotel penthouse suite.

My hotel suite. My mind raced to Lacey.

But no time for that now.

"Reid," I said, "someone killed Dad. We all know he was a bastard, but who the hell hated him enough to kill him?"

"You. For one."

"Luckily, I was in Montana."

"Yeah. And I was kidding, actually. Not that you didn't hate him. We all hated him. Who killed him? It's anyone's guess. It could have been a hundred different people. The cops have their work cut out for them."

"Maybe we should hire a PI."

"Why? I'm glad he's gone. I'd think you are too."

"Glad the world isn't being poisoned by his existence, sure. If Roy's right, though, and the cops are going to come after us, we need to keep our heads up."

"True enough."

"I can't believe he's forced me into this, but I have to do it for the rest of you."

Reid let out a soft chuckle. "Believe it or not, I've missed you, big brother."

I scoffed. "You're the only one."

"Not true. Roy and Riley missed you. Even Mom."

"Devil woman? I don't think so."

"Why do you hate Mom so much? She did the best she could under the circumstances. She was Dad's victim too."

"You're deluding yourself, man."

"What could she have done better? She took care of us."

"She hired nannies to take care of us."

"Well...yeah. But at least she didn't beat the hell out of us."

"We were all bigger than she was."

"Not always. Not until we hit eleven or so."

True. Our mother hadn't beaten us. She'd been indifferent, for the most part. I could have forgiven her that. I could have forgiven her almost anything, if not for that horrible conversation I'd overheard between her and Riley. But that wasn't my story to tell. It was Riley's.

"You're not at all curious who did Dad in?" I asked.

"Not in the slightest, and I can't for the life of me figure out why you are."

"Easy." I picked up the cup of brown water and took another sip. "I'd like to buy him dinner, complete with a Champagne toast."

That got another soft laugh out of my brother. "Man, I'd go in on that with you."

"Do you think Roy and Riley would?"

"Roy, yeah. In a heartbeat. Riley's tougher to figure out. She had a closeness with Dad that Roy and I didn't share. Maybe because she was the only girl. I don't know."

If I hadn't been sure Reid was in the dark about Dad and Riley, I was certain now. "What kind of closeness?"

"Dad would take her on trips. Big, lavish trips to places like Paris and Barcelona. They even went to Bangkok once. Roy and I finally stopped complaining about it. It didn't do any good."

"How old was Riley when she went on these trips with Dad?"

"It started when she was pretty young. Eight or so. They went on until she left for college. Or they might have continued, for all I know. I was already working here by then, and Roy was off in Soho painting."

Fucking bastard.

I knew exactly what had gone on during those trips.

"I'll tell you something, Reid. It's a good thing somebody else murdered that prick. If he hadn't, I might have."

18

LACEY

Finally, the day was over, and I couldn't wait to get home and into a hot bath. If Rock Wolfe was going to take up residence in my head, I might as well let him. I could fantasize while sitting in a luscious citrus steamy bath, a glass of wine next to me.

Why fight it? I'd get it out of my system. I'd even pull out my vibrator if I had to.

One evening ought to do it, and then I'd be freshly cleared out, kind of like doing a quick clean on my hard drive.

I was just about to leave when Charlie knocked and then opened my door.

"I thought you'd left," I said.

"No, I was getting caught up on some filing. A call came in for you."

"Crap. Who is it?"

"Riley Wolfe."

I arched my eyebrows. "Really? All right. Put her through." I picked up the buzzing phone. "This is Lacey."

"Hi, Lacey. I'm sorry to disturb you. This is Riley Wolfe, Derek Wolfe's daughter."

"Hi, Riley. What can I do for you?"

"Are you free for a drink tonight? Or even dinner? I'd like to talk to you about something."

"As a matter of fact, I'm not. I was just—"

"Please. Everything's on me. We can go to the most expensive restaurant in town, if you want. I *really* need to talk to you."

So much for my relaxing bath and glass of wine. I could still say no, but something in her voice sounded almost...desperate.

"No need to break the bank on my account. Just tell me where to meet you."

RILEY WOLFE HAD LONG dark hair, and curse her, she resembled Rock the most of her three brothers. Her eyes were brown, like Roy's, but the rest of her? Rock's male beauty in a female form would equal his little sister's. I'd originally thought Riley most resembled Roy, but that was before Rock Wolfe had come stalking into the conference room that first day. Rock might not be as pretty as Roy, but he had that windblown look that his sister shared.

I couldn't help thinking of him every time I looked at her.

She was quiet, which perplexed me, considering she'd invited me here to talk about...something. Something about her father's estate, I assumed. I wouldn't know about anything else.

She ordered a dry martini, double.

Yeah, she was serious about something.

I ordered a gin and tonic. Single.

She took a long sip of her drink when it came, and then finally looked at me. "Lacey, I know you're wondering why I asked you here."

"Yeah, it had occurred to me."

"It's going to take me a while to gear up to this, okay? Bear with me."

"Sure, Riley. Whatever you need." Now I was really confused.

"Tell me a little about what you do."

Clearly, she was trying to break the ice, feel more comfortable with me. But she knew what I did. I was a trusts and estates lawyer.

"I'm a trusts and estates lawyer."

"Interesting. I'm a model."

Yes, I know that.

"Riley, forget the small talk, okay? If you need some time, we don't have to talk. We can finish our drinks, order some food. Whatever works for you."

"Sorry. I'm just not very good at small talk. It's stupid. I know you're a lawyer, and you know I'm a model." She smiled timidly.

"I do." I took a sip of my gin and tonic. Refreshing. "But I don't know what kind of work you're doing. Are you still doing mostly runway work?"

She nodded. "I do a lot of it. But I do have some big news. I've just been signed to be the face of Dominique Cosmetics. It's a French brand."

An *expensive* French brand. I knew it well. "That's wonderful! Will you be traveling?"

"Yeah. I'm supposed to leave for Paris next week. I haven't told my brothers yet."

"They'll be thrilled for you."

"Yeah. Maybe."

"Maybe?"

"They're really protective of me. Except for Rock, of course. I hardly know him. He left when I was only six or seven."

Military school. Maybe Riley would have some answers.

"Reid told me he went to military school."

"He did. He and Dad had some kind of falling out. We never talked about it."

"Oh?"

"Well, if they did, I was too young to remember. No one even mentioned Rock after he left. Mom and Dad didn't, anyway. Sometimes Reid or Roy would reference times before he left, but it was always something I had no memory of."

Wow. This young woman had a brother she didn't even know. That was a shame.

"Rock seems like a good guy," I said. "A little brash, but a good guy."

"I honestly have no idea. The will was a complete surprise to all of us. We all thought Reid would be put in charge."

"I know. Like I've already told you, I tried to talk your father out of it, but he was determined."

"I don't understand it at all. Dad never even mentioned Rock. It was like he didn't exist. And then, to put him in charge of the company? It's crazy."

I nodded. Though I had come to believe that Rock, once he believed in himself, could accomplish anything.

Silence for a few moments. Clearly Riley wasn't quite ready to divulge why she'd invited me here, so maybe I could open her up a little by asking about her brothers.

"Tell me about your family. I know you and Rock don't really know each other. What about Roy and Reid?"

"You must know that Roy's an artist. He's a genius, really. His paintings hang all over my apartment."

"I'd like to see his work sometime."

"He has some work at the Gallery Galileo on Fifth."

Fat chance I'd get over there. "I'll try to pop in sometime."

"Anyway, he's a quiet and studious type. He spent most of his time alone in his room. He had very few friends when we were younger. Then Reid is the total opposite."

I'd heard stories about Reid Wolfe. He'd always been completely professional with me, but he was known as a womanizer. "He's definitely not shy."

"No. He's broken a lot of hearts, including some of my model friends." Riley smiled timidly. "I warned them all beforehand, but Reid has this bizarre effect on women. They love him."

"It's his charisma," I said. "He oozes it. Plus he's devastatingly good-looking, but so are your other two brothers."

"They are. Our family got blessed with good-looking genes, I guess."

"Are you kidding? All of you are beautiful. Even your father, at his age, was a very handsome man."

Riley's cheeks reddened a little. "He was."

"And your mother is still a beautiful woman."

"She is."

More silence. Family talk seemed to be over.

The waiter came to take our order. I chose a ten-ounce strip, rare—couldn't help thinking of Rock—with broccolini and rosemary polenta. Riley ordered a tilapia filet broiled without oil or butter with brown rice and carrots. Clearly a model's meal.

Still silence.

Until my phone buzzed in my purse. Normally I wouldn't check it during a dinner meeting, but we weren't talking. "Would you excuse me?" I fished my phone out of my purse.

A text from a number I didn't recognize. A number with a Montana area code.

19

ROCK

I 'm exhausted after my first day. Can I buy you a drink?

I texted those words to Lacey. I didn't tell her who I was, but I figured she'd know.

I waited.

And waited.

Then—

Are you kidding me?

I leaned back in my supple leather executive chair and couldn't help a laugh.

I started to text her back, when another from her came in.

I'm at a dinner meeting.

Where?

None of your business.

Is it a dinner meeting? Or a dinner date?

Again. None of your business.

She had a date. Damn her.

Not that I wanted any kind of exclusivity. We'd just met. But all I'd been able to think about all day was getting her back in my bed.

I typed into the phone. *Meet me later.*

No, thank you.

Playing hard to get, huh? That wouldn't fly with me. I had better things to do than chase women.

I texted back. *Have it your way.*

A few minutes passed.

I will. Have a good evening.

I sighed. A full wet bar lined one wall of my office—a spacious room that was nearly as big as my entire cabin in Montana. I could have a drink to relax, and then I'd make my way back to my empty hotel suite.

I fixed myself a bourbon on the rocks and sat back down behind my desk. I was actually more exhausted now than I'd ever been after a day of good old-fashioned manual labor. Crazy.

As fatigued as I was, I'd have no problem fucking Lacey Ward until the wee hours of the morning.

Aw, hell. I had to try again.

I picked up my phone, but it dinged with a text. From her.

Your sister wants you to join us. We're at Gramercy Tavern.

I HADN'T STOPPED to think about why Lacey was having dinner with Riley. I'd just hopped in the elevator, gone down the street, and hailed a cab as quickly as I could.

When I got to the restaurant, I hightailed it in.

"May I help you, sir?" the tight-assed maître d' asked.

"Yeah. I'm here to meet my sister and my...er...attorney."

"I'm sorry, sir, but we require a jacket and tie."

I was still clad in my jeans and my one decent shirt. "I don't have a jacket and tie. So if you'll kindly show me to my party—"

"If you could tell me whom you're supposed to meet, perhaps I could let them know that you won't be able to join them."

"Are you fu— serious? My sister is Riley Wolfe, the model. I'm Rock Wolfe, the new CEO of Wolfe Enterprises."

"Oh!" The man nearly fell into a bow. "I'm so sorry, Mr. Wolfe. Please follow me."

He led me to a small table in a dimly lit corner of the restaurant. Lacey looked amazing. She was all navy blazer but I knew what she was hiding underneath. My sister looked beautiful, as always. Too thin, though. I didn't like what modeling was doing to her. And her eyes...

I had to stop myself from gulping. I recognized that look in her big brown eyes. To me, she was still the six-year-old begging me not to hurt her daddy. My heart hurt just thinking about it.

So I decided not to think about it.

"Ms. Wolfe, your brother," the maître d' said.

"Great. Thank you. Sit down, Rock."

Lacey's cheeks were pink. Damn. Pink cheeks made for a hard cock. Crazy shit.

"I'll send your server over right away, but is there anything I can get you in the meantime, Mr. Wolfe?" He unfolded my napkin and placed it across my lap.

"Bourbon on the rocks. Thanks." *And don't come near my lap again.*

"Any particular bourbon?"

"I don't know. The first one the bartender can get his hands on works for me."

"Of course." He bowed again.

Being Derek Wolfe's spawn apparently made me royalty all of a sudden.

I opened my mouth to speak when the server appeared. "The ladies' meals are almost ready, so do you know what you'd like, sir? That way I can get it started and get it out as soon as possible." He handed me a menu.

I set it aside. "Just get me a T-bone, very rare. Baked potato with sour cream, and whatever vegetable you have."

"Very good, sir." He bowed and left.

Yeah. Fucking royalty.

"So, ladies, thank you for inviting me to join you." I grabbed the bread basket that was next to me. Nothing I recognized, but I took one anyway. "Could you pass the butter, please?" I said to Lacey.

She handed me the tray. "It was Riley's idea for you to join us."

That's what Lacey's text had said, which was strange, since my sister and I were virtually strangers.

My sister's cheeks turned pink. "Lacey mentioned that you texted her, and I thought it might be...nice. We could do some more catching up."

"Sure, that'd be great." I took a bite of my roll that appeared to have sunflower seeds and some kind of olive in it. Hmm. It was pretty good.

A few moments passed in silence.

"I figured since you invited me," I said to Riley, "that you'd start."

"Oh. Yeah. Sure." She cleared her throat. "How was your first day at the company?"

Something I didn't want to talk about. But as long as I stayed at the helm, the company was a quarter hers, and she had a right to know.

"Not bad." *Not good, either.*

"Reid showed you the ropes?"

"A few of them. It'll take a lot longer than one day for me to get the hang of this."

"I'm sure you'll do fine."

Silence again.

Why had my sister invited me here again? I was truly flummoxed. She didn't care how my day had gone. I could see it in her eyes. Again.

The server finally interrupted our silence, bringing our meals. Creamed spinach. The one vegetable I couldn't stand. My own fault. I'd told him to bring me whatever vegetable they had. Silly me. I thought vegetables meant vegetables, not vegetables drowning in white glop.

For what this dinner was costing my sister—I assumed she was paying—I ought to eat every bite. But no creamed spinach was crossing my lips.

I had my standards.

I cut a piece of my meat. Looked perfectly cooked. Nice and red. "How's yours?" I asked Lacey.

She swallowed, nodding. "Delicious."

"Rare?"

She reddened. "Yes. It's perfect."

I couldn't help smirking. I'd taught her how to enjoy a steak cooked to perfection. I'd like to teach her a lot more.

But that would wait.

I turned to my sister. This woman had once been the sweet little girl I'd tried with everything in me to protect from our deplorable father. I wanted more than anything for her to be happy. But she wasn't. I could tell.

"How was your day?"

She swallowed her bite of fish. "Good. I didn't have any bookings today, so I just did some reading."

"What are you reading?" Not that I'd have a clue. I hadn't read a book in a while, but I used to love reading. A long time ago, it had been an escape for me. Now—or rather, up until four days ago—my escape was big sky Montana and the outdoors.

"I'm trying to do the classics. I'm working on *Moby Dick*."

"Sis, I remember that from high school." We'd been forced to read it at that enslavement camp my father had sent me to. "It's about the most boring thing ever written. If you want to do the classics, try Dickens. You can't go wrong with any of them, but my favorite is *Great Expectations*. Or read *Dracula* or *Frankenstein*. Or anything by Robert Louis Stevenson."

Lacey turned to me, staring. "You've read the classics?"

"You find that surprising?" I arched an eyebrow at her.

"Well...no. Of course not. And I agree with you about *Moby Dick*. Are you enjoying it, Riley?"

"Not in the slightest," she said.

All three of us laughed at that, and for a minute, I saw the happy little girl my sister might have been.

Finally. Now I could relax a little.

20

LACEY

I had no doubt that Rock Wolfe was intelligent. I'd already surmised that during our first encounter. But well-read? That one surprised me.

Still, I wondered why Riley had invited him to join us. She'd obviously wanted to talk to me about something. Maybe she changed her mind and saw inviting Rock as an out.

I had no idea, but I was going to find out. I just had to wait for the right moment, and that wasn't going to happen with Rock sitting at our table.

My chance came when Riley excused herself to go to the ladies' room.

I stood. "I'll go with you."

When we were safely in the powder room, I said, "Riley, what did you invite me here for? Is it something you're okay talking about in front of your brother?"

She looked away, her cheeks red. "I... I changed my mind. I really don't want to talk to anyone about it."

"Are you sure?"

"Yes. Yes, I am." She went into a stall.

No need for me to stay. I did a quick makeup check and left.

As the bathroom door closed behind me, a retching sound came from inside. Was Riley making herself vomit? Did models really do that? Poor thing. Something was bothering her, but I couldn't force her to talk.

Rock had cleaned his plate, except for the spinach, when I returned to the table.

"She okay?" he asked.

Did he know something? I didn't know for sure she was puking, or that she was making herself do it, and I didn't want to spout off to Rock and cause him worry when I wasn't sure what was going on.

"Why shouldn't she be?" I said.

"I just didn't know you and my sister were that close."

"How would you know anything about her? Or about me?"

"Okay, okay. Calm down."

He was right, of course. Riley and I hardly knew each other. Something was bothering her—something she'd been willing to share with a stranger, but she'd lost her nerve. That was why she'd insisted on inviting Rock to join us. He'd given her an out.

"Truthfully, she—" I stopped when I saw Riley returning out of the corner of my eye.

"Truthfully what?"

"She's coming back," I whispered.

He nodded. "Everything okay, Sis?" he said once she'd sat down.

Riley looked a little pale. "Yeah. I'm fine."

"Good. Anyone up for dessert? I could go for a big slab of cheesecake myself." Rock smiled.

God, he was so good-looking.

"Nothing for me," Riley said, a little shakily.

He turned to me. "How about you? Or do I eat by myself?"

"I'll have a cup of coffee." I smiled. "And a bite of your cheesecake."

He gestured to our server, who came over instantly.

"Yes, sir?"

"Do you have any cheesecake tonight?"

"Yes, sir. We have a wonderful New York Cheesecake with raspberry coulis."

"Perfect. We'll take two slices, and two cups of coffee."

"Hey, I don't want—"

Rock stopped me. "Just bring two. She wants to taste mine, and once she tastes it, she's going to want her own."

I couldn't help smiling. He was probably right, though he had no way of knowing that. He must be used to women eating his dessert. Jealousy speared through me. Of course he was. A man like Rock Wolfe didn't live a celibate life.

Pissed me off just thinking about all the women he'd most likely been with.

Calm down, Lacey.

Riley looked at her phone. "If you two don't mind, I need to leave. I have an early shoot in the morning. I feel bad, since I invited you." She nodded to me. Then she pulled out her wallet and a couple one-hundred-dollar bills.

"Put that away. We'll just do it again sometime, and then it will be your turn. It's okay." Except that she was leaving me here with her gorgeous brother who'd try to lure me back into his bed.

And I'd probably go.

Still, I felt a concern for Riley as she mumbled her thanks and shoved the bills back into her purse. She was so young, and something had clearly been bothering her enough to want to talk to a stranger about it. A stranger who was also a lawyer.

She stood. "I'll call you."

"Of course."

She smiled weakly and left the table.

I doubted she'd call me. She'd gotten up her courage only to lose it. She'd have a hard time scraping it together again.

Rock took about two seconds to pounce on me about his sister. "Why were you having dinner with Riley?"

"I'm not really sure. She said she wanted to talk to me about something, but I guess she changed her mind."

He stared past me for a moment. I could almost see his mind working, wondering. But then he cleared his throat. "I guess it's just you and me, then, and here comes our dessert."

The cheesecake was rich and creamy, as I knew it would be. "Mmm," I said. "I might as well just paste this onto my waistline."

"Nothing at all wrong with your waistline." He eyed me lasciviously.

"Stop it," I said.

"Stop what?" he asked, wide-eyed.

"Looking at me like that."

"Like what?"

His feigned innocence was getting tedious.

"Like you'd rather eat me for dessert than this cheesecake."

"Hadn't thought of it. But it's a damned good idea, now that you mention it."

Already I could feel myself caving. But the way he'd walked out on me Friday evening had been obnoxious and rude. I wasn't about to set myself up for that again.

So I said nothing. Just took a bite of cheesecake.

And he watched me. Watched me place the fork between my lips, watched me chew, watched me swallow, watched me pull my napkin up from my lap and pat my mouth.

I was beginning to feel like I was putting on a show for him.

I took another bite, and he assessed me in the same way, his eyes fiery.

Talk about feeling self-conscious.

"Aren't you going to eat your dessert?" I asked.

"It's a lot more fun watching you eat yours." He licked his lips.

Oh. My. God.

Fine. I'd give him a show if he wanted a show. I sank my fork back down into the creamy cheesecake and then slowly brought it to my lips, never breaking eye contact with him. "It's so good," I said, doing my best to sound sultry. "Such a creamy texture on my tongue." I slid the fork through my lips. "Mmm."

"You're killing me here."

"You wanted to watch."

"I'll tell you what I want. I want to smear that cheesecake all over your naked body and lick it off."

I swallowed the bite of dessert with a gulp.

Already I was throbbing between my legs. Maybe this hadn't been such a good idea after all.

He gestured to our waiter. "I'm going to need a doggie bag for my dessert, *garcon*. I have other plans for it later."

"Right away, sir." The waiter took his dessert plate.

Rock turned to me, his gaze full of lust. "Let's get the hell out of here."

ROCK

"**N**o."

No? She said no?

"I'm not done with my cheesecake."

"We'll wrap yours up too. Take it with us. My hotel is only a few blocks away, baby. I can guarantee you a good time, as you know."

She took another bite of cheesecake. Did any woman know how to eat as sexily as this one did? I wasn't sure I'd ever gotten a major hard-on watching a woman eat cheesecake before.

She swallowed. "No," she said again.

"Christ, you're killing me here." I squirmed. My dick was way too big for these jeans right now.

"Oh, well." She took another bite—just to torment me, I was sure.

"Come on, baby. We had a good time, didn't we?"

"Who said we didn't?"

"Then why don't you want a repeat?"

She took one more bite of dessert and brought it to her lips achingly slowly. Once she swallowed, she said, "Because I don't appreciate being told I'm manipulative. And I don't appreciate being left alone in your hotel suite. So I'm done, Rock. It was fun, but I'm done."

"Damn, Lacey." My groin was on fire.

She fucking took another bite of that damned cheesecake, and then another.

One more, and she was done. Thank God. Then she took a sip of her coffee.

My cup sat, still full. Jacques—or whatever his name was—came back with my small box of cheesecake...and the check.

It would serve Lacey right if I left her with it. I didn't have any money. Not yet, anyway.

But she subtly slid it in front of her, pulled her wallet out of her purse, and placed a credit card in the folder.

"I'll get that," I said.

"Don't worry about it."

"But Riley invited me. You didn't."

"Riley invited me as well, but Riley's not here. I don't have any problem paying my own way."

"What about paying *my* way?"

"I don't have any problem with that either. This way I don't owe you anything."

Damn. That was a low blow. Would I seriously not be getting any tonight?

Then my phone buzzed.

Damn again.

"Yeah?" I said into it.

"Hey, Rock, it's Reid. You need to come back to the office. The cops found something about Dad."

～

IT WAS after nine o'clock when I got back up to the office. Reid was there with the cops. Roy walked in about two minutes after I did.

"What's going on? And how did you get here so quickly?" I asked Reid.

"I never left."

"Are you kidding me?"

"This is a round-the-clock job, brother. I thought I made that clear."

I had a feeling there were a *lot* of things that hadn't been made clear to me yet. "Yeah? Why didn't you bitch when I left, then?"

"I didn't realize you had left. It may surprise you, Rock, but I have way more important things to do to keep this company running smoothly than keep tabs on my new CEO."

"*Your* new CEO?"

He rolled his eyes. "The company's new CEO. Look. We both know I should have your job. Dad fucked us *all* over. Not just you."

"I get that. I do. But at least you weren't ripped out of a life you loved and forced into one you hate."

"Rock, the only way any of us are going to get through this is if you have a change of attitude. As long as you hate this, resent this, none of us will be happy. Get it?"

Oh, I got it, all right. "Fuck you, Reid."

"And fuck you right back. Thanks for listening, by the way."

"I heard every word you said."

"Did you? Then put them to use. For all our sakes."

I opened my mouth to respond, but two blues walked in before I could, followed by a plainclothesman.

The plainclothesman held out his hand. "I'm Detective Hank Morgan."

Reid shook his hand. "Reid Wolfe. My brothers Rock and Roy."

I shook his hand. Limp handshake. Great. Just who I wanted on this investigation. Not that I cared who offed my father, but I sure didn't want whoever it was coming after the rest of us.

"Will your sister be joining us?" the detective asked.

"I wasn't able to get hold of her," Reid said.

"But I just saw her at dinner." I rubbed my chin, worry for my sister churning through me. What was going on with her?

"All right. Let's all have a seat."

There weren't enough chairs for the two blues. "Why don't we go into a conference room?" I said.

"Good enough." Reid led the way.

Once we were seated at the table, Reid spoke again. "What's the news that couldn't wait until morning?"

"We got one set of prints from the gun we found at the scene, and we figured you'd want to know who they belonged to."

"Wait a minute," I said, shaking my head. "Whoever offed Derek Wolfe left the gun there?"

"Yup." Morgan pulled out his phone. "Most likely a plant."

"Meaning?" Roy asked.

"Meaning this weapon isn't registered anywhere or to anyone, which indicates the serial number has probably been tampered with. We're pretty sure the fingerprints on the gun don't belong to the shooter—"

"They were planted," I finished for him.

"Seems to be the case," Morgan said.

"Who do they belong to?" Reid asked.

The detective looked directly at me. "They belong to you. Rock Wolfe."

I stood, hot anger taking me over. "That's insane. I wasn't even in the state when this happened."

"Calm down," Morgan said.

"Wait, wait, wait," Reid said. "How do you know they're Rock's?"

"We ran them."

"But how—"

I stopped him with a gesture. "I was arrested a couple years ago for brawling in a bar, okay? The charges were dropped, but not before they took my prints and a mug shot. But I'll remind you again that I wasn't in this damned state when my father was killed."

"I know that, and it's been corroborated," Hank said. "But someone sure wants us to *think* you were there."

"Probably my bastard of a father," I said.

"Rock," Roy said, "why would Dad put you in charge of his company and then have himself killed and try to frame you for his murder? That doesn't make sense."

"Did the asshole ever make sense in his life?" I roared.

"Not as a father, no," Reid agreed. "But this is his business. If he left it in your hands, he sure as hell wouldn't want you hauled off to prison. Then what? According to his will, none of us would get anything."

I scoffed. "Maybe that was his plan the whole time."

Both my brothers' eyes widened. Yeah. I'd made them think. And while they didn't want to believe what I'd said, their eyes told me they weren't totally convinced.

"Do you have any enemies?" Hank asked me.

"Other than my dead father? No."

"You just said you were in a fight in a bar."

"With an asshole from out of town who tried something on one of my friends, but he was hardly the type who could have a billionaire murdered to frame me."

"How do you know? Do you remember his name?"

"Hell, no, I don't remember his name. I never saw him again. Go get the police report if you want details."

"I will. But for now, think back. You've been gone from New York a long time. Did you leave any unfinished business here? Or maybe in Montana? Did you have a falling out with anyone? Something major?"

I'd had more than that one brawl in biker bars, but none of those jerks were smart enough to plant my fingerprints on a weapon. "None that I can think of."

"How about women? A jilted lover, maybe?"

I hadn't had any serious relationships to speak of. I'd dated a few women, but everything had always ended amicably. At least I'd thought so. I only got serious with one. Of course I'd had my share of no-strings fucks as well. "No."

"Work problems?"

"No."

"All right. Good enough. We'll have to attack it from your father's angle then. There must be someone who wanted your father dead and wanted you blamed for it. Any ideas?"

"I'm sure a lot of people wanted my father dead," I said. *And I'm one of them.*

"I can't disagree with my brother," Reid said. "Derek Wolfe had plenty of enemies. But it was all business."

"Business with the wrong people can lead to things like this," Morgan said. "I don't have to educate you on that."

Reid nodded solemnly.

He knew something. Something he'd better fucking tell me when I could get him alone. I'd been thrown into this raging fire against my will, and I needed all the information available.

"I'm going to need access to all your father's business records. I need names of people he clashed with in business."

"You're going to be looking for a needle in a haystack," Reid said.

"Understood. But I've found those needles before. I intend to find it this time."

"I don't get it," I said. "I've been gone since I was eighteen years old. Not one of my father's business contacts would know anything about me. Who would want to drag me into this?"

"I don't know, Mr. Wolfe. But I will do my best to find out."

22

LACEY

The cab dropped me at my apartment. I whisked quickly past the doorman and stood, waiting for the elevator.

Horny and waiting for the elevator.

This was so crazy. Rock was a jerk. A really sexy and hot jerk, but a jerk, nonetheless. Oh, he was definitely his father's son, a comparison he'd hate.

Derek Wolfe had been a huge womanizer and had left a string of broken hearts in his wake. He'd cheated on his wife, Connie, and then on his girlfriend, Fonda. It was no secret at my firm. One of my partners handled the hush money, and it amounted to millions.

Rock Wolfe didn't have any money. Well, he did now. But before now, I had no doubt that he'd left a lot of broken hearts behind in Montana. Like father, like son.

God, he'd hate that.

No matter how true it was.

Time to forget about Rock Wolfe. The elevator dinged, and my neighbor, Paul Hansen, walked out.

"Hey, Lace. What are you up to tonight?"

"A hot bath."

Paul was dressed to kill in casual black pants, a red cotton button-down, and a black leather blazer. With his blond hair, hazel eyes, and fair skin, he was handsome and sexy. But he was nothing like Rock Wolfe. The anti-Rock.

"Are you kidding? The night is young. I'm meeting some friends for a drink. You should come."

I looked down at my wrinkled work clothes. "Maybe another time."

"You look like you could use some fun. Just one drink. I'm buying." He grabbed my arm. "Come on."

I sighed. Why not? "At least let me change first."

"Why? You look great, as always."

I could feel the bags under my eyes. I had to at least check my face. But before I could, he was pulling me out the door. We grabbed a cab, and within a few minutes, Paul was leading me into a bar.

Crowded, though not overly so. It was Monday night, not Friday night. A group of three waved us over to a table in the corner.

"Hey, guys," Paul said. "This is my neighbor, Lacey Ward. Lace, meet Jon Gregory, Lena Thomas, and Fox Monroe."

I smiled. "Fox? As in Mulder?"

He laughed. "I was named after him, actually."

Whoa. Young, then. No more than twenty-five at the most, and I'd put him younger. He had to be at least twenty-one to be here. I was suddenly feeling very ancient at thirty-one. He was gorgeous, though. They all were, including the woman. And dressed for a night out, which I so very wasn't.

"Have a seat." Fox patted the chair beside him.

What the heck? Paul took the spot on my other side, and our table was complete.

Fox signaled a server. When she arrived, he asked, "What

would you like?"

I had no idea. Then I thought of Rock. "Bourbon. On the rocks."

"Any particular bourbon?" the woman asked.

"The first one the bartender can get his hands on works for me," I said, mimicking Rock's statement at the restaurant.

"Now there's a woman after my own heart," Fox said, laughing. "Bring me the same."

The others placed their orders, and Fox turned back to me.

"What do you do, Lacey?"

"I'm an attorney. What do you do?"

"I'm a model."

Of course he was. His face was finely chiseled, not a single flaw, and his jawline sported a few days' growth of sandy brown hair. His eyes were clear and blue. Really beautiful and sparkling and very focused on me.

I squirmed a little. Why was this making me so uncomfortable? His age? Nah. I wasn't ageist or any -ist. Another time, I'd be loving his attention.

Why was he looking at me, anyway? My hair was no doubt a mess, my lipstick non-existent, and I was wearing clothes more suitable for a courtroom than a night out.

He continued staring at me, the silence becoming unbearable.

"A model?" *That was intelligent, Lacey.*

"Yup."

"I have a friend who's a model. Maybe you know her. Riley Wolfe?"

Riley was hardly my friend, but I had to say something.

"Oh, sure. I know Riley. She's gorgeous. Very talented. No one can navigate the runway quite like she can. She's as close as we have to an old-school supermodel these days. The way she moves is like a reincarnation of Cindy Crawford or Naomi

Campbell, except with her own twist. She'll be one of the classics. Amazing."

I nodded. Why did I bring up a gorgeous woman again?

"How is she doing?"

"Fine." As far as I could tell. Though I did think she was hiding something that she'd wanted to tell me but chickened out.

"That's good to hear. I'm glad she's doing better."

Better? So Riley *did* have some issues, one of which was no doubt anorexia or bulimia. I couldn't ask Fox about any of this, though. I'd said Riley was a friend, and if she were truly a friend, I'd know about whatever he was talking about.

Plus, this was so none of my business.

Our drinks arrived, which gave me something to do besides sit there saying nothing. I took a sip and gulped back a choke. The flavor was smoky and intense.

And damned good.

Why had I never tried bourbon before? To hell with cosmos and all those other frou-frou drinks I usually preferred. From here on, I was a bourbon girl.

"What brand do you suppose they gave us?" Fox asked me.

I had no idea. This was my first foray into bourbon. "I don't know," I said, "but it's really good."

"That it is. Nice and smooth. I'll bet it's a boutique bourbon from upstate. Some of those are amazing."

"Oh, yeah."

"What's your favorite?"

I took a sip. "This one, as of right now." Good save.

"Here, here." He clinked his glass to mine and took a sip.

I took another. Wowza. This was good stuff.

Fox signaled the server. "We're going to need another round here. I can tell already." Then he smiled at me. "This night is just getting started."

23

ROCK

"What can I get for you?"

"Bourbon on the rocks," I said.

"Any particular bourbon?"

"The first one the bartender can get his hands on works for me."

The waitress laughed. "You're the second person tonight who's said that to me. You realize that's an excuse for Johnny to give you the fifteen-year Pappy's. It's sixty-five dollars a shot."

"Whatever." Why should I worry about money now that I was CEO of Wolfe Enterprises? I was more interested in something else. "Who else said that to you?"

She nodded toward the left. "A lady over at that table."

I stared in that direction to a table in the corner. Three men and two women, one of whose back was to me but I'd recognize her anywhere. She was wearing the same jacket she'd had on during dinner, and the man sitting next to her had his hand on her forearm.

Jealousy lit up within me.

The server took Roy and Reid's orders while I continued to grit my teeth over that slug touching Lacey's arm.

Before the waitress left, I signaled her. "Just out of curiosity, did the bartender give the woman at the other table a sixty-five-dollar glass of bourbon?"

She laughed. "He sure did. Two, actually, as they ordered another. Four altogether, because the guy next to her ordered the same thing. They're going to be surprised when their bill comes."

I chuckled.

Reid looked over at the other table. "That's Lacey Ward. I didn't take her for a bourbon drinker, and certainly not an expensive bourbon drinker." He smiled. "You know what? Change my order to that bourbon, too. It's not usually my drink, but I'd like to try it."

Even Roy spoke up. "Mine too. You're going to have a good night tip-wise."

"Sure thing." She smiled and headed toward the bar.

I couldn't help chuckling softly to myself. Pretty boy with his hand on Lacey would no doubt get stuck with the bill. Served him right for touching her.

Reid was saying something, but all I could do was seethe at that jerk touching Lacey.

My Lacey.

Hell, no. Not my Lacey. She'd made that clear earlier, and I didn't want her anyway. At least not in any serious way.

The waitress—her name tag said Lisa—returned with our drinks.

"That's some quick service," Reid said jovially.

"When I get an order worth a couple hundred dollars, I step on it." She set our drinks down on the table. "Should I order you another round?"

"Let's see if we like it first," Reid said.

"You can get me another," I said. "Bourbon may not be my brothers' first choice, but it's mine."

"You got it, sweetheart." She winked.

Lisa was a pretty woman, curvy with red hair and freckles. Luscious lips that, any other time, I'd be dreaming about kissing.

Not tonight.

My thoughts were focused on the woman in the corner whose back was to me. She didn't even know my brothers and I had come into the bar. Hadn't turned around once.

And that damned guy's hand was still on her arm.

"What do you think, Rock?" Reid asked.

"What do I think about what?"

"What we're talking about."

"I have no idea what you're talking about."

"Christ. Haven't you been listening at all?"

"I guess not." No, I'd been watching the back of Lacey's head. Her arm being fondled by a pretty boy.

"He's been staring at Dad's lawyer," Roy said.

"You have the hots for Lacey," Reid said. "Can't say I blame you."

A sudden bolt jerked through me. Reid was known as a womanizer, was in all the celebrity magazines with different women on his arm. Had he and Lacey... Man, I couldn't even finish the sentence in my head.

All of a sudden I wanted to throttle my little brother into oblivion.

"Have you and she..."

He shook his head.

Damned lucky for him.

"Never had the pleasure," he said. "But I wouldn't kick her out of bed."

His comment made me seethe again, but I fought against it. "Do you happen to know any of those people she's with?"

"Only one. The guy on her right is Fox Monroe. He's a model. Riley introduced us once."

So pretty boy was a model. Made sense. And no pretty boy model was a match for me. I slid my chair backward. "I'm going over there."

"But we came here to talk about—"

I stopped listening to Reid. Rage boiled under my skin as I stalked toward the table in the corner. What would I say? I had no idea.

Right before I arrived, though, Lisa swooped in and laid their check on the table.

Pretty boy grabbed it. "Let me." Then his eyes widened as he looked at what must have been an exorbitant number he hadn't expected.

Lacey turned toward him and said something I couldn't make out. Her back was still toward me.

Pretty boy shook his head and grabbed his wallet out of his pants.

And I laughed uproariously.

A little louder than I'd meant to.

Lacey turned around, her beautiful eyes wide. "Rock! What are you doing here?"

24

LACEY

Rock Wolfe looked delicious. He always looked delicious, and I was already horny.

And a little bit drunk.

Three bourbons were a lot for me, apparently.

"Having a drink with my brothers. I thought I'd come over and say hi." He turned to Fox. "Mr. Monroe, I'd know you anywhere. Your face is all over the place. I'm Rock Wolfe. You probably know my sister, Riley."

Rock knew a male model? He had to be joking, and his tone was freakishly fanboy. So *not* Rock Wolfe. But he seemed to recognize Fox. *Was* his face everywhere? I hadn't recognized him. I doubted Rock followed men's fashion. But what the hell did I know?

"Yes, nice to meet you," Fox said, standing and taking Rock's outstretched hand. "I do know Riley. She's a wonderful model."

"Yes, she is. You look a little surprised. Is everything okay?"

Huh? Fox *had* looked a little unprepared for the check he'd offered to cover.

"Lisa told us you were drinking the fifteen-year Pappy's. So are we. It's smooth stuff."

Fox cleared his throat. "Yes, it is. Worth every penny." He slid a credit card on top of the check and pushed it toward the edge of the table.

Rock was still chuckling. How expensive was that bourbon, anyway? It would be rude to look at the check. I unhooked my purse from the back of my chair and fumbled for my wallet. I was the one who'd mimicked Rock's words and made the order. I'd had no idea the bartender would give us something ridiculously expensive. "I'll be happy to cover half."

Fox pushed my hand away. "I wouldn't think of it. I never let a lady pay."

"He's a high-paid model, Lacey," Rock said. "He can afford it."

Okay, that was enough. Rock was being an ass, as usual. I stood, but clumsily lost my balance. Rock's strong arms steadied me.

Damn that spark that hurtled through me at his touch.

"Easy, baby," he said. "How much have you had to drink?"

"Just three bourbons." Or did we have four?

"And a couple glasses of wine at dinner, if I remember correctly."

Fox stood then. "You had dinner with *him*?"

I opened my mouth, but only a squeak came out.

"Easy, pretty boy," Rock said. "It was just happenstance. But I'll tell you one thing that's for certain. Only one person is taking this lady home, and it isn't you."

Again I tried to speak but couldn't. I hadn't been planning to go anywhere with Fox. He was way too young for me and not my type at all. I didn't go for the fine-featured handsome types. No. I was much more interested in rugged handsome, strong handsome—kind of like the man who was ushering me out of the bar.

I didn't plan on going anywhere with him, either.

"Rock, I'm fine. Let me go. I'll get a cab."

"You're not going anywhere alone. You're completely obliterated."

"I don't get obliterated on three drinks." Or was it four? Even as I said the words, I was having trouble walking, and my vision was a little blurry. Good thing I hadn't driven.

Oh, wait. I didn't own a car.

"Are you used to bourbon?"

"Well...not really."

"Then why were you drinking it?"

"I don't know." But I did. I drank it because he drank it. Because Rock Wolfe had taken over my mind and apparently my body. I'd said the exact thing he'd said to the server at dinner.

Now I was paying for it.

And poor Fox was paying a— "How much is that bourbon, anyway?" I asked Rock, as he flagged down a cab.

"Sixty-five dollars a shot."

"Sixty-five dollars!" Nausea edged up my throat. I was going to be sick. Really sick. Fox and I had each had three, possibly four. And Paul and the others had joined us on the last round after we both sang its praises.

"Oh my God..."

"He'll get over it, Lace."

"But that's..." My mind wasn't calculating rapidly. Too much booze. "Over six hundred dollars for what we drank. Plus the other drinks." I rubbed my temples. Already a headache was forming. From the bourbon or leaving Fox with such a bill, I wasn't sure.

All because I'd mimicked Rock's words.

"Easy." Rock helped me into a cab and then slid in beside me. "Are you going to throw up?"

I rubbed my forehead. "No. I don't know. Maybe."

"Not in my cab," the driver said.

"We'll pay for any damage if she does," Rock said. "And I promise you a nice tip."

My stomach churned. I'd never be able to look Paul or Fox in the eye again. I'd have to pay Fox back somehow. *Oh my God.*

"Where to?" the driver asked.

"Where do you live?" Rock asked me.

But my mind wasn't working. I opened my mouth but all that came out was babbling.

Rock chuckled, grabbed my purse from me, pulled out my wallet, and looked at my driver's license. He gave the cabbie the address, and the car lurched forward.

Nearly taking the contents of my stomach with it.

"Easy," Rock said again, wrapping his strong arm around my shoulders. "Lean on me. We'll be there soon."

I swallowed back my nausea and nuzzled into his strong shoulder. He smelled so good. Still like pine and the outdoors, even though he'd been in an office all day. Or so I surmised. He'd have to update his wardrobe.

The cab driver jerked to a stop in front of my building, and I heaved against Rock but managed to keep everything down.

"Damn it!" Rock said. "Do you have to drive like a maniac?"

"You're not from New York, are you, man?" the cabbie said.

"No, I'm not. Not in this lifetime, anyway. But unfortunately I guess I'd better get used to it. Come on, Lacey." Rock helped me out of the cab, and then gave the driver a few bills. "Let's get you home."

Somehow, I managed to walk past the doorman and get into the building. Then Rock and I took the elevator to my small apartment on the top level. By the time we made it to my door, I was ready to give up and fall asleep in the hallway.

I fumbled with the keys again, until he took them from me and had the door unlocked in a matter of seconds. He guided me inside my apartment.

I turned to him.

He was so damned gorgeous!

But he had to leave now. I was about ready to blow big chunks, and I really didn't want Rock Wolfe to witness it. "Thanks for getting me home."

"Not a problem. Show me your bedroom—"

"Oh, no. Not going there tonight."

"So I can help you get to bed. You could actually let me finish a sentence, Lacey.

"Nope. I can take care of myself—" I ran into the bathroom, slamming the door behind me. I barely got the cover of the toilet up before I vomited.

Let me die now.

Two more heaves and my stomach was empty of the two hundred dollars plus worth of bourbon I'd put away. Not to mention the dinner I'd shared—and paid for—with Rock.

At least I felt a little bit better. But not much.

I fumbled for a bottle of ibuprofen in my medicine cabinet and swallowed four, followed by a glass of lukewarm water. Blech. But at least I probably wouldn't wake up with a headache. Then I brushed my teeth furiously and gargled some mouth-wash, which almost made me hurl again.

Rock pounded on the door, to the tune of a vibrating jack-hammer. "You okay in there?"

I wasn't the quietist puker in the world. If I could have disap-peared into thin air, I would have. How could I look him in the eye? Didn't matter, I assured myself. Rock and I were over. No way would I be going to bed with that douchebag again.

Though he *had* gotten me safely home.

Why did he keep doing things that endeared him to me?

But no. I was hardened. I splashed some cold water on my face and wiped the mascara raccoon eyes off with a cotton pad. Then I drew in a deep breath and opened my bathroom door.

There he stood, looking as magnificent as he had at dinner earlier.

"You okay?" he said again. "Can I get you anything?"

I let out a slow breath. "Just your absence. I'm going to bed."

"Hey, Lacey. Don't be that way."

"Look." I pushed him out of my way. "I have no intention of sleeping with you again. But even if I did, I am in no shape to get busy tonight. I'm exhausted—"

"And sick," he added.

"I *was* sick." Why deny it? He'd heard everything. "I'm okay now."

He chuckled. "That's a lot of money you just flushed down the toilet."

Ugh, don't remind me. "So if you'll be on your way," I said, "I'll be getting to bed. I have a busy workday tomorrow." Just thinking of my nine o'clock meeting had my heart pounding harder and my tummy doing somersaults.

"Let me tuck you in. I want to make sure you're all right."

My heart blipped a bit, but I was still not in the mood. I just needed my bed. I pushed him toward the door. "Please. Just go. Thank you for everything, but just go."

25

ROCK

I didn't want to go. The fact surprised me more than a little, given I knew she wasn't up for any kind of romp. I was feeling something new, something I wasn't altogether comfortable with. I wanted to take care of her, sleep next to her, and hold her. Get her to the bathroom if she got sick again.

This was so not me, and it was freaking me out.

What was the best thing to do, then?

Leave, like she'd asked me to.

But not before I got her into bed—to sleep.

I reached for her hand. "Come on. Let's get you to bed."

"I told you—"

"Do you really think I'm the kind of guy who would take advantage of a woman in your current state? Give me a little credit."

A giant yawn split her face, and I took her hand and led her through an open door that I assumed was her bedroom. I smiled. The bed was unmade, and laundry was strewn about. It was endearing. Most women I knew were such tidy freaks.

"Do you want to wash your face?" I asked.

"Too tired." She took off her blazer and hung it over a chair.

Then she turned to me, her cheeks red. "I'm going to get undressed now."

I chuckled. "If I see anything I haven't seen before, I'll scream."

"Not funny. Get out."

"Seriously? Lace, I'm trying to help you here."

"I am perfectly capable of undressing and putting on pajamas without your help."

I sighed. "Fine." I stepped outside the room.

About ten minutes passed. I sneaked back into the room, only to find her prone on her bed, topless, but her skirt and hose still on, snoring softly. I smiled and eased them off of her, leaving her only in her undies. Then I covered her, tucking the sheets around her gorgeous body.

I ought to get a medal for this. But strangely, as beautiful and enticing as she was, I still had no desire to take advantage of her. Odd.

I left the room, leaving the door open just a crack. Then I walked to the door of the apartment to leave.

"Crap," I said out loud as I looked at the door. I didn't have a key, and if I left, I'd have to leave the deadbolt unlocked. I knew enough about New York to know that was never a good idea. I could take Lacey's key, but what if she didn't have another?

No way was I leaving her unprotected.

I sighed, eyeing her living room. Her brocade couch looked mildly comfortable. Good thing, because that was clearly where I'd be spending the night. A crocheted afghan was folded on a nearby recliner. Hmm. That might be a better place to sleep. I removed my shoes, jeans, and shirt and settled in, pulling the afghan over me.

～

SUNLIGHT STREAMED IN THROUGH A WINDOW, waking me. For a moment I was disoriented. Where was I? Then I realized, as I cracked my neck. Lacey's living room. Her recliner. I stretched my arms over my head and yawned. I felt good. I'd slept strangely well for being on a recliner all night. I checked my wrist. Six a.m. Lacey would probably be up soon.

I stood and pulled my jeans on and then made my way into her small kitchen. A coffeemaker sat on the countertop. I ground some beans and started a pot, and then I looked around for something to make her for breakfast. She'd no doubt be achy and tired and still a little nauseated. Maybe just a piece of toast and some scrambled eggs. I got what I needed out of the refrigerator and began, when Lacey walked in, wearing nothing but her lacy red panties.

Her tits looked luscious, and her hair was a mass of unruly waves. She didn't seem to notice me at first as she ambled toward the coffeemaker and grabbed the carafe, nearly dropping it.

"Easy." I eased it out of her hands.

She jumped, nearly losing her footing. I steadied her.

"Why are you here?" She rubbed her temples. "Oh, God. We didn't..."

"No. We didn't. No offense, honey, but you weren't in any shape to do much of anything."

She looked down and clasped her arms over her chest. Too bad to cover up such great tits.

"Nice try, but I've seen them before."

"Just...leave, please, Rock."

"After I just made you a breakfast of champions? That's no way to treat me."

"I never asked you to—"

"Hey. There was no way for me to leave and to lock your deadbolt, so I stayed."

"Where did you..." She rubbed her temples again. "God. My head."

"In the recliner."

She eyed me. "You look so..."

She was staring at me like I was a side of prime beef. I couldn't help flexing my pecs just a little.

Then she turned around and ran back into her room.

Maybe I didn't look so great after all.

I set two plates on her small table and poured myself a cup of black coffee. The only way to drink it. After I cleaned my plate and she hadn't returned, I stood and walked into her room to check on her.

The bathroom door was shut. I knocked softly. "Baby? You all right?"

"Fine. Just go, please."

"You need some breakfast."

"Not hungry."

"It will make you feel better.

"Ugh. No, it won't."

"How about some strong coffee?"

"No. Please. Just go."

I didn't want to leave her alone, but what choice did I have? It was daylight now, so I didn't feel quite as bad about leaving her without deadbolting her door. She had a regular lock as well.

I went back out to the living room to gather my clothes, when my phone buzzed against my thigh.

26

LACEY

I wasn't nauseated. Just embarrassed with a hammering headache.

He looked like a god standing in my kitchen, spatula in hand, with nothing on but wrinkled jeans.

He'd been a perfect gentleman last night, which went against what I assumed to be his nature.

Maybe I was wrong about him.

Probably not, but I could hope.

I couldn't believe he'd seen me at my worst. There'd be no more passionate romps with Rock Wolfe. He'd never come near me again. Probably just as well. He was a complication I didn't need in my life. I was beginning to develop feelings for him, and he was not the type of man to fall in love with any woman. Plus, he had his work cut out for him at his father's—*his*—company.

I swallowed several ibuprofen tablets and turned on the shower. While I was waiting for it to heat up, I went back to the kitchen and poured myself a cup of the coffee Rock had made. My breakfast sat on the table across from his clean plate. I smiled. Just like a man. Couldn't be bothered to take his plate into the kitchen. I picked up both plates and inhaled. It actually smelled good. I took a bite of the eggs.

Cold, but nice. Rock didn't strike me as much of a cook, but then again, he'd lived alone in Montana for years. A man had to eat.

I took a few more bites and downed the coffee. Time for the shower. I had a freaking nine o'clock appointment.

I DRANK two more cups of coffee once I got to the office, only to have my nine o'clock cancel on me. A wave of relief swept through me. I told Charlie to hold all my calls and decided to take the day to catch up on emails and other stuff. No billing today. I didn't have it in me.

I'd answered my fourth email when Charlie peeked her head in. "Sorry, Lacey, but there's a Detective Morgan here to see you."

I groaned. "What for?"

"Something regarding the Derek Wolfe investigation."

There went my headache again. Derek Wolfe was determined to haunt me from beyond the grave. "Very well. Send him in."

Charlie led in a balding blond man.

"Ms. Ward, I'm Detective Hank Morgan." He held out his hand. "Thank you for seeing me."

"Not at all. Have a seat. What can I do for you?"

"I'm investigating the murder of Derek Wolfe. I understand you were his attorney?"

"One of them. I'm a trusts and estates attorney. I wrote and am in the process of probating his will."

"Did you think it was odd that he mandated that his oldest son move to New York to run his company?"

"I didn't think it was the best decision. I tried to talk him out of it."

Detective Morgan laughed.

"What's funny about that?"

"Just the idea of you trying to talk Derek Wolfe out of anything."

"Did you know Mr. Wolfe?" I asked.

"No, ma'am. I've just heard a lot about him. I imagine talking him out of it didn't work."

"I assume you're aware of the contents of the will, so you already know the answer to that question."

"I meant no disrespect," he said. "You're just..."

"A woman? A young woman?"

"Well...yeah."

"Mr. Wolfe trusted me with the writing and execution of his will. I was a woman when that happened."

His cheeks reddened. Typical male chauvinist cop. Probably been on the force for thirty years or more.

"I meant no disrespect," he said again.

"Why are you here, Detective?" I rubbed my temples. The sooner he left, the sooner I could see if I could get an appointment this afternoon with my massage therapist.

"We're questioning anyone who might have had a motive to kill Mr. Wolfe."

Say what? "Surely you don't think I had any motive. What would I have to gain?"

"That's what I'm here to find out."

Really not the day for this. My brain was throbbing. "In that case..." I picked up my phone. "Charlie? Could you see if Dane Richards is available? I'll need him to come in here. Thanks." I put down the receiver.

"Who is Dane Richards?"

"I'm surprised you don't know. He's one of my partners. He's also the best criminal defense attorney in the state."

"Ms. Ward, I think you've got the wrong idea. This isn't a formal interrogation. There's no need for you to have an attorney present."

"I see that a little differently than you do. If Mr. Richards isn't available, we'll be tabling this discussion for now."

My phone buzzed, and I picked it up. "Yeah, Charlie?"

"Dane's in a deposition, Lace."

"Okay. Thanks." I hung up and turned back to Morgan. "Mr. Richards isn't available, so I won't be answering any questions today." At least not until the jackhammer inside my head calmed down.

"Ms. Ward, as I told you, there's no need—"

"That determination is mine to make, Detective, not yours. I'll be happy to assist you in any way possible...when my attorney is present. Now, if you don't mind, I have work to do."

He made no move to stand.

Seconds passed.

"I can have you removed."

"By calling the police? I *am* the police, Ms. Ward. And by not cooperating—"

"I have told you I'm perfectly willing to cooperate, Detective Morgan. Just not right now. If this is not a formal interrogation."

"But—"

"Am I under arrest?"

"No, but—"

I stood, walked to my door, and opened it. "Then good day, Detective."

That finally got him. He stood and walked toward me. "This isn't over."

"It is for now."

As soon as he was out the door, I shut it, and then slid down the wood panel until I was sitting, my back against the door. My head continued to pound. I pulled my hair out of its ponytail and massaged my scalp, to no avail.

Never again was I drinking bourbon.

I understood why the police wanted to talk to me. I would be considered a "person of interest" in the case, since I'd had contact with the victim in the days right before his murder. I'd written his will. I had no problem being questioned. But in my current state, I wasn't about to answer anything without an attorney present. In fact, I'd be talking to Dane as soon as he was available to make sure he could attend any further meetings I had with Detective Morgan.

I made my way back to my desk and buzzed Charlie. I didn't usually ask her to do personal stuff for me, but today I needed it. "I need a spa day," I said. "Book me for the afternoon anywhere that's available."

27

ROCK

After getting Reid's call while I was still at Lacey's, I ran back to my hotel for a shower and barely made it to an impromptu meeting with marketing.

After that, I had an appointment with Dieter in my office. One suit was ready—money definitely talked—so that would be my uniform until the rest of my clothes were complete.

Oddly, there was a full-length mirror in my father's—*my*—office. Derek Wolfe must have spent a lot of time looking at his own reflection. Narcissus himself. The man was so busy being in love with himself that he couldn't see that the rest of the world hated him. I didn't envy Detective Morgan. Figuring out who might have offed my father wouldn't be like looking for a needle in a haystack. More like a needle in a landfill.

I stared at myself in my new and custom-tailored gray pinstripe.

It was no leather vest and chaps, but I didn't look half bad.

I walked toward my desk when my door opened abruptly.

I rolled my eyes when I saw who it was. "Hello, Mother."

"We need to talk, Rock."

"How did you get past Carla and Jarrod?"

"I ignored them, as I always have."

"From now on, you won't ignore them. This is my office."

"Only because your father insisted you be in charge. I have no idea why."

"Neither does anyone else, but you'll give me the same respect he commanded. You'll go through Carla or Jarrod the next time, or I'll have you banned from the building."

My mother smiled, and saccharine oozed from her lips. "I'm your mother. You won't ban me."

"My mother? In a biological sense only, Connie. You stopped being my mother the day I found out you were letting Derek Wolfe molest your only daughter. Your *baby* daughter."

"I never knew anything about that. Rock, whatever you think you saw—"

"What I *know* I saw," I said icily. What I also over*heard*. Apparently she wasn't aware of the latter.

"Whatever you *think* you saw," she repeated. "But the man *was* a bastard. You'll get no argument from me."

"Don't come in here all high and mighty and act like you don't know what went on. Why I got sent away. You not only sold out your only daughter, you sold out your oldest son."

Saccharine smile again. "Please, Rock. I didn't come here to argue with you."

Of course she hadn't. I already knew why she was here. Money. Her gravy train had ended with my father's death. "Spit it out, Connie. How much will it cost to get you out of my hair?"

"Really, do you think—"

"How fucking much?" I said through gritted teeth.

She sighed. "Half a million a month. I deserve no less for putting up with that man as long as I did."

I rolled my eyes. Well worth it not to have to deal with the one and only Mrs. Wolfe. "I'll have to run it by Reid and Roy."

"You're in charge here. Not them."

"Really? They like you a lot more than I do, Connie. I'd think you'd want their input."

The wheels were cranking in her head. I could almost see the cogs interlocking and then disengaging.

"Actually, Rock, I'd rather Reid and Roy didn't know about this arrangement."

I cocked my head. Interesting. "All right. Then why should I consent to give you anything? This business belongs equally to them and to Riley."

"I'm not asking for you to pay me out of business assets."

I lifted my eyebrows. "So this is to be between you and me. It's not Derek's money you want at all, is it? It's mine."

She smiled. Again with the saccharine. "Why should I care where the money comes from? Green is green. It all spends the same."

"Then why wouldn't you want your other children to know? You're confusing me, Connie, and I'm loath to give out money when I don't have all the facts."

"I really didn't want to resort to this, Rock."

"Resort to what?"

One more saccharine smile. "Let's just forget about it. Give me what I came for, and you won't hear a peep from me again."

"Not so fast. First you're going to tell me why you don't want my siblings to know you're asking for money. Surely they wouldn't find any of this surprising."

Connie Wolfe was up to something. Something that was no good.

"Rock...please."

"You come to me. The child who probably hates you the most, except possibly for your only daughter, whose father you let molest her."

"Leave your sister out of this."

"I'm sure Riley despises you as much as I do. Reid and Roy

are your only hope, but you don't want them to know you're here asking me for money. What are you up to?"

I'd been away too long. Or maybe it wouldn't have mattered. I'd never be as hateful and devious as my mother. Reid and Roy knew something. Something they were going to tell me.

"Get out!" I spat.

"Rock, I—"

"You won't get a penny from me, Mother. At least not until I know what you're hiding."

"I'm not hiding anything."

"Sell it to the Air Force. Do you really think I'm going to hand over money without consulting my brothers? I don't know shit about this business. I don't even know where all the assets are. I have zero in my bank accounts right now. Anything you get would have to come from the business funds."

"Rock—"

The phone on my desk buzzed. "We're done here, Mother." I punched the button. "Yeah?"

"Mr. Wolfe," Carla said, "Sergio is here."

"I don't know any Sergio."

"Your stylist. He's here to do your hair and eyebrows."

My eyebrows? No one was touching my eyebrows. "Tell him I'm busy."

"Mr. Wolfe made the appointment.

"Which one?"

"The other one. Reid."

"For Christ's sake," I muttered. "Send him on in."

Someone tapped on my door. "Yeah. Enter."

A more masculine man than I expected entered. He was tall and broad with blondish hair in a ponytail. Looked mildly normal. Except for the nose ring.

Another man, this one a little more flamboyant, and a skinny woman with pink hair followed him, carrying large bags.

"Mr. Wolfe," the large man said. "Pleased to meet you. I'm Sergio of Manhattan Hair Design. It's my pleasure to be of service to you."

"Yeah, yeah. Whatever." I turned back to my mother. "If you'll excuse me. Apparently I have a haircut."

"A cut and style. Plus a shave. Full grooming," Sergio said. "Mr. Wolfe's orders."

"Mr. Wolfe doesn't have a say in what I do, but that's fine. I could use a trim." My hair fell a little below my shoulders. Probably not the best look for the CEO of Wolfe Enterprises, according to my esteemed brother.

Not that I gave a shit, but at least it would get rid of my mother.

Connie Wolfe rose, turned abruptly, and then looked over her shoulder at me. "This isn't over, Rock."

"It is for now."

She harrumphed and left my office.

My office.

Still couldn't quite wrap my head around that one.

The two assistants—one female and one male—busied themselves setting tarps down and then setting up what appeared to be a foldable barber's chair. The man flipped open a tape measure and got a little too close as he measured me from my waist to the top of my head.

I eyeballed him.

"He needs to make sure the chair is at the right height for me," Sergio explained.

"Great." I rolled my eyes.

"Take off your jacket and shirt, please," Sergio said.

I removed my jacket.

"And the shirt."

"Why?"

"You don't want to risk getting any product on your expensive clothes, do you?"

That made sense. I guessed.

I removed my shirt, and both of the assistants sucked in a breath.

"You're not wearing an undershirt?" Sergio said.

"Do I look like I'm wearing an undershirt?"

"Have a seat."

I sat in the chair, which was oddly comfortable. The male assistant held a portable sink under my head as the woman shampooed my hair. Sergio was apparently setting up his little shop.

"Hey look," I said, my eyes closed as water splashed over my head. "I'm happy to come to your shop. This seems like a lot of trouble, you bringing everything here."

"No problem at all. I'm well compensated."

I'm sure you are.

Seeing my black curls on the plastic curtain at my feet saddened me a little. No more pulling the hair back in a tie for riding my Harley.

Where was my Harley, anyway? Back in Montana. I'd get Jarrod or someone to have it shipped out right away. That was one thing I wasn't doing without. Not in a million years.

Speaking of Jarrod, he walked in. "Sorry, Mr. Wolfe. Your brother's on the phone. Says it's urgent."

28

LACEY

Brent's hands had been cast by God. No other explanation. He kneaded my muscles just firmly enough so that I felt it but it didn't hurt.

Perfection.

Just what I needed today.

My bourbon headache had finally flown the coop, and after a gazillion cups of coffee, I no longer tasted the alcohol either. Now, as I relaxed under Brent's perfect touch, I couldn't help thinking about whose touch I'd really like to be feeling.

Rock Wolfe's.

That man had gotten under my skin, and he was slowly driving me crazy.

He'd taken care of me last night, and he could have easily taken advantage of me. No. A man like Rock Wolfe wouldn't do that. He was no gentleman, but he wasn't a criminal. And not because he had any kind of high moral ground. He just wanted a woman to be completely aware of everything he was doing to her.

I smiled into the massage pillow, watching Brent's feet as he moved around the table.

Brent was a nice looking guy. He wasn't my regular therapist, but he'd worked on me a few times before. He'd asked me out once, but I turned him down, thinking it wasn't a good idea to get involved with someone who'd already seen me naked.

Now, I was hoping he might ask again.

He wasn't Rock Wolfe, but he could ease the ache between my legs when I thought about the handsome biker turned CEO.

Because Rock and I weren't going to happen, no matter how much I wanted it. He was way too busy with his new responsibilities, and he'd made it pretty clear that I was only a fuck to him. A romp with someone else could perhaps ease the loss I felt.

Though he did make me breakfast this morning...

"Time to flip over, Lacey," Brent said, holding the sheet so I could turn onto my back.

I was so relaxed, I decided to give him an eyeful.

Instead of flipping over underneath the sheet, as was customary, I pulled my arms up, grabbed the cover, and tucked it around my waist. My breasts greeted him, hard nipples and all.

"Uh...here. Sorry. Let me cover you up."

"Mmm," I said. "You don't have to."

"I'm a professional, Lacey. Besides, you made it clear the one time I asked you out that you weren't interested."

"I wasn't interested then," I said. "Maybe I am now."

"Great," he said. "But not here. I could get fired."

"I'm not going to tell on you."

He whisked the sheet over me. "No way. You're beautiful, but no way. Not here. Now close your eyes." He covered my eyes with a weighted mask.

I sighed, holding back a pout. Was I still a little bit drunk? What I'd done was not me at all, but Rock Wolfe had me feeling like a sex siren. Lacey Ward would never expose her breasts to a handsome masseur.

But she just had.

The tingle between my legs was becoming unbearable, and the soft texture of the sheet tormented my aching nipples.

I sighed again.

"Do you want me to have someone else finish your treatment?" Brent asked.

"No. Of course not. I'm sorry." I'd embarrassed him...not to mention myself. What had I been thinking?

A romp with Brent might be fun, but it wouldn't make me forget Rock Wolfe.

I had a sad suspicion nothing would.

I relaxed into the massage, and when it was over, Brent left to get me some tea and I donned the fluffy spa robe. He stood in the hallway when I exited the treatment room.

"Here's your tea." He smiled. "Now, if you want, I'm off in an hour. You want to meet me next door at the Brook Tavern?"

Why not? That would give me time to shower and sit in the steam room. "Sure. I'd like that."

AFTER MY SHOWER AND STEAM, I dressed in my office clothes, wishing I had a pair of skinny jeans, stilettos, and a camisole to meet Brent next door. Oh, well. The black slacks and burgundy blazer would have to do.

I walked over to the tavern. Brent was already there, seated at the bar. His long blond hair was pulled back in a low ponytail, and he wore a few days of light brown scruff on his face. His jeans hung loose around his nice butt, and he wore a V-neck gray T-shirt that accented his biceps and triceps nicely.

Yeah, he was pretty. Really pretty. Not Fox Monroe pretty, but beautiful in a totally masculine way.

What was I doing here again?

I didn't want a fitness model. I wanted a rugged man in leather.

I wanted Rock Wolfe.

But I smiled. I'd accepted this date. He smiled back, holding up his bottle of beer.

God. Alcohol.

I definitely hadn't thought this through.

I sat down next to him and laid my purse on the bar.

"What do you want?" Brent asked me.

To have my head examined. Yeah, not really the right thing to say. "I think I'll have sparkling water to start. You know, hydrate after a massage and all."

"Good girl." He motioned to the bartender.

I scanned the rest of the bar as I waited for my drink and zeroed in on a loner at the end of the bar. He looked familiar. Familiar but refined instead of rugged, with hair as long as Brent's but dark where my date's was light.

Of course. Roy Wolfe.

Why would he be at the Brook Tavern? This was a modest little place, hardly up to Wolfe standards.

Roy was an artist, a loner, a renowned recluse. When he looked up, I smiled at him and waved.

He nodded slightly and then looked back down at his drink.

Was he okay?

Well, not my problem.

I took a drink of my water and tried to listen to what Brent was saying, when—

It became my problem.

Rock Wolfe walked in the Brook Tavern.

Our gazes met, and I glanced peripherally at Roy, who was waving Rock over.

Rock did not look happy.

I turned my attention back to Brent. He was the person

who'd invited me, after all. Still, Rock had taken care of me last night when he didn't have to. He was a good guy. A great guy. Not the douchebag I'd thought he was when we first met.

And man, he was a god in bed.

Why was he meeting his brother at Brook Tavern? They could be having drinks at The Four Seasons or the Marriott Marquis.

I focused again on Brent, forcing myself not to turn around and watch Rock sit down next to Roy. A few seconds later, in walked Reid Wolfe. How long before Riley joined them?

"So what do you think?" Brent asked.

"I'm sorry. Think about what?"

"Dinner. We can get a table. The food's pretty good here."

"I..." I hadn't eaten since the eggs Rock had fixed for me this morning. I opened my mouth to say no, but my stomach growled. I was indeed hungry. "Sure. Why not?"

"Great. I'll go see the hostess for a table." He stood and walked away.

I stared at my sparkling water, trying desperately not to look over at Rock. When I could no longer resist, I turned my head as nonchalantly as I could. Rock was engrossed in a conversation with his brothers. He couldn't care less that I was here with another man.

I shook my head and scoffed.

Good guy? Great guy?

Nope. Douchebag after all.

29

ROCK

nother fucking pretty boy. What the hell was she doing with him?

"Rock, would you stay focused, please?" Reid said to me. "This is important."

Yeah. Important. Roy had gotten a mysterious phone call from someone claiming to have information about our father's murder.

"Did the caller threaten you?" I asked Roy.

"No. Just said he had information, like I said. Then he hung up."

"Then why should I focus? Are you worried, Roy?"

"Not worried. Just curious. Why would someone call me and tell me that but then hang up?"

"Honestly? I don't give a shit." I was glad the bastard was dead. Right now I was much more concerned with the blond dude who looked like he wanted to undress Lacey.

I tensed when he rose and walked away. Everything in me screamed to go to her, grab her, kiss her.

Before I could, though, he returned and led her to a table.

This place was a dive. I liked it. It was actually classier than most of the biker havens I hung out at home in Montana—places where I could hang my helmet, grab a beer or a bourbon, and unwind a little. Meet a woman, maybe. Go to her place and have some no-strings-attached sex, and then be home before sunup.

"Damn it, Rock. Would you quit staring at that attorney and pay attention?" Roy this time, surprisingly. He didn't usually raise his voice.

"Why did you want to meet *here*?" I asked him.

"I didn't want us to be seen. Plus they make a good burger."

"You didn't want us to be seen? Why?"

"Because this is serious, man. The two of you have never taken me seriously. Christ."

I couldn't fault Roy's observation. He was the creative type, his head in the clouds most of the time. Quiet and brooding.

Reid and I—we were doers. Take hold and get it done. That's why Reid had gone into the family business.

That's why I had left.

"You just said you weren't threatened," I said. "But I'm sorry I said I didn't give a shit."

Reid put away his phone. "Sorry."

I wanted to take Roy seriously, but I couldn't seem to take my eyes off Lacey. Damn, first that male model in the bar last night and now this? Men flocked to her like flies to honey. Of course they did. She was fucking luscious.

"The call came this afternoon," he said. "To my personal cell, not my work one, which freaks me out more than a little."

"Who has that number?"

"Just family and friends," he said.

"No acquaintances?" I asked.

"I dated a woman a while back," he said.

I guffawed. "You dated? You? Mr. Loner?"

"This is why I don't tell you two when I date at all," Roy said.

"Yeah. A year ago I dated a woman for a few months. It was low-key and it didn't last, but I gave her the number. Other than her, I don't recall giving it to anyone outside family and close friends."

"Do you trust all your friends?" Reid asked.

"Since I have all of two, yeah, I trust them."

"Any reason the woman you dated would have for giving it out?" I asked.

"Not that I know of. She's an artist too. Quiet like me."

"And maybe ripe for the picking," I said.

"Tell us again exactly what the guy said," Reid said.

"He just said he had information about Dad's murder, and then he hung up. I tried calling back but it rang and rang and rang and never went to voicemail."

"Sounds like a hoax," I said.

"Let's get the number traced, first of all," Reid said.

"Already on it," Roy replied. "It's an area code in—get this—Montana."

Chills skittered across my skin. "Montana?"

"Yeah. Weird, huh? But that's where you were when Dad was killed, and somehow, someone got your prints on the gun that did it."

"We should tell that detective who's working on the case," Reid said.

My stomach dropped. I wasn't sure why, but I didn't want Roy running to that cop with this information. "Why should we do that? Let him do his own damned job."

"He can find out if this is a hoax," Reid said.

"Look," I said. "I hope it is a hoax. But what if it's not? What if someone is trying to frame me for murdering Dad?"

"They can't frame you, Rock," Reid said. "You weren't in New York when it happened."

"I know that, and you know that. But what if they decide to say I ordered it or something?"

"Then why would your prints be on the gun?"

"Maybe it was my gun."

Reid shook his head. "Fuck. You own a gun?"

"I own several, actually." Including one identical to what had offed my father. I wasn't quite ready to voice that little tidbit yet. "I was joking, for God's sake. If my gun had offed him, the cops would know it. All of my weapons are registered to me in the state of Montana."

"Was one of them recently stolen?" Roy asked.

"I have no idea. I keep most of them in a gun safe, and I don't look at them every day. The last time I went shooting was over a month ago."

"Doesn't matter," Reid said. "If the murder weapon was registered to you, the cops would know it."

I rolled my eyes. "I think I just said that. Except that gun at the scene wasn't registered to anyone, and there's a problem with the serial number. Whatever the hell that's supposed to mean."

"So your prints are on it," Reid said, "but the gun isn't registered to anyone."

"Good job, Holmes." I rolled my eyes again.

"Chill, Rock," he said. "I'm just trying to figure this out."

"I don't want the cops involved any more than they already are," I said.

"You got something to hide?" Reid asked.

"Of course not."

I was innocent. That I knew for a fact. But there was a lot my brothers didn't know, not the least of which was that I'd tried to off my father when I was fourteen.

My mother did, though.

Fucking Mommie Dearest.

Of course. I should have known. That was why she was in my office earlier demanding one point two million dollars per year in an agreement just between us.

She was going to go to the cops with her story about my past.

Would she, though? Would she frame her own son just to get money?

I wasn't about to find out.

If she relayed that story to the cops, it wouldn't be hard for them to put together a case against me. Despite the prints, they wouldn't be able to prove I'd pulled the trigger. They could easily prove a motive, though, and make a case that I'd hired the killer to use a gun I'd handled.

First thing tomorrow, I'd make arrangements for her to be paid. Anything to keep her off my back. Besides, I knew this woman. If I didn't act soon, the price would go up. Then up some more.

Connie herself was innocent as a lamb when it came to Derek's murder. She wouldn't off her meal ticket.

But she was damned angry at whomever had, and determined enough to restore her financial status that she'd blackmail her firstborn to keep the green flowing.

Anger boiled in me. Maternal instincts were definitely missing in Connie Larson Wolfe.

Reid was nursing his whiskey, but Roy looked visibly rattled. From one phone call?

What was my reclusive brother not telling me?

I'd been gone for a while, but I could read my brother as if it were yesterday. He was hiding something.

Who was I to talk? I was hiding a ton, not the least of which was what my mother had to hold over my head.

I'd cut Roy some slack. This phone call had him seriously spooked. More spooked than it should, but I'd give him time.

"...might get cold," Reid was saying.

"Sorry...what?" I said.

"If we don't jump on this, the trail might get cold."

"Oh." I nodded. Whoever had offed Derek Wolfe had done the world a favor. I honestly hadn't cared about the trail.

Until now.

We needed to figure out who had killed my father before someone found my secrets and the cops came after me.

And I had the distinct feeling that Roy had secrets of his own.

30

LACEY

My God, this man was boring. Brent Hedstrom was delicious to look at, and his hands were works of art that could soothe the tension out of anything, but could he talk about anything other than holistic stuff? I was all about massage and yoga and even color therapy. But cupping? Crystals? Psychic healing?

Yeah, drawing the line there. No way would I pay someone to heal me with his thoughts. I didn't have that kind of spare change lying around.

I glanced over at Rock still sitting at the bar with his brothers. Rock Wolfe would be laughing his ass off at the idea of psychic healing.

And I'd be right there with him.

I held back my belly laugh, though. I was not a rude person. Besides, Brent was buying me dinner.

At least I thought he was, until he ordered a bottle of wine and then instructed the server to issue separate checks.

Seriously? I was a partner in a Manhattan law firm and could certainly afford my own dinner. And yes, I probably made ten times what he did as a massage therapist. But he had invited *me*.

I'd decided not to drink tonight, but when the server brought the wine and poured me a glass, I took a drink. Hell, I was paying for half of it, might as well get my money's worth. After one sip, though, I knew I wouldn't be finishing it. It was a German Riesling and was just too sweet for me. I'd be buying half of his bottle of wine. He'd probably cork it and take it home.

This would *so* be our only date. To think I'd actually had the idea that I'd sleep with him to get Rock off my mind.

Brent kept talking about Zen and aromatherapy and how he'd backpacked and hitchhiked through the back ass of nowhere for a year. He was a chatterbox, especially for a man. Not that men couldn't enjoy conversation, but this guy *was* the conversation.

"When I met my spirit animal, that's when I really found myself. He's with me all the time now."

For real? I nodded.

Again.

"What about you?"

I lifted my brow. Was he actually asking me to speak? I hoped he didn't think my spirit animal was with me at the moment.

"Never backpacked," I said. And never would, thanks very much.

"You should try it. It's such an amazing experience. Pure Zen."

Good thing I didn't like the wine he'd chosen, or I'd be getting drunk again tonight. Anything to make his stories more interesting. I'd just had a great massage and a shower and steam. I should be more relaxed than I was.

Probably because my body was hyperaware of the handsome man still sitting at the bar with his equally handsome brothers.

I itched to dump Brent and walk over to Rock. If he sat me down on a bar stool and took me right here in public, I doubted I'd object. I was squirming already just thinking about it.

Which meant I had to get out of here.

"I'm sorry, Brent. I've got an early day tomorrow, and I need to go over a lot of depositions tonight."

"Oh. I'm not quite finished."

Of course he wasn't. He'd been talking the entire time I was eating. "I'm sorry. I really do have to go." I flagged down our server. "Could I get my check, please?"

"No need," she said. "Both of your tabs have been paid."

I widened my eyes. "What?"

"Mr. Wolfe over at the bar took care of it."

"Mine too?" Brent lifted his brow.

"For the table," she said. "Gave me a very generous tip too. I hope I earned it."

"Of course. You've been great." I stood. "Goodbye, Brent."

"Wait," he said. "Do you know that guy?"

"He's a friend," I said.

"We should go thank him."

"Uh...I'll thank him. You go ahead and finish your dinner. I'll be sure to tell him how grateful you are." *And how cheap.*

"I thought you had to leave?"

"I do. I'll just pop over and say thanks first. Thank you for a lovely time, Brent." I tried not to sound too sarcastic.

I didn't want to interrupt Rock and his brothers, but I did need to say thank you. And to tell him never to undermine my date again. Not that I'd ever go out with Brent and his spirit animal again. Threesomes weren't my jam.

The three Wolfes were deep in conversation when I approached.

I touched Rock's hard shoulder. Tingles shot through me at the contact.

He turned to face me, his emerald eyes burning. "Lacey."

I cleared my throat. "Thank you. You didn't need to do that."

"I heard your date ask for separate checks."

"I'm perfectly able to pay for my own dinner, as you well know."

He smiled. Damn, he was gorgeous. Those green eyes twinkled like no others. He stood, took my arm, and walked me out of earshot of his brothers.

"I'm taking you to dinner tomorrow," he whispered in my ear. "And we won't be getting separate checks."

A warm shudder ran through me. His breath on my ear, his husky voice, his nearness. Everything about him put me on high alert. Everything about him made me want to forget all logic and hop into bed.

Still, I resisted. "I might be busy tomorrow night."

"Get unbusy."

My knees weakened. "I might be able to do that."

"Make it happen."

A jolt landed between my legs. "Rock, I—"

"Just do it, Lacey."

I gulped. I was never one to take orders, but everything in me screamed to take this one. To obey him without question. To cancel anything and everything to accommodate his needs, wants, and desires.

"All right, Rock." I smiled. "I guess I'll see you tomorrow."

"Wrong," he said huskily. "You'll see me tonight. As soon as I get done with those two bozos."

"But you—"

He cut me off with a quick kiss to my lips. "I won't be long."

31

ROCK

"So Dad's attorney is still your flavor of the week?" Reid said when I returned.

Lacey Ward had me hot and bothered. Damn, I could still smell her. Her fresh fragrance was all over me. For some reason, Reid's comment irked me. "I'm not you, Reid. I don't have flavors of the week."

"Sorry. Flavor of the month, then?" He gestured for the bartender to bring another round.

"No more for me, thanks," I said.

"We're not done talking about this," Roy said. "This has me freaked."

"I get that," I said, "but I don't think it's anything to worry about."

My brother didn't look convinced.

And then something dawned on me. Did Roy have anything to do with our father's murder? No. Not even in the realm of possibility. Roy was an old soul. A gentle soul.

Still, he'd taken the same beatings the rest of us had, and God only knew what had occurred after I'd left at fourteen.

Had Derek Wolfe broken Roy? Had our middle brother gone rogue?

Roy Wolfe was anything but rogue. I'd never believe he had anything to do with Dad's death. But I had to ask.

"Is there something you're not telling us, Roy?"

He shook his head as he sipped the last of his drink, not meeting my gaze. "Just the call."

"If that's it," Reid said, "I agree with Rock. We find out what we can, but there's no reason to go running to the cops or to even be worried."

"Why me?" Roy asked. "Why didn't they call one of you?"

"My guess is someone got hold of your private cell number and is playing some dumbass game," I said.

"Agreed." Reid nodded.

"I don't know. I have a weird feeling about it," Roy said. "I feel like something shady is going on."

"Something shady probably *is* going on," Reid said. "Our dad had a lot of enemies out there. But none of that has anything to do with us."

"How do you know that for sure?"

"Because the three of us aren't Dad," Reid said. "Hell, Rock hasn't even been here in over a decade. I haven't made any enemies in business. Well...not any that would resort to murder."

"But it's Dad's business. By extension, you *are* Dad." Roy set his glass down and picked up the filled one the barkeep had set in front of him.

"Don't," Reid said. "Just don't. I'm not anything like Dad."

"I don't mean it that way," Roy said. "But you were his right-hand man in the company."

"You're making me feel pretty shitty right about now, bro," Reid said. "Besides, if someone's after me, why did *you* get the call?"

Roy went pale.

Yeah, he knew something.

Was he involved?

I doubted it. Roy was a good man. But was he hiding something?

Absolutely.

"Look, Roy," I said. "You need to be straight with us. If there's something you're not telling us, we can't help you."

"Nothing," he said again—again not meeting my gaze. "Just the phone call."

I nodded, though I didn't believe him. But now was not the time to push. He wasn't in any immediate danger that I could see, and I had a hot woman waiting for me at her place. "All right. You call me if you need anything. Got it?"

"Me too, bro," Reid said. "I'm with you, Rock. I have an international conference call in about"—he checked his phone—"an hour, and I need to prepare some stuff. Let's go. You okay here, Roy?"

He took another sip of his drink. "I'm good."

"You call," I said again. "Anytime."

Roy nodded. Reid and I walked through the tavern and outside.

"What do you think?" Reid asked.

"He's hiding something," I said. "I haven't been around for a while, but he's still the brother I remember. Quiet and studious, and something's got him freaked."

"I agree. Too bad we're both busy tonight. I wouldn't mind getting him completely blasted to get him talking."

"Another time," I said, hailing a cab. "Where's Riley tonight?"

"I don't know. I just assumed he didn't call her."

"You're probably right." I got into the cab. "See you later."

～

MY COCK WAS ALREADY HARD as I rode the elevator up to Lacey's floor. What that woman did to me. She made me think things I had no right thinking.

We'd keep it casual, Lacey and I. No need to complicate things with feelings and such. I'd been there, done that, and I wasn't up for it again.

Nieves and I had shared some great times, but when it got serious between us, things fell apart, and I learned she wasn't the woman I thought she was. I had no desire to repeat it.

I knocked on the door harder than I intended.

Lacey opened the door wearing a silk robe and holding a glass of red wine.

Nothing underneath that I could see. Her nipples protruded against the red silk like two round berries.

Fuck.

"What took you so long?" she asked.

"Sorry, baby, but I'm here now." I entered, closing the door behind me.

"Wine?" she asked.

"I'm surprised you're drinking, after last night."

"Just one glass. I didn't drink any of the Riesling at dinner. Too sweet."

"Riesling's a pretty boy wine. Perfect for your date."

"Hey, don't disparage my—" She laughed and shook her head. "Who am I kidding? He was a complete flake. I accepted his invitation on a whim. He actually gave me a massage this afternoon. When my appointment was over, he asked me out, and I figured, what the hell?"

"Not a good fit, huh?"

"Let me put it this way. His spirit animal was apparently with him on our date."

"His what?"

"Don't ask. I get that he's really spiritual and all that, but he went so overboard talking about Zen this and Zen that. Then when he said his spirit animal was always with him, I knew I had to get out of there."

"Three's a crowd," I said.

"Exactly." She handed me a glass of wine. "Make yourself comfortable."

She sat down on her couch and patted the seat next to her. "Can we get to know each other a little?"

"Nothing you don't already know about me." Well, there was a lot she didn't know about me, but nothing necessary for her to know to accomplish the task at hand, which was hot monkey fucking.

"What do you do in your spare time?"

"In the last few days? I've been fucking you."

She rolled her eyes. "Come on, Rock. I'm serious."

"I'm a biker and construction worker from Montana, Lacey. You know that already. Life as I knew it a week ago is over. Now I'm an uptight businessman who wears uncomfortable clothes and has no clue what he's doing."

"Hobbies? Likes? Dislikes?"

"Hmm." I took the glass out of her hand and set it on the coffee table next to my own. "I like fucking you. I dislike talking when I could be fucking you."

She stood and let out an indignant—and really cute—huff. "Get out."

"Come on, baby. You don't answer the door wearing nothing but a short red silk robe if you don't want to fuck."

"Get out," she said again, this time angrier.

My cock was having none of that. "Don't be that way, Lace."

"If you can't even sit and talk to me for ten minutes, what kind of relationship is this?"

I stood and glided my fingers down one of her silk-clad arms. "You are beautiful, Lacey Ward. Beautiful and brilliant and a fucking spitfire in bed. I've enjoyed every second we've shared. But, sweetheart, what makes you think we have a *relationship*?"

She yanked her arm away, picked up one of the wine glasses, and splashed the wine in my face.

I gasped, closing my eyes against the burgundy attack. "Why you—"

"Get out of here!" she yelled.

I shed my suit jacket and quickly untucked my shirt, wiping my face with the tail.

"Get out," she said again, seething.

Her anger was only making me hornier. Damn it to hell. I wasn't going anywhere.

"Aren't you going to offer to help me clean up? You just ruined my—"

"Like you give a rat's ass." She shook her head. "You know, as I was sitting with Brent tonight, listening to his lame stories, I was thinking about what a good guy you are, doing all of this for your brothers and sister. How could I have been so wrong? You're a grade A asshole."

"I suppose that's better than being a grade B asshole."

"Yeah." She let out a sarcastic chuckle. "You would never settle for being less than the best asshole out there."

I laughed. "I do my best."

"Great. Now I'm serious. Get the hell out of my house."

"I don't think so." I stalked toward her.

"I mean it, Rock. Leave."

I grabbed her and pulled her to me. Her body was already heated with arousal, and I swore her nipples were poking into my soiled shirt.

"I'm warning you," she said.

"Warning me about what?" I growled. "About how turned on you are right now? Guess what? I already know."

"This isn't happening."

"All right. You win." I let her go and then removed the soiled shirt. "You got anything I can put on?"

Her gaze drifted to my chest.

Yeah, I wasn't going anywhere.

Then her gaze dropped.

To the bulge in my trousers.

"See something you like?"

"You're a complete jerk," she said. "A complete and total jerk."

"Who's hard as a fucking rock for you, Lacey."

"Damn you," she said. "Damn you, Rock Wolfe."

"I'm sure I'm already damned, baby."

Her nipples poked through the red silk even further. Fuck. I was done for. I had to have her. Had to—

I picked up my jacket from the couch and put it on. I couldn't look at her again, or I'd grab her and fuck her senseless. If she wanted me to leave, I'd better do it now.

I closed my eyes and cleared my throat. "Remember, we have a dinner date tomorrow night."

She widened her eyes. "Are you kidding me?"

"Not at all, sweetheart. You can have my dry-cleaned shirt delivered to the office."

"You are something."

I smiled. "Nothing I haven't heard before. Now I need to get the hell out of here before I bend you over the back of your couch." I headed toward the door.

But she stepped in front of me.

32

LACEY

I was nuts. Completely nuts. Rock Wolfe was being a class A douche, and I was blocking him from the door.

After I'd told him—how many times?—to get out of my apartment.

My entire body quaked. He was hard as a rock. His bulge was impressive, and I knew what lay beneath that fabric. I knew it. And I wanted it.

Maybe we didn't have a relationship. Maybe we'd *never* have a relationship. I could at least fuck him. I was already ripe for the picking. I had to squeeze my thighs together to ease the ache in my pussy.

I felt so empty, and I longed to be filled.

By Rock Wolfe.

This was a guy I'd let screw me in my office after I'd known him for about two minutes. Lacey Ward didn't do things like that.

Except that she did.

When Rock Wolfe was involved.

I wanted him. Ached for him. I'd never known a longing so

intense. It scared the hell out of me, especially when the object of my longing was such a shithead.

God, but he was a gorgeous shithead—a gorgeous shithead who knew how to rock my world in bed.

He'd had a haircut. I missed his longer locks, but now he looked like he could be walking the runway wearing the latest Dolce & Gabbana. Or sailing in a black speedo in a cologne ad. David Gandy had nothing on Rock Wolfe.

Those shoulders, so bronze and toned, so broad. His biceps large, but not from the gym. I'd bet Rock Wolfe had never set foot in one. No, his muscles came from honest labor in the outdoors. He'd earned them. His forearms were corded and sexy. And that chest...

Without thinking, I walked to him and brushed his jacket over his shoulders, letting it land in a puddle on the floor.

His skin was warm.

Hot.

That chest, those abs, and the trail of black hair leading to...
The bulge.

"You're giving me some serious mixed signals here. Do you still want me to get out?"

I licked my lower lip and then bit it gently.

No. I didn't want him to get out. I wanted to drop to my knees, take that cock out and deep throat him until he couldn't stand it.

"Lace?"

That voice. Low and husky and seductive to a fault.
I'm going to do it.

I dropped to my knees and freed his erection, letting his trousers fall over his hips and brushing his boxer briefs down his rock-hard thighs.

"I'll take that as a no," he said gruffly with a swift inhalation.

His dick was a work of art. A shade darker than the rest of

him, it was curved only slightly upward with two blue veins marbling around it. A drop of fluid oozed from the tip. I darted my tongue out and licked it off.

"Fuck, baby," he groaned.

Yes, he was a beautiful man. Every part of him was physically appealing. Every. Single. Part.

I'd already thrown caution to the wind tonight. I would suck this gorgeous cock, and then I'd let him do whatever he wanted to me.

Whatever. He. Wanted.

He wanted no relationship? I'd give him no relationship. But first, I'd give him a night he'd never forget.

And then I'd say goodbye to Rock Wolfe.

Forever.

I darted my tongue out once more and twirled it over his cockhead. He groaned again, and I couldn't help smiling. He might be a jerk, but right now, I held a bit of power over him.

I was going to revel in that power.

I teased him with tiny licks and kisses all the way down his shaft until I reached his balls. I gave them a quick nip and then went back to his dick.

I wrapped my lips around his knobby head and applied some suction. He groaned again.

I continued to tease him this way, moving my hands to his hips to hold steady. But I was going to be in control here, at least while I sucked him.

He tasted like cinnamon and salt, and he smelled like hot musky man. My senses were on overload. I closed my eyes for a moment, erasing the visual to concentrate on the spicy scent, the salty flavor, and the feel of his hardness in my mouth. I could only take little more than half of him before he nudged the back of my throat.

"Baby, you suck cock like a champion."

I smiled in my mind since my lips were otherwise occupied. Oh, yeah. I was going to make this one night he would never forget. Then, when I refused to see him again, maybe he would feel a slight twinge of the hurt I felt when he said there was no chance of a relationship.

Revenge wasn't normally my style. What the hell? I was enjoying every minute of this. We would both be satisfied. Just because I intended never to be with him again after tonight didn't mean anything. We would still enjoy ourselves this last time.

I wanted to make him come in my mouth, but I didn't want the night to be over. I choked back a laugh, my mouth still full of cock. What was I thinking? This was Rock Wolfe. Not some inexperienced teenager. I'd bet he had two or three orgasms in him per night at least.

Yeah, he was going to come in my mouth.

I gripped him at his base, adding my hand so that the sensation would be that I was taking him all the way. I increased my rhythm.

"Slow down, baby."

I increased my pace.

"Now. Don't want to come yet."

Oh, then he was *definitely* going to come. I continued plunging my mouth over him, my hand adding to the sensation. Once. Twice. One more time... And then—

"Damn!" He exploded.

I pulled back so I could feel every spurt, let his essence trickle over my tongue, flow down my throat.

I sat back, licking my lips and smiling.

"I think you're pretty pleased with yourself right about now," Rock said, his voice breathless.

I said nothing. Just kept smiling.

"You stay right there on the floor, baby. I'm going to suck that pussy dry."

He spread my legs roughly, and I gasped when he lifted me —yes, he lifted me—off the floor and secured my knees over his shoulders. I was completely bared to him, my pussy hanging around his neck.

He breathed in audibly. "You smell great, baby. And you look beautiful. All wet and swollen and glistening. I'd like to eat you like this, but I don't want all the blood to flow into your head. So I'm going to take you into your bedroom, lay you on your bed, and then I'm going to eat that cunt until you can't take it anymore."

He walked gently, more gently than I expected. Seeing everything upside down was disorienting, but soon we were in the bedroom and I was on the bed, flat on my back. He spread my legs and lifted my hips.

"Beautiful," he said softly.

I let out a blissful sigh.

He gazed down at my pussy for what seemed like an eternity. I watched him, his green eyes burning. He was enjoying this. Enjoying the tease. But the look in his eyes... Was he also enjoying just staring at me?

"Beautiful," he said again.

Yes, apparently he was enjoying it.

I bit my lip, keeping begging words from tumbling out of my mouth. A few more seconds passed, and finally I could hold out no longer. "Please. Please, eat my pussy."

He met my gaze, and I shivered all over. His green eyes were heavy-lidded. Seductive. He knew what he was doing to me, but I was also doing it to him. The thought made me happy.

Something about him. Why was I so attracted to such a jerk? Yes, he was physically a very appealing specimen, and clearly we had amazing sexual chemistry.

But I was feeling something more. Something I didn't want to be feeling.

Before I could dwell on it too much longer, he clamped his mouth onto my pussy.

And that was all it took. I soared into a climax. Just from the touch of his lips on my most sensitive tissue.

He groaned, the vibration spurring me further into climax.

I bit my lip to keep from crying his name.

Couldn't give him that satisfaction. Couldn't—

"Yes, Rock! Yes!"

He moved his mouth away for a second. "Good, baby. That's good. Come. Come for me." Then clamped it back down, sucking on my clit.

I grabbed fistfuls of my comforter and arched my back. The sensation was all too much, all too—

Two of his thick fingers breached my heat, massaging my G-spot, and I flew again.

Two orgasms in about two minutes.

Crazy.

He continued to groan as he devoured me.

"I could eat you all night, baby," he said against my folds. "All fucking night."

Fine by me. Though I'd be a puddle of butter by morning. Which also sounded fine.

He tugged on my labia as he continued to fuck me with his fingers. I closed my eyes, reveling in the intensity, the sensation, the emotion swirling through me.

Emotion I didn't want.

I tumbled into another climax and then another.

Another.

Another.

Until my body sank into the bed.

"More," he said. "Give me one more."

"Can't."

"*Can.*" He swirled his tongue over my clit and pressed his finger into a spot so deep that I rocketed skyward once more.

So intense, so... God, like nothing I'd ever felt before. I sank down this time, sank into the depths of the ocean where nothing existed except the two of us and this orgasm.

When I finally stopped spasming, I lay limp, whimpering.

"That was hot, baby," he said. "Did you know you could squirt?"

"I... What?"

"Squirt. A G-spot orgasm. I've never been with a woman who could do it."

"I... What?"

He laughed and crawled up next to me. "You've never squirted before?"

"Not that I know of," I said weakly.

"I'd love to talk about it some more, but I really need to get my cock inside you."

"Yeah. Okay."

He climbed on top of me and thrust into me.

33

ROCK

Home. Sweet. Home.

Damn.

Damn it all to hell.

This woman was pure paradise with heaven between her legs.

She seemed a little dazed. I'd be dazed too after that many orgasms in a row. Women didn't know how lucky they were.

The squirting had been a major turn-on. I'd seen it in the occasional porn flick—I honestly didn't watch a lot of porn—but had never encountered it in real life, despite my pretty impressive track record with the ladies.

That said, I wouldn't mind encountering it again and again.

With the woman beneath me.

She had a magic pussy. Or so it seemed to me, at least.

She closed her eyes, biting her lower lip as I thrust into her.

"Open your eyes, baby. I want you to see me fucking you."

"Mmm." She opened her eyes halfway. "Feels good."

"Sure does."

Thrust.

Thrust.

Thrust.

I was close. Damn. I'd just come in her mouth, and already I was ready to release inside her sweet heat.

Thrust.

Thrust.

And once more...

"God! Lacey. God." I plunged into her balls deep, letting go.

Letting go.

A wave of emotion swept over me, nearly bringing a tear to my eye.

Strange.

I didn't cry. Couldn't remember the last time I had. Certainly never after a fuck.

I felt so complete, though, still embedded in Lacey's warmth. So fulfilled. So...

I pulled out.

This was way too much "feeling" for me.

I rolled over onto my back, my arm over my forehead. I lay tense for a moment. Would she want to talk? Of course she would. Women always wanted to talk.

A few minutes later, though, she let out a soft snore. I smiled. No talking. Good. Hell, if I'd had that many orgasms, I'd be out cold too. I yawned, stretching.

I should get out of here. Go home. God himself only knew what awaited me at the office tomorrow.

But I didn't move. Didn't want to move.

And that scared the shit out of me.

I ENDED UP TAKING OFF, but I left a note.

Damn. I'd never left a woman a note before in my life. But I had already asked her to dinner the next night, so I figured a note was appropriate. I kept it simple.

Had a great time. I'll pick you up tomorrow at seven for dinner.
Rock

Perfect. No one could read anything into that, right?

Back to the hotel for me. My father's Manhattan penthouse was still a crime scene. Who knew when I'd be able to move in? After grabbing a cab, I took the elevator up to my suite, my soiled shirt in hand. I didn't actually expect Lacey to have it dry-cleaned. I'd kind of had the wine in the face thing coming.

Why had I been such a dick?

I huffed to myself as I inserted the key card to open the door to my suite.

I knew damned well why, and I didn't want to even think it. Still, it bubbled to the surface of my mind despite my desire to block it out.

I was feeling something for this woman. Something I'd never felt. Something I'd been pretty sure I'd never feel in this lifetime.

And I wasn't ready for it, especially not now with all these new responsibilities facing me.

I inhaled. I could still smell her—her coconutty hair, her citrusy fragrance, her musky arousal—as if she'd imprinted on me. Was her scent all over me? Or was it just in my memory?

Most likely a little of both.

I needed to watch myself. This woman could have me by the balls so easily, and I couldn't let that happen. I could cancel dinner tomorrow. I quickly looked at my watch. Correction... tonight. It was after midnight. I should cancel dinner.

But I didn't want to.

I felt like a kid. I'd just left her, and I couldn't wait to see her again.

I closed the door behind me and stripped off my suit jacket and trousers. I stuffed them plus my soiled shirt into the laundry bag and left it outside the door. Wearing only my socks and boxer briefs, I yawned, stretching my arms over my head, and made my way into the bedroom.

"That's a nice look on a man."

I jerked slightly. The voice was female. And familiar. I waited for my eyes to adjust to the darkness. "Who the hell is there? And how'd you get in here?"

The click of the night table light. I squinted against the onslaught of illumination.

"It's me, hon."

Raven black hair tumbled over milky shoulders and onto two pert breasts, brown nipples hard and taut.

"Nieves. What are you doing here?"

"Thought I'd come visit."

"Put some clothes on, for God's sake. How'd you get in here?"

"I told the night manager that I'm your wife. He didn't question it at all."

Interesting. That was one night manager who'd no longer have a job in the morning. I was too tired to deal with it now.

"Get the hell out of my bed."

"I have a better idea. Why don't you join me?" She pulled the covers back.

Nothing. Not one stir in my cock, and Nieves was a gorgeous woman. Half Mexican, half Irish, she had the milky white skin and sprays of light freckles from her mother and the raven hair and black eyes of her father.

We'd had a good time, but I'd bailed when she started to get serious. That was nearly a year ago. Why was she here now?

"I don't think so," I said. "I'll sleep on the pullout in the living room. We'll deal with why you're here in the morning. I'm beat at the moment."

"Let me take care of you then, handsome." She leaned forward, her nipples protruding through the black curtain of her hair. Her shoulder tattoo of a skull and rose drew my focus.

I'd kissed that spot a thousand times, running my lips over the lines of the work. It was beautiful, and the red of the rose was a shade I'd never seen on another tattoo. It had been my favorite place to kiss her.

Which should have told me something right there.

Now? Nothing. Not one budge of my cock.

Maybe because I'd already had two orgasms.

Or maybe because I was infatuated with another woman.

No, I'd been infatuated before. I was feeling something more profound for Lacey.

Something more...

I shook my head to clear it. Not going there.

Right now I had a woman in my bed...and not the one I wanted there.

"Goodnight, Nieves." I walked out the door.

Uncomfortable sofa bed for me tonight.

34

LACEY

Riley Wolfe is missing.

That was the message waiting for me when I got to the office the next morning.

The message hadn't come from Rock or either of his brothers. It had come from my associate who was handling the transfer of the Wolfe family jewelry, most of which had been left to Riley.

This wasn't really my problem. Ordinarily, I'd leave it to the family to find their missing member. But Riley Wolfe niggled at me. Something was bothering her. And if she was missing? She wouldn't show up in Paris for her contract in several days. Fox Mulder—or whatever his name was—had mentioned that she had some issues. Maybe he could shed some light on where she might be.

I picked up my phone. "Charlie, see if you can find any contact information for Fox Mul—" What was his last name? I sighed. "First name Fox, last name starts with M. He's a model."

"You mean Fox Monroe?"

"Yeah, that's it. See if you can find him. He might have information on Riley Wolfe."

"Will do."

I checked my calendar and then grabbed my purse. I pulled out the small piece of paper with Rock's handwriting on it. It had a slightly right slant, and his writing was very masculine. At least that's how I perceived it.

Had a great time. I'll pick you up tomorrow at seven for dinner.
Rock

Why had I kept the note? And why had I put it in my purse and brought it to work with me?

I sighed, remembering the previous night. Orgasm after orgasm after orgasm, until that last one that had taken me to another planet. Rock said I'd squirted. Damn. Whatever I'd done, it had been amazing.

Quickly I typed "squirting orgasm" into my search bar. Time to learn a little bit abou—

My phone buzzed. "Yeah?"

"I found him," Charlie said. "Got his cellphone number off his Facebook page, of all things. I can't believe he made it public."

"He's just starting to get into modeling. He'll realize his mistake soon enough." I laughed. "Yeah, get him on the phone, if you can."

A minute later, I was talking to Fox Monroe.

"I'm glad you called, Lacey," he said.

I cleared my throat. How did I let him know this was not a pleasure call?

"It was nice meeting you the other night," I said.

"I enjoyed it too."

I cleared my throat again. "I have a question for you. I represent the estate of Derek Wolfe, and he left significant assets to Riley Wolfe, his daughter. But we can't seem to find her. Do you know where she might be?"

"Well...no. I don't. I thought you said Riley was a friend of yours."

"More like an acquaintance. Have you seen her recently?"

"I haven't talked to Riley in the last month or so."

"You said she'd had some issues. Is that anything you might feel comfortable discussing with me?"

"What does this have to do with her father's estate?" he asked.

Smart man. I hadn't given Fox enough credit. "We can't get the property distributed if she's not here. If I know what these issues are that she's struggling with, I might have a better idea of where to find her."

"Just some depression and stuff like that. She missed a few shoots earlier this year. That doesn't bode well. But she's so fantastic at what she does that the industry cuts her some slack."

"I see."

Riley had seemed a little off when she and I had dinner. She'd definitely wanted to talk to me about something, but then she'd reneged.

"Did she ever mention anyone who lives out of town? Anyone she might be visiting?"

"We aren't really that close, Lacey. We've done a few runway shows together, but that's the extent of my relationship with her."

"All right. Thank you, Fox."

"I am really glad you called, though. I enjoyed meeting you and would love to see you again for a drink. This time just the two of us?"

When it rained, it poured. I seemed to be a magnet for pretty boys—as Rock would call them—lately.

How to let him down gently...

"I'm flattered. Really. But I think I'm a little old for you, Fox."

"Age is only a number."

"Really? How old are you, then?"

"Twenty-one."

God. Even younger than I'd imagined. "I'm thirty-one. That's a decade."

"Yeah, thanks. I can do the math, Lacey."

"The math says no dice. I'm sorry. You're a really nice guy. You certainly shouldn't be lacking attention from women."

"Most of them are too young," he said, laughing.

"The right one will come along. In the meantime, you're twenty-one. Have fun. You deserve it. Enjoy the money you're making."

"Oh, I get it. You're looking for a relationship."

I wasn't really, but if that would send him packing... "Right. And you're way too young to be settling down."

"I guess you're right about that. Oh!"

"What?"

"I'm so stupid. You're dating Riley's brother, aren't you? He sure wanted to take care of you the other night."

"Actually, no. We're not dating." *Just fucking.*

"That's good. No offense, but he seemed like kind of a dick."

Yeah, he didn't do a great job of hiding that. "He has his moments," was all I said.

"I'm sorry you're not up for some fun," Fox said, "but I respect your decision. Maybe we'll see each other around."

"Maybe." Though I doubted it. "Thanks for the information, Fox. Have a great day."

"You too. Bye."

That hadn't yielded much information at all. Did Rock know his sister was missing? He hadn't mentioned her last night. Was it even my place to tell him?

I bit my lip. He'd been a complete shithead last night but then had given me incredible pleasure, and he was taking me to dinner tonight.

Still, he'd made it damned clear that he didn't want a relationship. Were we friends? Not really. I didn't know any more about him than I did when I first met him. We weren't in a relationship, and we weren't even friends. What the hell were we?

Fuck buddies?

I'd never had a fuck buddy before.

Rock Wolfe was a terrific fuck buddy, if that was what I was looking for.

I'd told Fox I was looking for a relationship, and I thought I'd been lying. Was I? Maybe I *did* want a relationship. I loved the idea of children, and I was thirty-one already. The biological clock was ticking away, almost like a time bomb.

If I wanted a relationship, I couldn't be with Rock Wolfe. He'd made that clear. Anything with him would be a waste of time. A fun waste of time, but a waste nonetheless.

In fact, it might be best to call off dinner tonight. Should I tell him Riley seemed to be missing?

No. Best to stay out of family business. I cared about Riley. I cared about all of them, but I couldn't get in any deeper. Rock would find out soon enough.

I grabbed my cell and then realized I didn't know his number. We'd never talked on the phone. No matter. It would be in the Wolfe file, which was sitting on the corner of my desk. I located the number quickly and called.

"Rock Wolfe," said his deep husky voice.

Already my skin tingled.

"Hi, Rock, this is Lacey."

"Hey, sweetheart."

"I'm going to have to cancel our dinner plans this evening."

"No, you're not."

Exactly why I was canceling. He was a dick, as Fox had said.

"Yeah, I *am*, actually."

"Nope. I'm picking you up. See you at your place."

"Rock, you need to listen to me."

Nothing.

"Rock?"

Had he really just ended the call?

Fine then. I wouldn't be home when he picked me up.

35

ROCK

Lacey Ward was feisty, I'd give her that. But she and I *were* having dinner tonight. I'd show her how a man should truly treat a lady of her caliber. After her split check with pretty boy yogini, she'd be impressed.

Impressed? I laughed aloud. Why was I so intent on impressing Lacey Ward? I'd never worried about impressing a woman before now. Especially not the one who was currently hogging my bathroom. Nieves had gone in nearly an hour ago to shower. Did she not realize I had a company to run?

A brick hit my head. How could I have been so obtuse? Of course. That was why she was here. She'd heard I'd inherited a billion dollar company, and she wanted to get back in my good graces.

I'd felt something for her once, but if she wanted me back, she'd have come by before now. Nieves was all about Nieves, which was a big part of why I'd ended things.

I pounded on the bathroom door. "Time's up. I've got things to do today, all of which require me to be showered."

The door opened, and there she stood, buck naked, the

mermaid tattoo snaking around her midriff as it always had. I didn't like that one near as well as the one on her shoulder.

"Come on in," she said. "Nothing stopping you."

"For God's sake." I yanked a towel off the brass rack. "Cover yourself."

"You never minded looking at me."

"I mind now. I booked you your own room for the next two nights. That will give you time to make plans to go home."

"I'm not going home."

"The hell you're not."

"I've decided to move here, Rock. I want us to try again." She sauntered toward me, wiggling her hips. "Haven't you missed me at all?"

"We ended things over a year ago. I'm over it."

"I'm not." She grazed her hand over my bare chest.

Again, nothing from my cock. Just a look from Lacey got me hard.

I wrapped the towel around her and led her out the door. "Get dressed. I need to wash."

I locked the door. Knowing Nieves, she'd try to hijack my shower.

"CARLA," I said, walking into the office. "Get my mother on the phone."

"Actually, she's in your office, Mr. Wolfe."

Of course she was. "From now on, she can wait out here unless she has an appointment, which she doesn't."

"Yes, Mr. Wolfe. I'm sorry."

"No reason to be. Now you know the procedure." I walked into my office and closed the door behind me. "Hello, Mother."

"Rock, good morning."

"I have good news for you."

"I figured you would." She smiled.

My mother had been beautiful once. Dark hair and blue eyes, high cheekbones and classic beauty.

Now she looked plastic. Bleached blond and plastic.

"I've decided to give you the allowance you requested. I'm not exactly sure where all the money is at the moment, but I'll get it taken care of as soon as possible."

And it would stop as soon as my father's murder was solved, but I didn't add that little tidbit.

"I knew you'd see reason, darling." She stood and patted my cheek.

Her touch burned. Not in a good way.

"Now get out of my office."

"I'll need some cash to tide me over. You know, to get back on my feet?"

"You were never off your feet, Connie. Dad has only been dead a little over a week."

"Whatever you have in your wallet should be fine." She smiled.

"I've got nothing." True words.

"Goodness. I guess I could go down the hall and see Reid, then. I just hope I don't talk too much."

"Don't threaten me. I know what you're up to. I've got no cash on me, so you'll have to make do. It's not my fault you managed your millions so poorly."

"I didn't get near what I earned, putting up with your father all those years."

"Cry me a river. Now if you'll excuse me. I've got work to do."

She exited with a huff.

～

THE DAY WAS ROUGH. Meetings and more meetings, and I didn't understand anything Reid and the others talked about. This wasn't going to be easy. But I'd do it. I'd cursed my father more than once today for putting me in this position. I could bail. But screwing over my siblings like that?

No, couldn't do it.

"You thought I'd bail, didn't you?" I said out loud to my dead father. "That way you could fuck all four of us over."

I'd decided long ago never to have children. I sure didn't want to be a father like my own old man. He'd had no love for any of us, and this final straw from the grave was proof of that.

I'd show him. I wouldn't bail on my brothers and sister. We'd all have what was rightfully ours.

I walked out of the elevator and toward Lacey's door, an adolescent spring in my step. I was looking forward to this. To being with her. Yeah, we'd fuck later, but I was actually looking forward to spending time with her.

Damn.

And I'd told her we didn't have a relationship. I didn't think I wanted one. Could I have been wrong?

I slid down the wall right by her door into a sit.

Damn.

Damn. Damn. Damn.

She was right behind that door, waiting.

The elevator door dinged, and she stepped out.

She *wasn't* behind the door waiting. My heart quickened just seeing her.

"Rock, what are you doing here?"

"I came to pick you up for dinner."

"You're late. And I already told you I'm not going."

"I said eight o'clock."

"Your note said seven, genius."

"Shit. Well, you're here and I'm here, and our reservation is for eight thirty. Let's go. I've got a cab waiting."

"Uh...no. I canceled, remember?"

"You're obviously not busy." I took the grocery bags from her.

"I am, actually."

"Yeah? Doing what?"

"None of your business."

I peeked into one of her bags. "Microwave popcorn. I see. You're busy watching TV tonight."

She gripped the handle of the other bag with white knuckles. "You're such an ass!"

"Doing what I do best, baby." I grinned.

"Go home, Rock."

"I no longer have a home."

"You have a luxury hotel suite. Go there."

"Come on. Let's go to dinner. You look great."

"I'm in my work clothes."

"So? You still look great. Here, let me." I took the key from her hand and opened the door, went in, and set the groceries in the kitchen. "Any of this perishable?"

"Just the milk."

I located the quart of milk and put it in Lacey's refrigerator. "All done then. Let's go."

"You do speak English, right? You understand what 'no' means?"

I split my face with a grin. "I do. It means 'let's go.'"

She shook her head, but her lips were curving upward. She was trying to stop it, but she was melting.

"Come on. I'm going to show you how a real man treats a lady for dinner."

36

LACEY

I went.

I couldn't explain why, but I went.

Fact was, I wanted to be with Rock. I was in for heartache, I knew, but I couldn't help myself.

"Reservations for two. Wolfe," Rock told the maître d'.

"You two?" The man darted his gaze to me.

"Yeah."

"But your date has already arrived, sir."

I lifted my brow.

"My date is right here beside me," Rock said.

"She arrived ten minutes ago. Black hair, gorgeous?"

"For God's sake."

"This is my cue to leave," I said.

"No. You're not leaving. *She* is." Rock walked into the restaurant.

Five minutes later he walked back out. "She's not my date, but she's refusing to leave without making a scene. Do you have another table for the two of us? I'll make it worth your while."

"I'm sorry, Mr. Wolfe. We're booked solid."

Rock went rigid. "Let me tell you something. This is the last time my family comes to this place. You screwed up. She's *not* my date."

I tugged on his arm. "Then how did she know you'd be here?"

"She saw it on my calendar, apparently."

"And how did some strange woman have access to your calendar?"

He sighed. "It's a long story."

"Apparently we're not going to have dinner, so start talking. Seems we've got all evening."

"No. Fucking no. Set another place at the table," he said. "My date and I are going to eat. Then, call the police and have Ms. Romero escorted out."

"That would cause a scene," the maître d' said.

"Do I look like I care?" he asked, seething. "She will leave. She can't afford to eat here."

"Who is this woman, Rock?"

"A blast from the past," he said. "One I really don't want to deal with."

"I think you're going to have to deal with her."

"Unfortunately, you're right, but trust me. This won't take long." He headed into the restaurant.

Should I follow? I had no idea. In the end, though, my curiosity won. I wanted a look at this "blast from the past."

"Ma'am," the maître d' said, "was he serious when he asked me to call the police?"

"I've never known him not to be serious. And he *will* boycott this place, I assure you. He and his entire family. I'd do what he asks."

The man nodded. "Very well, then."

I headed into the restaurant.

Rock stood at the edge of a table secluded in a corner. A very private table. I smiled. He'd arranged this for us, and at the moment, another woman was in my seat.

Not for long.

The woman was indeed beautiful. Fair skin, dark hair, and an emerald sequined dress with a plunging neckline. Bigger breasts than I ever hoped to have, and a biker tat on her shoulder.

It worked for her.

I was still in my work clothes, and God himself only knew what my hair looked like.

This woman was everything I wasn't at the moment.

"The police are on their way, Nieves," Rock was saying. "You can either leave now or be escorted out."

The woman simply shrugged and then lifted her brow when she met my gaze. "Is this your lovely date?"

"She is. Have a seat, Lacey."

What the hell? "Thank you," I said sweetly, and sat down across from the woman he'd called Nieves.

The other woman smiled, her dark pink lips framing perfectly straight, white teeth. "Nieves Romero. Nice to meet you."

She actually sounded sincere.

"Ms. Romero is just leaving," Rock said.

"Why?" I asked. "Why don't the three of us have dinner?"

Rock sent me a dark glare.

I simply smiled. I'd called him to cancel, but he hadn't taken me seriously. Then I'd come along anyway like a lapdog. So why not throw him for a loop now? I found the idea oddly exciting, plus this woman offered me a glimpse into Rock's past—something he hadn't been overly forthcoming about.

"That's not what I had in mind tonight," Rock said gruffly. "Besides, the cops have already been called."

"You can take care of that," I said.

"Sure you can," Nieves agreed. "Call off the dogs."

The maître d' approached the table and addressed Nieves. "I'm sorry, ma'am, but I made a mistake. This table is reserved for Mr. Wolfe and his guest. You erroneously told me *you* were his guest. I'm going to have to ask you to leave."

"I'll be joining Mr. Wolfe and his guest," she said.

"No, she won't be," Rock insisted.

"I've had to summon the police at Mr. Wolfe's insistence," the man continued. "If you'd like to leave now, we can avoid you being escorted out."

Rock glared at her.

He was serious.

Bummer. I was hoping to get some information about Rock.

"Fine." Nieves stood with a huff. "I'll be in touch, Rock."

"Please, don't be." He thanked the maître d' and then sat down in the vacated seat. "I'm sorry about that."

"So tell me," I said. "Who exactly is she?"

"I told you. A blast from the past."

"I'm looking for a little more detail here, Rock."

He sighed. "We dated, okay? I'm sure you already figured that out."

"Yeah. I guess I'm looking for more specific information. I mean, she must have meant a lot to you if she thinks she can hijack your dinner plans."

"It meant more to her," he said. "When things got serious, I ended it. This all happened almost a year ago. I haven't heard from her since, until she showed up in my room last night."

"She was in your room last night?"

"Yeah. She got someone to let her in. I had the night manager fired this morning."

"Hmm. Normally I wouldn't condone getting someone fired, but he shouldn't have let her in your room."

"Damn right."

The waiter came by to take our drink orders. Rock ordered the expensive bourbon he'd had at the bar that night. I stayed with sparkling water.

"Tell me about her," I said.

"Do you really want to spend the evening talking about Nieves Romero?"

"No, not really. I'd like to learn more about you, but you're incredibly tight-lipped about that. If I learn about your former girlfriend, maybe I'll learn a little something about you."

"She's a cosmetologist. She does hair."

"How did you meet her?"

"On a ride. Her bike was in the shop, and she was looking for someone to ride with, so I offered to let her ride bitch with me."

"Wait a second. Ride bitch?"

"Ride on the back. That's all it means."

"It's a little demeaning, don't you think?"

"Lacey, for God's sake. It's just a term." He smiled. "I'll let you ride bitch with me whenever you want."

"Yeah. No thanks."

"You ever ride before?"

"Big no on that."

"You don't know what you're missing. This weekend, we go riding."

"That's in two days."

"Yeah. You got plans?"

I didn't, but truthfully, getting on the back of a bike with Rock scared the hell out of me. So why did I want to do it so badly?

"Lace?"

"No. But I'm not riding with you."

"Not here, that's for sure. We'll fly home."

"Home?"

"Yeah. To Montana."

"I can't just pick up and fly to Montana in two days."

"One day, actually. We'll leave tomorrow evening. That way we'll have all day Saturday to ride. We can stay at my place."

I squirmed, my skin tingling all over. This was so unlike me...and I wanted it more than my next breath of air.

"You haven't lived until you've ridden under the big sky." He sighed. "Man, I miss it."

"You haven't been here that long, Rock."

"No, but riding is like breathing to me. You'll see what I mean."

"You don't think I'm actually considering this," I said. Though I was.

In fact, I'd already decided.

I was going.

If I wanted to learn more about Rock Wolfe, Montana was the place to do it.

37

ROCK

Lacey took a long sip of her sparkling water. Then, "Fine."

"Fine what?"

"Fine, I'll go to Montana with you."

"Great. I can't wait to get back to the fresh air of big sky country." I took a drink of bourbon. "Man, this is good stuff. Expensive bourbon really is better than rotgut. Do you think pretty boy appreciated it after paying that big bill the other night?"

Lacey shook her head. "Can you be not an asshole for more than a few seconds at a time?"

"Not sure. Never tried." True enough.

"What do you want from me, then?" she asked.

"Your company. Your tight little body for that great sex we have together."

She huffed. "I'm serious. You can have any woman you want. Nieves just traveled halfway across the country to be with you, and she's gorgeous."

"She's a pain in the ass."

"And I'm not?"

"You have your moments," I said. Didn't matter. I hadn't

given a thought to any other woman since I'd laid eyes on Lacey Ward.

"Then why me, Rock?"

What could I say to that, except to be honest? A first for me, but why not?

"Because I haven't been able to stop thinking about you since I first laid eyes on you."

Her mouth dropped open.

"Surprise you?" I asked.

She cleared her throat. "Yeah. More than a little."

"Just telling the truth. We've had our share of good times in the short time we've known each other. You have to admit that."

"I admit it. But we still don't really know each other. Every time I ask you—"

"Stop." I held up my hand. "I don't get personal, Lacey. It's not who I am."

She finished off her sparkling water and stood. "You've made that clear. You've also made it clear that we don't have a relationship. Sorry, Rock. That's not enough for me. I enjoy sex as much as the next person, but I'm not looking for a fuck buddy."

"Lace, sit down. Please." The thought of her leaving tied my insides in knots. I had to resist. I had no other choice. There were things she didn't know about me—would never know about me—and if she did, she'd run away as fast as she could.

If I were a better man, I'd let her run away.

But I was not a better man, unfortunately. I wanted her. I wanted to take her to Montana and show her the beauty of the outdoors.

I wanted to sleep with her in my own bed.

I wanted to wake up next to her and fry her some bacon and eggs in my cast-iron skillet, make her a pot of coffee.

I wanted to make love with her in front of my crackling fireplace, though that would have to wait since summer was nearly here.

I wanted to make her a pot of beef stew or barbeque steaks on my grill for her.

Take her hunting, show her how to pluck and skin a pheasant and then enjoy it together with my famous cognac cream sauce.

"You going to say anything?" she asked. "You asked me to sit."

I itched to tell her everything racing through my mind, everything I wanted to share with her.

But I couldn't. Just couldn't.

She rolled her eyes. "That's what I thought."

"Please. Let's have dinner. And go with me to Montana this weekend. I promise you'll have an amazing time."

"I'm not denying that our sex is great, Rock."

I wasn't talking about sex, actually. Surprising even to me. Words floated through my head, but somehow they never made it to my vocal cords.

"Yeah, our sex is great."

"We can have sex here," she said. "We don't need Montana for that."

I sighed. "I do. I want to go home. I want to..."

What the hell did I want?

Things I had no business wanting.

She didn't miss the opportunity to badger me.

"What *do* you want, Rock?"

I sighed. "You. I want you."

"Meaning...?"

She wasn't going to let this go.

I wasn't falling in love. I couldn't be. I didn't have it in me. But I wanted something from this beautiful woman—something I couldn't put into words.

"I want you to spend the weekend with me. In Montana. It's perfect. Monday's a holiday so we can make it a long weekend."

"Memorial Day," she said. "I usually volunteer with homeless veterans on Memorial Day."

Could she be any more perfect? "What if I make a sizable donation to the organization to make up for the loss of you for one day?"

She smiled. "It's not about money, Rock. It's about doing something I believe in. I don't have a lot of time to do volunteer work, so I do what I can, and I take it seriously."

Beauty, brains, honesty, integrity, and selflessness.

If I had the capacity to love, I'd love Lacey Ward.

"All right," I said. "We'll come back on Sunday evening. That way you can—"

She reached across the table and laid her hand over mine. A bolt of lightning shot through me at her touch.

"I'll find another way to help this year," she said. "I'll go with you for the long weekend."

Elation filled me. I felt like a school boy who just found out the girl I had a crush on liked me back.

Ridiculous.

"You won't regret it."

"Call me or text me with the flight information," she said. "I'll have to pack tonight because I have a full day of appointments tomorrow."

"What time is your last appointment?" I asked.

She checked her phone. "Three thirty."

"And how long will it take?"

"About forty-five minutes at most. Why?"

"Great. I'll pick you up at your office at five to give you some cushion."

"Are you sure you'll be able to get a flight by tomorrow?"

"Very sure," I said, winking. "We'll be taking the Wolfe jet."

Her eyes widened into circles. "What?"

"I'm the CEO of the company. All I need to do is make a call."

"You can use the jet for personal business?"

"Of course. I'd bet my father took it all over the place, and I know Reid has used it to go to the Caribbean on more than one occasion."

Her gorgeous lips dropped into an O.

I reached across the table and touched the bottom of her chin, closing her mouth. "Never flown in a private jet before?"

"Not once."

"Well, tomorrow you can take that off your bucket list."

"It wasn't ever on my bucket list."

"Oh? What is, then?"

She pinked up.

Interesting. She definitely had a bucket list, then.

"Come on, baby. Spill it."

She closed her eyes and then opened them. "It's silly, really."

"Nah. Bucket lists aren't silly."

Her cheeks were fiery now. This was going to be good.

"Well...I've always wanted to go to a nudist place."

This time my jaw dropped. "Really?"

"Yeah. Too weird for you?"

"Not at all. The idea is intriguing. I just wouldn't have guessed that for you."

"That's because you don't know me yet, just like I don't know you."

Oh, she was good. She found every tiny way to try to get information out of me. I wasn't falling for it.

"I can probably arrange that nudist thing," I said. Yeah, I'd be on that first thing in the morning.

If possible, she reddened even further. Fuck. She'd never been so enticing. My cock hardened right there at the table. I squirmed, adjusting myself.

When the waiter came to take our dinner orders, I said, "Wrap it up. We're getting out of here."

"What?" Lacey said.

"Sorry, baby," I said, after the server left, "but I'm hard as a rock right now. I need to get you home. I'm going to eat you for dinner tonight."

38

LACEY

He'd promised me a dinner. Told me he'd show me how a man was supposed to treat a date.

Instead, we ended up in his suite, our dinner in Styrofoam takeout containers. Rock called room service and had them bring up china, silverware, and a table complete with linens. He even had the server put our food out. Then he signed what I assumed was a huge tip and escorted him out the door.

Just as well we'd left the restaurant. I was still in my work clothes and I felt stiff and ridiculous.

I couldn't take my eyes off of Rock. I missed his long hair, but now he looked like a male model walking the runway at an Armani fashion show. So unassumingly gorgeous. The man acted like he was nothing special, nothing spectacular.

But he was.

He'd already removed his suitcoat when we arrived, and now he loosened his tie and removed it, unbuttoning the first two buttons of his shirt.

"Get comfortable, Lace."

My skin prickled, sending a racing tingle down my spine and straight to my pussy. Get comfortable. Comfortable would mean out of my work clothes. I stood and headed into the bathroom. Sure enough, a robe hung on the inside of the door. I quickly stripped and covered myself with the lush white robe. Then I pulled my hair out of its French roll, fluffed it with my fingers, and went back out.

Rock's eyes nearly popped out of his head. "Wow."

"You said get comfortable."

"I did, didn't I?" He smiled as he removed his shirt. He stood wearing only his suit trousers, and the bulge inside them was very apparent.

I couldn't help a smile. "Our dinner will get cold."

"It's probably already cold. Take off that robe."

I obeyed, untying it and letting it slip over my shoulders before it fell to the floor.

He stared at me, and his gaze hardened my nipples. They stuck out like ripe berries, yearning for his touch. Meanwhile, I throbbed between my legs.

"I can see why you want to visit a nude beach," he said. "You seem very comfortable naked."

My body wasn't nearly as beautiful as I imagined Nieves's to be, but right now, the way he was looking at me, I felt like Helen of Troy herself.

He slid one lone finger over the apple of my cheek, down my neck, and over my shoulder. "So beautiful."

I reached forward and touched his shoulder as well. "You are too."

He smiled. "No one's called me that before."

"Beautiful? Then anyone who's seen that chest is blind. It's beautiful. You are beautiful, Rock Wolfe."

"God, Lace." He grabbed me and smashed our mouths together.

I opened, letting him in, surrendering to the passion of his kiss, the raw need in his groan as he devoured my mouth.

He tasted of the crisp bourbon he'd drunk at the restaurant. Bourbon and spice and the unique flavor that was Rock Wolfe.

Our tongues tangled and dueled, our moans answered each other. His cock poked into my belly, and I reached down to cup the hard bulge.

I wanted him.

Not just his body but all of him.

All of Rock Wolfe.

I knew next to nothing about this man, but emotion bubbled in me—emotion that was foreign to me.

Love.

I was falling in love.

God, I was headed for heartbreak. This man was a closed book. He shared his body with me but nothing else. How could I love him? It made no sense, but love him I did. I knew it as I knew the most basic tenets of life.

I love you, Rock Wolfe.

How I longed to break the kiss, panting, and admit those feelings. Fear, though, prevented that. Fear of rejection. He wouldn't say it back. He didn't feel it. If we didn't have a relationship, he certainly wasn't falling in love.

Could I do this? Could I spend the weekend with a man who wanted me but would never give me his heart?

As he continued to kiss me with such force and passion, I realized I already knew the answer.

Yes.

Yes, I could.

When this ended—and it inevitably would—I'd be devastated.

But until then, I'd enjoy what I could have of Rock Wolfe. His body. His attention. His warm mouth on mine.

He pushed his cock into my belly and his leg between mine.

I ground into his hard thigh, my clit pounding in time with my rapid heartbeat.

He broke the kiss, and we both inhaled heavily.

"Damn, Lace. I could kiss you forever."

I shivered, my nipples hard and aching. He was caught up in the moment. That was all. He didn't mean he literally wanted to kiss me forever.

How I wished it were true, though! How I wished he could love me.

Before I could think much more, he turned me around, yanked the robe off me, freed his cock, and pushed it into me.

This was how he'd taken me that first day in my office. Hard and fast and from behind. I'd been slick as aloe then, and I'd bet I was even wetter now. I couldn't get enough of Rock, of his raw maleness, of his massive cock.

"You're so tight, baby. So fucking tight. You've got the sweetest pussy on earth."

His words made me hotter. They weren't the words I longed to hear, but they spurred me on anyway, and soon I was jumping into orgasm.

"Rock!" I pushed backward, trying to force him farther and farther into me, so deep into me that we became one.

"That's it, baby. Come all over my hard cock. Come all over *me*." He plunged into me again and again.

Again and again and again.

Until he jammed into me one last time, groaning. "Lacey, my God!"

When I pulled out after he finished, I held back the whimper that threatened. I pasted a smile on my face and turned to face him. "Hungry? We'd better eat before the food gets any colder."

"Hungry for you, baby."

I let out a little laugh that was supposed to sound nonchalant but instead sounded forced. "There's plenty of time for that. Let's eat."

"You okay?"

"Fine. I'm fine." And I was. Sort of. He hadn't promised me anything past this weekend.

I was okay with that.

I had to be.

39

ROCK

No one had heard from my sister since she left dinner that night with Lacey and me. When Reid mentioned it at work the next morning, my skin went cold.

"Let's find her then," I said to him. "We've got Daddy's resources. Put the best PIs on her tail."

"Already done," Reid said. "I called it in this morning. Nothing so far."

I nodded, my heart racing. I loved my little sister. Protecting her was what had sent my life down the shithole. I'd do it again, though. I only wished I'd been more successful the first time.

I wouldn't fail my baby sister again.

"I was planning to go to Montana for the weekend," I said, "but I'll cancel. Riley's more important."

"No need to do that," Reid said. "There's nothing either of us can do. We've got the best people on it."

"*We* need to be on it."

"I get it, Rock. She's my little sister too. But we're doing all we can. Go on your trip. You need to pack all your stuff up and ship it back here anyway."

He was right about that, though packing wasn't what this

weekend was about. This weekend was about taking Lacey on a ride she'd never forget, no pun intended.

But my sister trumped that.

"I don't feel right going away right now. We need to find her."

"We will, but you have to understand." He paused a moment. "This isn't the first time Riley has taken off."

I lifted my eyebrows. "It's not?"

He shook his head. "The third time, actually, and when she goes, she doesn't want to be found. She's an adult, Rock. An adult with...issues."

Issues? Of course she had issues. Our esteemed father had violated her for God knew how long. Did Reid seriously not know that had happened?

"Then we should get her help," I said.

"We've tried. Dad tried while he was alive."

"Dad? Dad's the reason she's fucked up!"

"I know he wasn't the most attentive father in the world, but—"

"Attentive? He was a little *too* attentive to Riley."

"What the hell are you talking about?"

"Oh my God. You really don't know. Did you and Roy just close your eyes to everything going on in that godforsaken house?"

"You're one to talk. You weren't even there once you turned fourteen. Roy and I kept to ourselves. We sure as hell didn't want to be shipped off to military school."

Man. My brothers didn't have a clue. "Military school wasn't my choice."

"Of course it wasn't. You were a pain in the ass, Rock. Mom and Dad couldn't handle you."

"That's what they told you, huh?"

"It wasn't hard to believe. You were..."

"I was what, Reid? How much do you even remember? You

were nine when I left, and Roy was eleven. Roy spent all his time in his room anyway. What exactly do you remember about how I acted before I left?"

"You were...you know. Boisterous."

"So were you, as I recall."

"You came in late. You missed curfew."

"Uh-huh. It might surprise you to know that most kids don't get sent to military school for missing curfew."

"I guess... I guess I was too young to remember."

"Exactly. And Roy doesn't remember because he didn't pay much attention to the rest of us. What exactly did Mom and Dad tell you about why I was sent away?"

"They said you were caught stealing, and that..."

I resisted the urge to grab my brother's shoulders and shake him. "That *what*?"

"You got into a fight and nearly killed another guy. With a knife."

I curled my hands into fists. "Those assholes."

"You're saying you didn't pull a knife on someone?"

"I'm saying I never did what they told you I did."

"They lied?"

"Hard to believe, isn't it?" I scoffed sarcastically.

"I know Dad was no saint, but—"

"Dad was an evil piece of shit," I said.

"Why did they send you away, then?" Reid asked.

"That's not my story to tell," I said.

"Whose is it, then?"

I didn't respond. Instead, "Suffice it to say that while you and Roy got pampered at prep school, I got the shit kicked out of me by wannabe heroes who liked to pummel the students to make themselves feel better for being military school failures."

That was the first year. After that, I took part in the pummeling. Not my finest moments.

"First of all, we weren't exactly pampered. Roy had it especially hard. He was a huge target for bullies."

"A Wolfe heir was a target at a fine prep school?"

"You really think being a Wolfe meant anything there? They were all from powerful families. The first-year hazing was brutal."

I shook my head. I could tell him horror stories about hazing at military school, but I didn't particularly want to relive it at the moment.

"But I'm sor—"

I held up a hand. "Don't. Just don't. It's over, and I try not to think about it."

Reid nodded. "I get it. I do. Don't worry about Riley. She'll turn up when she's ready. I hate to see her fuck up her career like this, though."

"Yeah, I do too." I sighed. "I still think we should look for her."

"We're using our resources in the best way," my brother said. "If these PIs can't find her, she doesn't want to be found. Go ahead on your trip. There's nothing else we can do here. I wish there were, but there isn't."

I nodded. I still felt shitty about leaving, but the reality was that I hadn't had a clue the two other times my baby sister had gone missing. I'd divorced myself from this family long ago—something I deeply regretted now. I had reason to hate my parents, but my brothers and sister had done nothing wrong.

I owed them my loyalty. I'd go to Montana with Lacey as I'd promised.

Then I'd leave my beautiful home behind for the last time.

40

LACEY

The Wolfe private jet was even more luxurious than I'd imagined.

And yes, there was a bed.

Rock, though, was oddly distant. He hadn't mentioned the bed, or joining the mile high club, which, from the little I knew about him, seemed out of character.

I sipped Champagne from a crystal flute and ate strawberries dipped in chocolate.

Rock sat next to me, his drink sitting on the table in front of us, and he hadn't touched the fruit.

"Are you okay?" I asked.

"I'm good. Just a lot on my mind."

"Anything I can help with?"

He smiled. "No. I want to have a nice weekend with you."

"I'd like that too." I returned his smile and took another sip of Champagne. "This is delicious."

"Only the best for the Wolfes," he said, a little sardonically.

The attendant walked toward us. "Mr. Wolfe, the pilot says we're going to start our descent soon, so you'll need to fasten your seatbelts. I'll clear away these dishes."

Rock nodded. "Thank you."

I clicked my seatbelt closed.

Montana, here I come.

~

ONE LIMO RIDE LATER, we arrived at Rock's secluded cabin. It was small and cozy, and I loved it immediately.

"Make yourself at home," he said. "I'm going to take your suitcase into the bedroom."

"Thanks."

Yes, he was definitely off. I still knew so little about him, so I didn't feel comfortable pushing it. The living area was furnished with a leather sofa and two recliners flanking an oak coffee table. The fireplace was huge, and the mantle above it was made of white granite.

"Too bad we can't have a fire," Rock said.

"Probably not in spring." I smiled.

"Would you like anything? A drink? Something to eat?"

"No. I'm good for now. I think I'll change, though. Get out of these work clothes."

"Help yourself." He pointed toward the room where he'd taken my things.

I left, and he made no move to follow me. Again, odd. Was he sorry he'd brought me? I doubted it. This was Rock Wolfe. If he'd wanted to bail, he would have.

If only I didn't love him. This was starting to hurt a little.

I changed into some loose jeans and a tank top and walked barefoot back out to the living room. Rock had poured himself a drink and was sitting on the couch. I sat down next to him.

"Everything okay?" I said, and then wanted to take back the words. The last thing I wanted to be was a nag.

"Fine. Just a rough day. I'm worried about Riley."

I placed my hand over his. "I'm sorry. Is she still missing?"

He lifted his brow. "You *know*?"

Uh-oh. He didn't sound pleased.

"Yeah. I guess I just assumed you knew, and I didn't think it was any of my business."

The spark of anger in him dissipated, and I silently thanked the universe.

"We've got PIs looking for her, but according to my brother, this isn't the first time she's gone AWOL."

"It isn't?" Her Paris trip crossed my mind briefly. Was she really going to walk out on Dominique Cosmetics?

He shook his head. "Apparently she's struggling. And I haven't been here. I feel helpless right now, Lacey. This is my little sister. How could I have stayed gone all those years?"

I caressed his forearm, wanting to go further but not sure what to do. This was the most he'd ever opened up to me. I didn't want to jinx it.

"She seemed like she wanted to talk to me about something that night we went to dinner, but then she ended up leaving."

"That's the last time I saw her," he said.

"Me too. She was supposed to meet with me regarding the transfer of personal items from the will, but she didn't show."

He nodded. "She's been through a lot."

"I think you all have."

He pursed his lips into a flat line. "I don't want to talk about this."

I squeezed his hand. "Okay."

"How was your day?"

"Busy, but fine."

He nodded but said nothing.

I wasn't sure what to do, so I did nothing. A few minutes passed, and then he held up his arm. "Come here."

I smiled and snuggled into his shoulder.

He kissed the top of my head.

We stayed there, silently, the only sound our breathing.

ROCK WAS in a better mood the next morning. We'd gone to bed together, and he held me, but we hadn't made love.

Really weird, but it was also nice. I was feeling closer to him, which was what I wanted, but I fought myself. I didn't want to enjoy it too much and end up heartbroken.

I took a quick shower and then found him in the kitchen, frying up bacon and hash browns in a cast-iron skillet. He was wearing a pair of old jeans and nothing else, his newly cut hair was in disarray, and he looked absolutely edible.

We hadn't so much as kissed since we'd gotten on the plane. He must really be worried about his sister.

"Hey." I put my arms around him and kissed the back of his shoulder. "Anything I can do to help?"

"Nope. Coffee's done, and the mugs are in the cupboard above the brewer."

"Great. You need a cup?"

"Already got one. I hope you're hungry. I make a great breakfast."

"I know. You left me eggs the morning after my overindulgence, remember?"

"Lace, this is going to be so much better than cold, clammy eggs."

I inhaled. "It smells divine." I took a drink of coffee. "So where are we riding today?"

"Everywhere," he said. "I can't wait to get back on my bike."

"Sounds good." I hoped I sounded sincere. The bike still scared me a little, but I had no doubt that Rock would be in solid command of it. The man could take solid command of everything, including Wolfe Enterprises.

Including my body.

Including *me*, God help me.

I missed the furious lovemaking, but I was also enjoying this side of Rock. He seemed more real to me, and I liked it.

I liked it a lot.

I took a seat at the small oak table in the kitchen and inhaled again.

"Ready?" he asked. He handed me a plate of what appeared to be a breakfast casserole.

"Hash browns and bacon topped with two eggs over easy and green chile."

"It looks amazing," I said, "but I'll never be able to eat all of this."

"Sure you will, once you see how good it tastes."

I laughed and brought a forkful to my mouth. It was indeed delicious, but a little spicier than I had anticipated. I took a sip of coffee.

"Best chile in Montana," he said.

"Where'd you learn to make it?"

He looked at his plate. "Nieves, actually."

Did he expect me to react? I'd show him. "Well, she must come from a line of good cooks."

"True. Just because she's a pain in the ass doesn't mean we can't enjoy her chile."

I tried to ignore the stab of jealousy. Nieves wasn't here. I was, and Rock had made it clear which one of us he preferred. I could have done without him mentioning her, though I was the one who'd asked about the chile.

And Rock was right. Before I knew it, I'd gobbled up the whole plateful.

He laughed. "Told you."

"It was amazing. You'll have to give me that recipe."

"Good luck finding chile peppers like that in New York."

Did that mean he wasn't going to give me the recipe? I wasn't getting a good read on Rock at all this morning. Then again, when had I ever? The only time I'd ever read him accurately was when we were having sex, and that hadn't occurred yet, which was in itself really weird.

Rock finished his plate and took the dishes to the sink. "I need to shower, and then we'll be off. Jeans today for sure, and long sleeves if you don't want to get sunburned. And no open-toed shoes."

I dropped my mouth open. "That's all I brought."

"We're going riding, Lace."

"You didn't tell me I needed anything special."

"I assumed you knew."

"Why would you assume that? I've never been riding in my life."

"For Christ's sake!" He raked his fingers through his hair. "We'll stop at the Harley shop and get you what you need."

I sighed. This weekend wasn't turning out at all as I'd imagined.

When Rock's phone buzzed, and he narrowed his eyes and left the room to speak privately, I felt it get a little worse.

41

ROCK

"Any news?" I asked Reid.

"Not about Riley, no. I'm calling about something else."

"What?"

Silence on the other end. I counted to ten.

"For God's sake, Reid. What?"

"That detective is sniffing around. He called me at home this morning, at six fucking a.m."

"So?"

"He has questions," he said, "about Roy."

"Roy? What about him?"

"I have no idea."

"Shit. I told you I shouldn't have left town."

"I know. You were right. But we had no idea this guy would be in my face this morning. Has he called you?"

"Not that I know of." I took a quick look at my phone. "No, I don't see any missed calls."

"He'll get to you eventually. I told him you were out of town until Tuesday."

I cleared my throat, thinking. "Do you think Roy is hiding something?"

"I don't know. He's really hard to read. Always has been."

"Agreed, but I've been gone for so long anyway, I wouldn't know how to read any of you. I did get the feeling, though, that he was hiding something the other night in the bar. What was the guy asking you about him?"

"Mostly about his mental state. Weird shit, like had he ever had any psychotic tendencies."

Roy? Psychotic? "Seems pretty far off."

"I know. Roy's an introvert for sure, but psychotic? Not in this lifetime. Also, he was asking me about Roy's art. He seems to think some of his paintings show signs of psychosis."

"I'm no art expert, but I think the detective is the one who's psychotic."

Reid chuckled but then said, "This isn't a laughing matter, Rock."

"Then why are you laughing? And as far as Roy's art goes, I haven't seen any of it. I assume you have. Do you think it's psychotic?"

"No. But I'm no art expert, either. He does a lot of portraits, but he also does abstracts. Some of it is pretty dark, but some isn't."

"I'm not sure this detective has a clue," I said. "I do think Roy knows something—something he wanted to tell us at the bar the other night. But our brother is no psycho. That's a term reserved for the bastard who fathered us."

"You think Dad was a psycho? I don't know, Rock. He was an asshole for sure, but I don't think you could call him psychotic."

Of course Reid didn't. He didn't know what he'd done to our sister. Did that make him psychotic? Probably not. Sociopathic, for sure.

"Reid," I said. "You were nine when I got shipped off. What happened during those years?"

Silence met my ear.

"Reid?"

"We don't talk about it."

"We meaning who?"

"Roy and I."

"What about Riley?"

"Riley was fine. She was Daddy's little girl. He doted on her."

Wow. A lot my brother didn't know. "He did, huh?"

"Yeah. Nothing was too good for her. She had the best of everything. He even took her on special trips. He called them princess trips. Roy and I didn't get anything like that."

My brother didn't know how lucky he'd been. I knew exactly what went on during those princess trips. Damn. My poor baby sister. But my brothers? How could they have missed everything? Had they seriously been too preoccupied with envy that they couldn't see what he was doing to her? Unreal.

"Have you ever wondered why Riley struggles so much?" I asked. "Why she runs away from time to time?"

"She's a spoiled brat, Rock. I know she's had her issues with depression and all, but damn, if she didn't live such a coddled life, she wouldn't have time for such self-indulgence. God knows I don't."

Wow again. Reid was truly ignorant. And naïve.

"Dad used to beat the shit out of me, Reid. Many times because I took it when he went after you. Did you know that?"

"I know. I suppose I should thank you, but after you left, who do you think he took it out on? Roy some, but mostly me. Roy was always closed up in his room working on some painting. I was the one who tried to gain favor with Dad, the only one of us who was truly interested in learning the family business. And for that I was punished."

I cleared my throat. "I'm sorry."

And I was. I should have been there to protect not only my sister but my brothers as well.

Instead, I was banished for my efforts.

"I'm over it. Though I suffered quite a few black eyes and bruises courtesy of Daddy."

I paused a moment. Then, "Were there ever any marks on Riley?"

"Are you kidding? Of course not. She was his angel."

No marks. At least not where he would have seen them. Nausea clawed up my throat. Reid and Roy truly didn't know what he'd done to our sister. Or perhaps they didn't want to know. Perhaps they were so clouded with their own envy that they refused to see.

But I saw. The bastard had beat me black and blue many times before I found him sneaking into Riley's room at night. I *hadn't* refused to see. In fact, I'd taken the situation into my own hands.

That had been my downfall.

A fourteen-year-old on the cusp of maturity, testosterone coursing through my veins. I'd let the rage and anger take control, and I'd acted without thinking.

I'd paid dearly for it...and so had my baby sister.

Apparently so had my brothers.

Because of my rash decision in the heat of the moment, all four of us had suffered.

And Derek Wolfe was never going to let me forget that. He made sure of that with his last earthly action—forcing me to take control of his company or my siblings would suffer.

He knew I'd do it, because he knew my actions had already caused them to suffer. I wouldn't allow it to happen again.

He knew I'd do it because I was a good man at heart.

And that meant...

Holy shit.

That meant Derek Wolfe thought I was a good man. Better than he had ever been.

I'll be damned.

Lacey had once said that maybe he'd put me in charge because he felt I was the best person for the job. She was still wrong. But my father *had* been sure of one thing. The choice would be mine. Either I would suffer, or my siblings would. He didn't care one way or the other, but he was betting on me. He knew what I'd done for my baby sister all those years ago, and what it had cost me. He assumed I'd pay the price again to save my siblings.

My father might be a malicious bastard, but surely he didn't want his company sold off.

On the other hand, he didn't seem to really give a crap about any of his children, even his little princess. If he had, he wouldn't have abused her the way he did.

I rolled my eyes. I was overthinking this. Here I was, trying to make sense of what my father had done and why he'd done it, when the task was impossible. The man had been a weasel. He'd done it because it would fuck us all over.

He'd done it because he *could.*

How such a sociopathic freak had been an A-plus businessman was beyond me.

But he had been. The best. Big shoes for me to fill.

The thought made me nauseated all over again. I was a week in, and I still had no clue what I was doing. Thank God for Reid.

Reid. He was so misguided. He'd called Riley a spoiled brat, for God's sake. In his mind she was, just taking off whenever she wanted, everything else be damned. Maybe it was time to tell him the truth. Tell him why I'd really been sent away.

It all sat on the tip of my tongue...

But it was Riley's story to tell. Not mine.

"Listen," I finally said to Reid. "We'll figure this all out. Roy knows something, and we'll have to get him to tell us. But I'm absolutely sure he had nothing to do with Dad's death."

"I'm sure too," Reid agreed.

"Then tell the detective to go fuck himself. If he wants information from Roy, he can go to Roy. If he wants information from me, he can wait until I get back to town."

"Good enough," Reid said. "Sorry to bug you on a Saturday morning, bro. Have a nice time."

"I'll try. See you." I ended the call and returned to the kitchen.

Lacey wasn't there. Her empty plate was in the sink but her cup was missing. Had she gone to take a shower? No, her hair had been wet when she came in to breakfast. Where was she? This cabin wasn't that big.

I walked outside in my bare feet. There she was, roaming around the cabin in her jeans and flip flops and sipping her cup of coffee. She looked relaxed. Relaxed and beautiful, as if she belonged here.

But Lacey was a city girl. This was all new to her. Strange, because she looked as at home here as I felt.

If only...

If only we never had to go back. If only we could stay here forever, just the two of us, escape the rat race life of Manhattan.

Why was I thinking in terms of "we"? I was an "I" type of guy. I'd already told Lacey we didn't have a relationship. Truth was, though, I'd lied to her. Moreover, I'd lied to myself. I wanted to be with her. With Lacey.

She wasn't as beautiful as Nieves, but Lacey's allure was inside as well as outside. And she was strong. Strong and brilliant and challenging. All of those virtues added to her simple beauty.

I watched her as she stooped to pick a wildflower. I watched as she brought it to her nose and inhaled. I watched as she tucked it behind her ear.

I watched, mesmerized.

She turned then, and smiled when our gazes met. "I can see why you love it here so much. It's simply beautiful."

I nodded and walked to her, taking her hand. "You're beautiful."

Rosiness swept over her cheeks.

"You must know how beautiful you are, Lacey."

"Not like Nieves."

"Nieves is nothing compared to you." I knelt down, picked another blue flower, and placed this one behind her other ear. "You look like a garden nymph, with your hair down around your shoulders. You should be wearing a wreath of baby's breath on your head and a long flowing skirt over those amazing hips."

"You think I look like a hippie?"

"No, not a hippie." Hadn't she heard me? "A garden nymph. Or a goddess of the woods."

"That's sweet." She giggled. "But you don't look like a god of the woods. You look like a dark god. A god of war or something like that."

"Do I? You think I look evil?"

"No. Not at all." She giggled again. "But your tan skin and your nearly black hair, and then those piercing green eyes that stare at me as if they're dissolving my clothes with some kind of laser ray but could also stare down anything in the universe. You're so strong, Rock. You look like you could overcome anything in your way."

"You see all that in me? Because I have dark hair?"

"It's not just your hair, silly. It's your looks, yes, but it's all of you. Your personality, your demeanor, the way you make me want to do anything to please you." She blushed again. "I shouldn't have said that last part."

My heart raced, and my cock hardened. But more than either of those, emotion burst through me like holiday carols.

I felt good.

More than good.

I felt...*happy*.

Damn.

Even in the face of the shitstorm that had currently overtaken my life, I fucking felt *happy*.

Not that I hadn't been content before. I loved my life here. Working outdoors, riding, hunting, sitting by my fire on a chilly evening.

I'd been content since I'd arrived in Montana all those years ago.

But happiness, true happiness, had eluded me.

Until now.

Now, when I had to leave my home and do a job I hated, deal with my family, worry over my little sister...I'd found happiness.

I never thought another person could be the key to happiness.

Indeed, I still didn't think that. It wasn't Lacey so much as Lacey and me together. The two of us. That made me happy. I'd been worried about Riley, and I'd hardly touched Lacey since we arrived here, yet still I felt complete in a strange and content way, just because of her presence.

Damn.

I wasn't sure I had it in me to actually do a relationship. I'd been holding back. I knew that. I wanted her so much, ached for her...

Loved her.

I fucking loved this woman who I'd known for so little time.

I opened my mouth to actually say the words, but before I could, a police car drove up.

42

LACEY

Warmth coursed through me. Rock was staring at me with something new in his eyes. The lust, yes, but something almost...reverent.

I shivered, tensed, and shivered again, until he opened his mouth.

"What the...?" he said.

I turned. A police car drove slowly up Rock's cobblestone driveway. My heart sank. We'd been about to have a moment. I was sure of it.

I sighed. Probably something to do with his father's murder. But why here in Montana? The crime had occurred in New York.

"Wait here," Rock said and walked toward the squad car.

A uniformed deputy stepped out. "Mr. Wolfe? Rock Wolfe?"

"Yes, that's me. What can I do for you?"

"We're looking for a Lacey Ward."

My stomach dropped. What did they want with me?

"Is that her?" the officer asked.

"Maybe it is and maybe it isn't," Rock said. "What do you want with her?"

"She's wanted for questioning in a murder case in New York.

We've been asked to make sure she returns to New York right away."

"I'm Lacey Ward," I said, approaching. "Unless you're here to arrest me, you can tell the department in New York that I'll be back on Tuesday."

"We're not here to arrest you, ma'am, but apparently you've become a person of interest in the murder of Derek Wolfe."

"That's my father," Rock said. "Lacey had nothing to do with anything. You heard her. She'll be back on Tuesday, and I'm sure she'll cooperate with the NYPD at that time."

"Ma'am, they need to talk to you right away."

"Have they heard of a phone?"

"They've asked—"

I held up my hand to stop his words. "I won't be talking to anyone without an attorney present, and I won't be able to get counsel until Tuesday anyway, since this is a holiday weekend."

"Listen," Rock said. "Lacey here is an attorney herself, and I know a setup when I see it. This has my mother written all over it."

"Your mother?" I said.

"Yeah. Connie's trying to pull something here. She got the NYPD to call the county sheriff out here to harass us. I haven't quite figured out why yet. I already agreed to give her the money she wanted. After all, she was married to the louse."

"Look," the deputy said. "All I know is I'm supposed to get you back for questioning."

"Not without arresting me," I said adamantly.

"You heard the lady," Rock said.

"Then I'll have to arrest you."

"On what grounds?"

"Accessory to murder."

My mouth dropped open. "What?"

"You heard me, ma'am." He pulled out his handcuffs. "You have the right to remain silent—"

"This is bullshit," Rock said. "Who paid you off? My mother?"

"Are you suggesting I've been bribed, sir?"

"That's exactly what I'm suggesting. Whatever she paid you, I'll double it. Lacey had nothing to do with any of this."

"He's right. I drew up Derek Wolfe's will," I said. "That's it. Ask anyone. You have no probable cause to arrest me on any grounds."

"You look like a nice person," he said. "I'm just doing my job."

My heart beat like rapid thunderclaps against my sternum. Why was this happening? Numbly, I held out my hands. As the cuffs clicked in place, I held back a heave.

"You have the right to remain silent," he said again. "Anything you choose to say can and will be held against you. You have the right to an attorney. If you can't afford an attorney, one will be appointed to represent you. Do you understand these rights as I've stated them?"

"Uncuff her." Rock's low voice came from behind me.

The deputy's eyes widened and his eyebrows nearly flew off his forehead.

I turned.

Rock was pointing a pistol right at the deputy. When had he gone in to get it? I'd been so busy freaking out over the potential arrest, I hadn't noticed.

"Sir, put that gun down."

"I will not. Uncuff her. She'll be back in New York on Tuesday. Until then, she's not going anywhere."

"I'll have to arrest both of you, then."

"You're funny. Give it your best shot. I'm the one holding the gun here."

The deputy twitched his hand slightly.

"Don't even think about going for your own," Rock said. "I'll have a bullet in your shoulder before you're halfway there."

"Rock," I said swiftly. "Think about what you're doing here."

I said no more. I didn't want to give the deputy any more ideas. Although there were no grounds for arresting me, Rock had just given them grounds to arrest *him*.

Pulling a gun on a cop. What was he thinking?

"Lacey is as innocent as a lamb. Now what's it going to take for you to walk out of here and pretend no one was home?"

"More than you've got, living out here."

"I knew you were dirty." Rock snickered. "I've got way more than my mother, who I'm pretty sure is the brains behind this stupidity."

"Don't insinuate—"

"Please. This lady is a lawyer and a damned good one. She'd never get involved in killing my father on any level. How much did my mother pay you?"

The deputy sighed and unlocked my handcuffs. "I don't know what you're talking about."

"Sure, you don't." Once I was free of the cuffs, Rock continued. "Step back, Lacey."

"Rock, I—"

"Step back," he said again, this time more commanding.

"You know I'm calling for backup as soon as I get back into my car."

"Do I look like a moron to you? Of course you will. And whoever comes this way will get an earful about how you were bribed."

"That's your word against mine."

"I think I'll get them to see my side of things," Rock said. "Depends on how much of a chance you want to take."

"Rock—"

"Lacey, I'm not going to say it again. Get in the cabin."

Anger swirled within me. Who the hell did he think he was? "I'm not going anywhere. This clearly involves me more than it does you."

"Look," the deputy said. "Let's just call it a day, okay? I won't call for backup. Forget I was ever here."

Rock chuckled, still holding the gun. "I won't forget it, Deputy"—he eyed the cop's name badge—"Gore. I'll have your badge. Now get the fuck out of here."

He walked slowly to his car, never taking his gaze from Rock, got in, and drove away.

Rock turned to me. "Are you all right?"

My heart hammered. "Please, Rock. Put down the gun."

"Sorry." He laid the pistol on the ground. "Do guns scare you?"

"Not as a rule, but *you* scared me, Rock. You pulled a gun on an officer of the law."

"He was dirty, Lace. I've been around this block more than a few times. I've seen dirty cops before, and he had the look. I swear to you."

"He may have been dirty, but you still just pulled a gun on him. You could be arrested."

"Don't worry about me. I'll just call Reid and have him take care of all of it. You'd be amazed what money can buy. I didn't learn much this first week at my new position, but I sure as hell learned that." He pulled out his cellphone and soon was talking to his brother.

I sat down on one of the redwood Adirondack chairs on his front porch, my heart still thundering. What had just happened here? Someone tried to have me arrested for accessory to Derek Wolfe's murder. I'd been home alone when the crime occurred.

I knew that.

But no one else did.

I lived alone. I had no alibi.

Nausea welled within me. If someone chose to push this...

But he was killed with a gun. I didn't own a gun. Had never even shot a gun. The sight of Rock wielding a pistol still made me feel sick. He'd been protecting me, and I loved him for it, but he'd probably made things worse for both of us.

He returned in about ten minutes. "Reid is on it. Deputy Gore will be unemployed within the hour."

I nodded numbly.

"You sure you're okay, Lace?"

I gulped. "No. I'm not sure of anything at all right now."

"Hey. We'll hop on my bike and disappear if you want. All you have to do is say the word."

I stared at him. "What?"

"I mean it. I'll make it happen. Neither of us has to deal with any more of this bullshit."

"But your brothers. Your sister. My law firm."

"I love my siblings, but I don't know them. I've been away too long. Roy has his art. Reid will bounce back in no time. The man's a genius businessman. And Riley...well, she doesn't want to be found right now, according to my brothers. As much as I want to help her, there's nothing I can do."

"But the company..."

"Will be sold. I get it. I've always gotten it, but..." His eyes softened. "You're more important than all of that."

Had I heard him right? "What?" I said again.

"I know. I can't believe it myself. And I hope you don't turn around and run away when I tell you this, but I'm in love with you, Lacey. I'm totally and completely in love with you."

43

ROCK

Elation filled me, as if a giant cement block had been lifted off my shoulders. How could professing love to a woman make me feel so light inside? So happy? So completely fulfilled?

All I knew was, when that dirty deputy had cuffed her and she paled with fear, I was ready to do anything—*anything*—to protect her, to keep her out of harm's way.

I loved her. I totally loved her.

She hadn't said it back. She just stared at me, her eyes wide.

I wanted to hear her say the words, but even more, I wanted her to *feel* them.

But if she didn't? I'd said them. I'd opened myself up to another human being, something I'd never done.

It was miraculously freeing.

"What?"

I smiled. "That's the third time you've said what. I'm pretty sure you don't have a hearing problem."

"I... I..."

"You don't usually have a speaking problem, either." I touched her cheek, her skin like the softest velvet.

"You... You're...in love with me?"

"Why is that so surprising?"

She shook her head. "Only for about a dozen or more reasons, not the least of which is that you made it very clear that we didn't have a relationship."

"I know. I apologize. I was burying the feelings I was developing for you. They scared the shit out of me, Lace."

"We've known each other a week."

"A week and three days." I smiled.

"Oh, okay," she said sarcastically.

"Look. I don't have any experience in this kind of stuff. That's for sure. But I sure hated seeing you with both of those pretty boys. I wasn't sure what that meant, but when I came out here this morning and saw you pick that flower and put it behind your ear, I knew. And if I had any lingering doubts at all, they were erased when I watched that bozo cuff you. I was willing to do anything to protect you. I would have shot the motherfucker dead if I'd thought he was going to harm you in any way."

She gulped audibly. "Rock, I—"

I touched my finger to her lips to silence her. "You don't have to say anything. But I'm glad I told you. In fact, I don't think I've ever been happier to utter three words in my life."

"No," she said, brushing my hand away. "I'm glad you said it. Surprised...but very, very glad. Because... I love you too, Rock."

Warmth spread through me like the joy of a child on Christmas morning. I'd never known such wonder, such happiness. I wanted to shout to the world that I was in love and then take her inside and make passionate love to her for the rest of my life.

"You have the most beautiful smile," she said. "It lights up your whole face."

"Nothing about me is anywhere near as radiant as you are."

No truer words. She stood before me in her simple clothes, no makeup, wildflowers behind her ears.

She was the most beautiful thing I'd ever seen.

"Are you sure?" she asked. "I mean, you said—"

"Forget what I said. I was scared. I love you, Lacey Ward. I love you so damned much." I pulled her to me and crushed my lips to hers.

As many times as I'd kissed her, this one was different. Different and amazing and wonderful. The soft moan from the back of her throat hummed, and I felt more than heard it. The kiss was so raw, so powerful, and my cock throbbed.

I was wearing only the jeans, so the denim rubbed against me as I hardened. I pushed into her, trying to ease the ache, but only one thing would crush this yearning.

To be inside her. Inside that hot little pussy that gripped me so tightly.

I broke the kiss abruptly. "Inside," I said. "Now."

Her lips, red and swollen, trembled as she nodded. Then I scooped her into my arms and carried her through the door and into the cabin.

We'd been here since last night and I hadn't made love to her.

Something had stopped me. Worry about my sister. About my responsibilities. About everything.

Those thoughts still niggled at me, but what better way to relax than to make love with my woman?

My woman.

I stopped in the living room and laid her gently on the couch. Then, not so gently, I pulled off her jeans and inhaled. Her musk was already in the air, so fruity and feminine. As much as I wanted to dive between her legs and taste her, that would have to wait.

I needed to be inside her. Inside her warmth and sweetness.

I pulled off my jeans quickly and my cock sprang out. Her eyes widened as she licked her lips. Had I been with someone else, I'd make a smartass comment. Not now. Not with this woman who I loved.

I mounted her, rubbed my cock head between her slick folds, and then thrust into her balls deep. "Ah, God," I groaned.

She clamped her hands onto my butt cheeks and pulled me even closer so I was so far into her we were nearly one.

Nearly one.

Why had I fought this? Everything about Lacey Ward interested me, intrigued me.

Enthralled me.

I pulled out and thrust back in. Her eyes were closed, her long lashes a soft curtain over her cheeks.

"Open your eyes, Lacey. Please. Open your eyes and look at me. Watch me making love to you."

She obeyed, her blue eyes sparkling.

I pulled out, missing her tightness already. "Get on top of me, baby. I want to show you something."

She got up, and I lay down on my back.

"Ride me. Sink your pussy down onto my cock."

She obeyed, a soft sigh escaping her throat like a spring breeze.

I watched. I watched her pussy eat up my cock.

"Look down," I said. "Watch me go into you. It's beautiful."

She obeyed once more. "It is. So beautiful."

The rhythm mesmerized me. She set the pace, but soon I was rushing, couldn't go quickly enough. I pushed my hips upward, taking over the rhythm.

"God, baby," I said through clenched teeth. "My God. You feel so good. So fucking good."

She whimpered, and when she trailed her right hand over

the swell of her breast, down her perfectly shaped belly, and to her swollen clit, I nearly exploded.

"God, yeah. Touch yourself, baby. You're so hot."

She moaned as she gently rubbed at her clit, and when her nipples puckered and her pussy clamped down, I could hold out no longer.

I came.

I came harder than I ever had in my life. Shudders racked my body as my world became my cock inside her pussy, the two of us joined together.

Lacey.

Me.

Lacey and me.

I filled her with my hot come. I filled her with my everlasting love.

I filled her.

But truly? She filled *me*.

When we both finally slowed down our breathing, she collapsed on top of me.

My arms went around her and I held her.

Such new feelings. Such amazing feelings that I could almost forget...

I was a fucking mess.

She knew nothing about me.

Would she still love me when she finally knew everything? All my secrets?

I tightened my grip on her. Never wanted to let go.

I'd hold on to her for as long as I could.

Because eventually she would find out the truth.

Eventually she would leave.

44

LACEY

Mrs. *Rock Wolfe.*
   Mrs. Lacey Wolfe.
   Rock and Lacey Wolfe.

Rock Wolfe, CEO of Wolfe Enterprises, and his wife, Manhattan Attorney Lacey Ward Wolfe, attend a charitable gala at the Waldorf Astoria.

Rock and Lacey Ward Wolfe proudly announce the birth of...

God help me.

I'd regressed to fifth grade in my head, doodling names on the cover of my three-ring binder.

He was in love with me.

Rock Wolfe was in love with me.

Me.

He could have a beautiful supermodel. Or an exotic cosmetologist named Nieves. Or any starlet in Hollywood. They'd all be proud to be seen on his arm.

He chose me.

Me.

It was all too unreal to be true. Any minute I'd wake up. It would be all over. He'd be telling me we didn't have a relationship.

And I'd be hauled off for questioning in his father's murder.

An anvil hit my gut.

That last part—it was true.

"Baby?" He cupped my cheek. "You're shivering. What's wrong?"

"It just hit me. I was handcuffed and nearly arrested today."

"Don't worry about that. My mother was behind it."

"Why? Why would she want me arrested? And what if she *wasn't*, Rock? What if, somehow, I've been implicated in your father's murder?"

"Honey, please don't worry." He pressed his lips to mine in a soft kiss. "I won't let anything happen to you. I meant it when I said we could leave today. Hop on my bike and never look back."

"Running away isn't the answer."

"It worked pretty well for me the first time." His eyes took on a haunted look.

I wanted to ask him what he meant by that. Yes, I knew he'd left his family and come here to Montana, but I didn't know why.

Something kept me from asking, though. He hadn't been forthcoming with information in the past, and just because we'd professed our love for each other, I still didn't feel he would be. As much as I wanted to know, this was something Rock kept private.

Very private.

I wasn't about to push him. I had to let him go at his own pace.

I cupped his cheek, his stubble rough under my fingertips. "I can't run away. It's not who I am."

"Sometimes it's the only choice, baby. We can't control other people or what they choose to do to us. The only thing we can control is whether we stick around to let them continue."

I couldn't fault his logic, but still I shook my head. "We need to go home."

"We will. Monday evening as planned."

I shook my head more vehemently. "No. We need to go now. I'll never be able to relax without knowing what's going on. An officer was ready to arrest me as an accessory to your father's murder."

"But he didn't, Lacey. He didn't because he had no grounds. I'm telling you. This is Connie's work."

"Why would your mother have anything against me?"

"Why do birds sing?" He shook his head. "I gave up trying to figure my mother out years ago. She made decisions I didn't understand then, and she continues to now."

"She's truly that bad?"

He chuckled. "I don't have a mommy complex, baby. I'm not looking for someone to fill her shoes."

"That's not what I meant."

"I know that. I'm just saying that I don't see her through rose-colored glasses. She's not a good person, Lace. I wish she were, but she's not. I suppose she's not as bad as my father was, but truly, is the witness to the crime just as guilty if she says nothing?"

"What are you talking about, Rock?"

"Nothing." He clammed up and stood, replacing his jeans. "I'm going to shower, and then I'm taking you out on the bike. It's what we came here for. I'm not letting some dirty cop or my mother or anyone else ruin this weekend for us." He stalked off.

Rock Wolfe might think he didn't have mommy issues, but he had some kind of issue, something he'd buried so deep that he ran all the way to Montana to escape it. He'd tell me when he was ready.

I just wasn't sure I wanted to know.

45

ROCK

My mother.

I had one good memory, and it was the earliest thing I could recall. I was barely three, and my nanny, Alexandria, brought me to the hospital to meet my new little brother. My mother smiled at me. She was beautiful when she smiled, at least when she *really* smiled. I climbed into her hospital bed next to her, and she let me hold baby Roy. He had a mop of black hair and his face was red, but I loved him just the same.

He was my baby.

"He's your baby, Rock," she said. "Yours to help and protect. He'll always look up to you."

Roy hadn't needed my protection, though. He was a recluse who kept to himself. I did protect Reid from a few beatings courtesy of our father, and God knew I'd tried to protect Riley.

I'd been successful with Reid—until I was banished.

Unsuccessful with Riley.

At fourteen, I was the victim of risk-taking testosterone.

In that moment, I had truly wanted to end my father's life.

Looking back, I was glad I'd failed. I wouldn't be able to live with myself, even though the asshole had deserved what I'd planned.

But Riley...

She didn't deserve what had continued after I was gone. My brothers hadn't protected her because they hadn't known what was going on. I felt sure they would have intervened had they known.

How could they not have known?

It had been so obvious to me.

But my room was next to Riley's. We had the two biggest bedrooms, next to our father's. Mom and Dad had separate rooms. Mom gave Riley the second largest room in our new mansion. Reid and Roy had grumbled, but she'd said a girl needed more space. As the oldest, I still got the biggest room. I wasn't sure why, and I didn't ask at the time.

Riley's was the farthest away from my mother's.

Maybe my mother had truly thought she needed more space.

Or maybe she knew what was coming, and she didn't want to hear it. That way, she could pretend it wasn't happening.

Sounded like vintage Connie Wolfe to me.

On the other hand, though, why would she want her oldest son closest to her daughter? Surely she'd—

Unless...

My mother was hoping I'd do something to stop it.

That was a hell of a burden to put on a fourteen-year-old boy—a burden she herself should have borne to protect her daughter.

She just wasn't strong enough.

Or she didn't care enough.

Or maybe that was why my mother hated me so much. I hadn't just failed Riley. In her mind, I'd failed her as well.

I scoffed. I'd wanted more than anything to protect my sister, but I was a kid myself. My mother had placed the burden on a kid, a rebellious kid who was likely to pull out a knife and attempt to kill his own father.

Which was exactly what I'd done.

If my father had died while my parents were still married, everything would have gone to her. Had she been hoping I'd kill him? And take the blame? She'd be off scot-free. Rich and rid of him.

And rid of me.

She and I had always been like oil and water. I wasn't sure why, but we never did click. Not since that day when Roy came into the world. That was the fondest memory I had of Connie Wolfe.

I finished washing my hair and body and stood under the stream of hot water, letting it cleanse me of the memories of my youth. My life had been one fucked up mess, and I wasn't going to let my mother or anyone else screw up what I could have with Lacey.

Which meant one thing.

I had to take the reins.

I had to solve my father's murder myself, before someone could frame Lacey or anyone else I cared about.

I scoffed again. The only other three people I cared about were Reid, Roy, and Riley.

My mother hadn't murdered my father. She wouldn't get her manicured hands dirty. In fact, she probably hadn't hired it out. She was too smart for that. No, Connie Wolfe was simply doing what she always did, taking advantage of the situation at hand.

She wasn't a killer.

Neither was I, despite my rash actions as a teen.

And neither was Lacey.

Why would anyone want to implicate Lacey? Was there something I didn't know about her?

I laughed out loud. Funny. There was a *lot* I didn't know about her.

Of course, there was a lot I *did* know about her too. I knew she had a tiny raised mole at the top of her right thigh and an angel's kiss birthmark on the back of her neck. I knew she had the sweetest natural fragrance. I couldn't get enough of it when I was kissing her neck. I knew her hair smelled like pineapple and coconut, and that her nipples got hard when I so much as looked at her.

But I didn't know her favorite ice cream. I didn't know what she liked to read for pleasure. I didn't know why she'd chosen to go into law as a career.

Still, there was no doubt in my mind that I loved her.

Loved her so damned much.

The thought of my life without her in it...well, it would be no life at all.

I couldn't let my mother or anyone else drag her into this murder investigation. I'd figure it out myself. My brothers would help me. I already knew Roy was hiding something. He was going to tell me what it was, whether he wanted to or not.

The water continued to pelt me.

Wouldn't life be so much simpler if Lacey had taken me up on my offer to ride off into the sunset? We'd have a simple life, but a good life. Only the two of us with no one to answer to. It was a life I was accustomed to, a life I loved.

A life I wished I could get back.

A life I could have gotten back. The only cost would have been my siblings.

And Lacey.

I wouldn't have met Lacey.

Or I would have met her, but I would have told all of them to fuck off and hightailed it back here. To my home. It would have been a much simpler decision.

A soft knock on the door. "Rock?"

I cleared my throat. "Yeah?"

"Everything okay? You've been in there a while."

The water had indeed gone from steamy to tepid. I turned it off and wiped my face on a towel. "Yeah. I'm good."

But was I?

I could do it. I could take off on my bike, Lacey on the back, and never return. I didn't even have to tell her what I was up to. By the time she figured it out, we'd be across the Canadian border. I knew exactly where to cross. I even knew a guy who could get us Canadian passports.

It was tempting. So tempting.

As much as I desired it, I knew I'd never do it. I wouldn't double-cross Lacey. I couldn't double-cross my brothers and sister.

I wouldn't let whoever was attempting to double-cross Lacey win.

My mother may well have implicated Lacey. She'd tried extortion with me, and I'd succumbed rather than deal with the truth coming out about my past. But Connie Wolfe hadn't murdered my father. She was manipulative, petty, and liked to turn a blind eye to things she didn't want to deal with, but she was not a killer.

There was only one way for me to get Lacey out of this. I had to find out who had offed Derek Wolfe.

And I couldn't do that from Canada.

Lacey wasn't in the bedroom when I left the bathroom. I got dressed quickly in my riding garb, and then I went to my gun safe. I kept most of my guns there, all but the Smith & Wesson nine millimeter that I'd pulled on ex-Deputy Gore.

My Glock 23—the one I could easily conceal—was in the safe. It was going with me wherever I went from now on. Funny. It was the same model that had killed my father.

I carefully dialed the combination, and—

"Mother fuck."

The Glock was missing.

46

LACEY

I knocked on the bedroom door again. "Rock?"

No answer. Was he still in the bathroom? I entered. Rock stood facing the wall. The painting on the wall facing the bed sat on the floor, and a wall safe was opened. Rock stared into it.

I approached. Several small guns sat in the safe. My heart jumped as a sliver of fear sliced into me.

"Rock?" I said again, this time more timidly. "Everything okay?"

He shook his head. "Everything's not okay. Not even close."

I gulped. "That's a lot of guns."

"One less than should be here."

"Why would you— Oh. Shit."

"Someone stole my Glock. The exact model that was used to kill my dad."

"But your gun didn't kill your dad, Rock. You'd know that by now."

"You're right. I know. But still, this doesn't look good. Especially with my prints—"

"Your prints?"

"I know. It's crazy."

"You weren't even in the state of New York when your father was murdered."

He nodded. "I have an ironclad alibi. Except that no one was here with me."

"Rock, you were on a plane the next day. That's easily traceable."

"I know that, damn it! I'm not a moron, Lacey."

"Easy."

"Sorry, baby. But this is a fucking mess."

"No, it's not. I'm sorry someone stole your gun, but you weren't in New York. They can't possibly implicate you. I'm clearly the one who's been implicated, and I was in Manhattan that night. I'm the one without an alibi, Rock. I was alone in my apartment. I have no alibi."

"Your doorman?"

"Maybe."

"Someone is trying to get to me through you. Damned if I know why, though. Maybe I was wrong. Maybe my mother isn't behind this. Who else would want me to rot for the murder of my father?"

"Do you have any enemies?"

"Only my father, and even he isn't stupid enough to plan his own death to get me from beyond the grave. Though he did do just that with that damned will of his."

I cleared my throat. I had to ask, though I knew he wouldn't answer. "Just why is your father an enemy, Rock? What happened between you two?"

His lips were a flat line.

No response. Not that I expected one.

I cupped his cheek. "It's okay. You don't have to talk about it. But if someone is implicating me—"

"I'll protect you."

I sighed. If only he could. Not even Wolfe money could get me out of this mess if someone had decided to frame me.

Why would anyone want to frame me?

Rock thought his mother might be behind this, but I didn't even know his mother. She couldn't possibly know Rock and I were together. We'd kept it pretty hush hush. Though if Roy and Reid knew…

Still, it didn't make any sense.

Every lawyer instinct in me told me his mother wasn't behind this. Of course, I'd never met the woman, and according to Rock, she was no saint.

My father had once cautioned me never to get involved with a man who had a bad relationship with his mother. "The way he treats his mother is an indication of how he'll treat you," he'd said on more than one occasion.

Boy, had I not heeded that advice.

Rock seemed to dislike his mother nearly as much as he disliked his father.

And there had been times in the few days since I'd met him that Rock had treated me less than nicely.

Oh, God…

"First thing we do is check with your doorman," he said. "He'll know when you came in and when you left. My father was killed during the night, so if you got home from work and then didn't leave until morning, and the doorman knows that, you're in the clear."

"Someone could pay the doorman off."

"I'll pay more."

"Damn it, I don't want anyone paying anyone! This is crazy! I'm not guilty of anything."

"I know, baby. I know. I'm going to make my mother or whoever it turns out to be pay for this."

"Rock, I've been thinking. Why would your mother want to frame me?"

"Why does Connie Wolfe do anything? She's a nut job."

"She's your mother. She created you. She can't be all bad."

He shook his head, chuckling. "She's a mercenary, Lacey. She married my father for the money, lay in his bed for the money, and then, when he divorced her, she made sure she got plenty of his money for her troubles."

"Does she even know about me? About you and me, I mean?"

"I don't know."

"If she doesn't know about us, why would she have any interest in framing me?"

"She's not trying to frame you, Lace. She's trying to fuck with me."

"Why would she do that?"

"Because it's what she does. If it made any sense, she wouldn't be Connie Wolfe."

I sighed. "Maybe we *should* fly home. This is a mess. I feel so out of control here. And now with your gun gone..."

"I'll take you home if it's what you truly want, but I promised you the ride of your life. You'll love it."

I kissed his lips. "All right. Let's take that ride. I'd love to get my mind off of all of this."

AFTER A QUICK DRIVE into the small Montana town to pick up riding gear for me, Rock strapped a helmet on my head, and we were off.

I held on to Rock for dear life at first, especially when he took hairpin turns around the windy back road. But soon I was looking above at the big sky, enjoying the wind on my face and the beautiful scenery around me.

We stopped for a late lunch at a biker bar.

Yes, a biker bar. I, Lacey Nicole Ward, good girl extraordinaire, went into a biker bar.

"Rock Wolfe! Good to see you!" A burly and bearded man wearing a black Harley vest greeted us.

"Hey, Burke, good to see you too. Though I think you just saw me two weeks ago."

"True that. But I heard you went off to New York."

"Where'd you hear that?"

"Word gets around," he said. "How about a beer?"

"Not while I'm riding. But we'll look at the menu for lunch."

"Good enough." He sauntered away.

"That's odd," Rock said.

"What?"

"That he knows I went to New York. I never talk about my family with these guys. They have no idea I'm part of *that* Wolfe family."

"It wouldn't be too hard to find out," I said. "Just do a search for Derek Wolfe, and his children will be listed. How many Rock Wolfes are there in the world?"

He shook his head. "I smell a rat somewhere. Like I told Burke, I was just in here two weeks ago, before my father died. There was no reason for him to even know I'd been out of town."

A tattooed server with three nose rings brought us water and menus.

"Honey, could you send Burke back over here?" Rock said.

I didn't relish him calling her honey, but if he was attracted to me, no way would he be attracted to her. She was pretty, but I was as strait-laced as they came. No ink, no piercings. Well, my ears, but that didn't count.

"Sure, Rock."

"You know her?"

"That's Honey. She's Burke's sister."

I nearly spit out the drink of water I'd taken. "Honey is her name?"

"Yeah..." Then he guffawed. "You thought I was calling her honey?"

"What else was I supposed to think?"

Rock continued to laugh.

"I don't see anything funny from where I'm sitting." I took another drink of water.

"Sorry, Lace. But Honey and I..." He continued laughing. "It's just too much to even think about. Besides, she lives with two men. They share her."

"They what?"

"It's a threesome. A permanent ménage a trois."

"Do the guys...? With each other?"

"I have no idea." He shook his head. "Don't want to know. But if they do, you can bet no one gives them any shit. They're both the size of tanks."

"And her brother...?"

"Burke looks the other way. What else can he do?"

"Oh my God..."

"Sweet little Lace. You're so sheltered."

"I'm not..." I stopped. "I can't pull that off. I'm a Manhattan attorney. I was raised on Long Island. My parents are still married. I had a normal childhood. Yeah, I guess I'm a little sheltered."

"You are, but that's part of what makes you *you*." Rock smiled.

God, that smile. It could melt the polar ice caps.

Burke sauntered back over. "Honey said you wanted to talk?"

"Yeah." Rock cleared his throat. "I was just wondering... How did you know I was in New York?"

"Heard it from...Manny, I think? Or maybe Hoss."

I couldn't help a smile. "Manny and Hoss? Are we trapped in an old episode of *Bonanza*?"

Burke erupted in laughter. "That's some funny little lady you got there. Sweetheart, Hoss is an attorney in Billings. Real name is Horace Stiers the third. Manny is Parker Manfred, a gynecologist. The two of them come down on the weekends."

"Weekend bikers?" I said.

"Sure. Doctors and lawyers who pretend to be bikers on the weekend. Hoss and Manny are good guys, though. They're around. I expect them in for lunch any time now."

"How would they know I'd gone to Manhattan?" Rock eyed the menu.

"Don't know," Burke said. "But you can ask them yourself. They're walking in the door."

47

ROCK

Manny's broad shoulders and short, stocky build were a stark contrast to Hoss's height and lankiness. We sometimes called them Mutt and Jeff. Both were bald as cue balls, Manny by choice, Hoss by genetics.

"Hey, guys," Burke said, motioning them over. "Look who's back!"

"Jesus, Burke. I wasn't gone for long."

"Hey, Rock." Manny held out his hand. "Good to see you. Nice do."

Right. My short hair. "Ha! Funny, coming from you. Sit down, guys."

"Don't mind if we do." Hoss grabbed a chair, turned it, and straddled it. "Who's this lovely lady?"

"Lacey Ward. She's an attorney too."

Hoss held out a hand to Lacey, and she shook it tentatively.

"You're way prettier than any of the old stodges at my firm. We've got some juicy associates, though."

Lacey reddened. She wouldn't find Hoss's sexist talk particularly amusing.

"Knock it off, Hoss," I said. "I need to talk to you two."

"Yeah? What about?"

"Burke says one of you guys told him I'd gone to New York."

"That'd be me," Manny said.

"Interesting. Exactly how did you know that? I didn't tell anyone when I left."

"A new patient," Manny said. "She came in, and we were doing the requisite small talk while I was examining her. Anyway, she asked if I knew you, and I said yes. Then she said you were in New York."

"Do you remember her name?"

"Not offhand," he said. "But I wouldn't be able to tell you anyway. Doctor-patient confidentiality and all."

"I'll make it worth your while," I said.

"Rock, if you think I'm the kind of guy who'd sell his integrity—"

"Then you're right!" Hoss slapped his knee.

"Thanks, ass munch. Nice, coming from my lawyer." Manny chuckled. "I can't help you, Rock. I'm sorry."

"Fuck." I shook my head. "This was a new patient, you say? A woman?"

"Men don't usually have gynecological issues," Manny said.

"Funny." I searched my mind. It couldn't have been my mother. She only let her own personal physician and plastic surgeon near her. One look at Manny's shaved head and beer belly, and she'd have hightailed it out of there. Besides, I'd interacted with her on a nearly daily basis since I'd returned to New York.

Who else would know I'd gone to New York? And why would she mention it to her gynecologist?

"Look, Manny," I said. "I get the confidentiality thing, but I need to know who this person is. I'm investigating my father's murder."

Manny reddened.

"Shit," I said. "She told you something else, didn't she?"

"I'm sorry." Manny shook his head. "I can't. It's not worth my license. I shouldn't have told Burke you were in New York. It has nothing to do with her treatment, so I'm probably in the clear, but I should have kept mum."

"Agreed," Hoss said.

I turned to Lacey. "Is there any way around the confidentiality thing?"

She shook her head. "I'm afraid not, unless you subpoena his records. But to do that the records would need to be relevant to some sort of legal claim. A civil lawsuit or a workers comp case, for example."

"Damn."

"I'm real sorry, man," Manny said. "I should've kept my big trap shut."

"You're not going to lose your license over this," Hoss said. "Hell, I've seen doctors who fuck their patients get off. Gotten a few off myself, as long as they pay their bills."

"What does it matter, anyway?" Manny asked.

"I told you," I said. "I'm investigating my father's murder."

"And that has to do with my patient...why?"

"Maybe nothing, but I'm following every lead. Why would some new patient of yours know anything about me?"

"Maybe she read about your father's death." Manny took a drink of the beer Honey had set in front of him.

"No," I said. "You said she asked you if *you* knew me."

"Look," Manny said. "Can we just not talk anymore about this? I'm really uncomfortable."

"Damn," I said again.

A woman. And she'd told Manny something else, something he was loath to tell me. Manny was a good guy. He probably was truly concerned about doctor-patient confidentiality.

Who the hell was it?

Nieves? She'd found out somehow. But Manny knew Nieves. She wouldn't be a "new" patient. And Nieves would never let Manny near her.

No, this was someone else.

Someone here in Montana—or who'd come to Montana— knew I'd gone to New York when I hadn't told anyone I was leaving.

It could be completely innocent.

Yeah, right. There was something more here—something only Manny and his patient knew.

And I aimed to find out.

I opened my wallet and slid a hundred dollar bill—courtesy of my new ATM card that accessed the Wolfe troves—over to Manny. "There's a lot more where that came from. We've known each other for years, Manny. You know I wouldn't ask if it wasn't important."

"I get it, but I'm sorry. I can't."

"Especially not in front of his attorney," Lacey said. "And yours."

Easy enough to read between the lines. I needed to get Manny alone. If I promised to be discreet, I might be able to convince him to give me the woman's name. I didn't relish the idea of leaving Lacey in the company of Hoss, a serial misogynist, but I had to try.

"Care to step outside, Manny?" I said.

"Not at the moment."

Okay. So much for that idea.

Honey brought our meals, and we ate in silence, my mind churning. This could be nothing. A complete dead-end.

Or it could be a clue I needed.

Lacey clearly thought Manny could be bought, but she didn't know him. I did. He was a good guy, but even the best guys could sometimes be persuaded by the green god himself. Money.

Manny made a great living, but he had no idea the kind of money I now wielded.

I signaled Honey for the check. "It's on me today." I placed bills on the table.

"Thank you, Rock," Hoss said.

"Obliged," Manny agreed.

I stood, offering my hand to Lacey. "You know where I am if you change your mind." I led Lacey out the door.

"Okay, baby," I said. "We're taking another ride. A long one. A gorgeous one. I want you to free your mind and enjoy it. Because tonight I need you to use that beautiful brain of yours and figure out how we can get Manny to spill his guts."

"I don't think he will," she said. "He seems pretty principled. His attorney, on the other hand…"

"Hoss?"

"Yeah. I don't get a good vibe from him."

"Probably because he's a sexist pig."

"Well, that. Yeah." She smiled. "But more that he admits to defending doctors who screw their patients."

"He's an attorney. It's what he does."

"True. Part of the reason why I went into trusts and estates. I can't stand working with shitty people."

"You worked with my father."

"Yeah. When I got into the trusts and estates, I realized my error. There's no area of the law where you don't deal with shitty people, but I do see less than some."

"Hoss, huh?"

"I'm not telling you to bribe someone," she said. "But if you choose to do something like that without my knowledge, Hoss is where I'd start."

48

LACEY

The landscape deprived me of breath, it was so gorgeous. And the ride… Holding on to Rock's strong body while we nearly flew over the road held me captive.

Still, though, the thought of what had occurred this morning didn't completely leave my mind. I'd nearly been arrested.

As an accessory to a murder I knew nothing about.

In law school, we'd read cases about false arrest and imprisonment. There were even cases where an innocent person had been executed. They were rare, but they did occur. Statistically, they were insignificant.

They no longer seemed so insignificant now that I was starring in one.

Someone wanted me to pay for Derek Wolfe's murder. Why? I had no idea. All I'd done was draw up his will. I hadn't handled any of his other trust work. Robert had handed Derek over to me when he stopped practicing less than a year ago. Maybe Robert would know something. I made a mental note to get in touch with him when I returned to Manhattan.

When we finally arrived back at Rock's cabin, he stared at me.

"What?"

"You look so beautiful. You're glowing."

I attempted a smile. "I'm sure I've got a bad case of helmet head."

"You look perfect, Lacey." He feathered his fingers over my cheek.

My nipples hardened against my bra.

"I wish I could bottle up this moment," he continued.

I nodded. "Me too."

"But I can't. I need to find Hoss. I know where he and Manny hang out at night. If you think he's the one—"

"Only a hunch," I said. "I can't make any guarantees. I could be wrong, and he'll be pissed as hell that you're asking."

"Old Hoss won't be pissed. He'll respect me for trying."

"He'll respect you for bribing him?"

"Well," he laughed. "Maybe not. But I have to try. I need to find out what's going on. Someone has been keeping tabs on me, and someone is trying to drag you into this. That means someone knows what you mean to me. I'm beginning to think..."

"What, babe?"

"My father's had someone watching me this whole time. Here I thought I was alone in this cabin. Away from his vileness. Damn!" He looked up at the light fixture in his kitchen. "You son of a bitch! You were watching me the whole time, weren't you? You fucked up S.O.B.!"

I stroked his arm. "Rock, that's just a light."

He eased away from me. "You don't get it, Lace. Derek Wolfe could do anything he wanted."

"Why would he want to have you watched all this time?"

"Hell if I know. Why would he want to fuck me over from his grave?" He let out a sarcastic laugh. "That part I know. Because he was a dickhead. Because he wanted to control me. To punish me."

"Punish you? For what?"

He clammed up then, riffling his fingers through his short hair.

"What, Rock?" I persisted.

"Nothing. I need to go see Hoss."

"Where?" I asked, picturing another biker bar in my mind.

"Lucia's."

"Is that a bar?"

"Yeah...sort of. I mean, it *has* a bar."

"Get to the point, Rock. Where are you going?"

"I don't need to leave for a few hours. Besides, we haven't eaten yet. We should shower and get the bike grime off of us, and then I'll take you out for the best steak you'll ever eat."

I had to hand it to him. Rock Wolfe was a master at avoiding the subject. I wasn't born yesterday, though.

"What is Lucia's, Rock?"

"Fuck, Lacey. It's a strip club, okay?"

A brick hit me in the stomach. "Oh."

"I don't find any of those women remotely attractive. I never go there myself."

"Then how do you know about it?"

"Because I'm not a moron. I live here. Well, *lived* here."

"So you've never been there?"

"I didn't say that."

"You did. You said you never go there."

"Anymore. I never go there any*more*. I moved here when I was eighteen, Lace. Give me a break."

"When's the last time you went there?" I cringed at my own words. I sounded like a jealous teenager.

"I don't know. A year ago, maybe?"

"A year ago?"

"Yeah. For a bachelor party. For fuck's sake, Lace. Are you really upset about this? You?"

I inhaled and let the air slowly out of my lungs. I was being a complete child. "I'm sorry. This isn't me. I've just... I've never felt this way about anyone, Rock. I'm not quite sure I'm ready to deal with it."

"The first thing is trust, Lace."

"I know. I know."

But did I know? I'd had two significant relationships in my life, and both had ended with infidelity on their parts. I didn't talk about it. I didn't have any close friends. Instead, I threw myself into my work.

"Do you trust me?"

Did I? He could have run off with Nieves easily. She made me look like liverwurst. "We don't know each other very well yet."

"So you're saying you don't trust me?" He raked his fingers through his hair once more.

"That's not what I'm saying. But this all happened so quickly."

"Yeah, it did, but that doesn't make it any less real." He grabbed me and pulled me against his body. "I'm hard for you even now."

"That's physical, Rock. What about—"

He crushed his mouth to mine before I could finish my sentence. I opened instantly, giving him my tongue and then sucking on his. He tasted of the ride today, of the wild prairie, of the big Montana blue sky. Of wildflowers and leather. Of sunshine and cinnamon.

Of trust.

Silly, I knew. What did I know of trust? I'd been betrayed twice, and though I hadn't physically betrayed my previous lovers, I had in my mind.

He consumed me with the kiss, and soon I couldn't think at all. Only emotion bubbled through me.

Love, passion, desire.

Everything and nothing. All at once, from the pit of my belly to the tips of my fingers and toes. I knew nothing except this moment. This kiss.

This man.

He swept me into his arms, not breaking our kiss, and walked into the bedroom. There he finally broke the kiss with a loud smack.

"We're sweaty and dirty from riding all day, but I can't wait for a shower." He pushed my leather jacket over my shoulders, and it fell to the floor. Then he met my gaze with his searing green eyes. "I burn for you, Lacey. I fucking burn for you. I was hard all day just from having you hold on to me as we rode. I've never burned this way for a woman before."

I scraped my fingers across his stubbly cheek, letting my thumb fall over his full lower lip. He kissed it gently.

"Trust me," he said, his voice low and husky. "Trust me, Lacey."

In that moment I'd have promised him anything, if he'd only kiss me again.

Instead, he stared at me, heating me, nearly melting my clothes away. Even the leather chaps I wore seemed to melt under his gaze.

"I never imagined I could feel the way I feel about you. You've awakened something in me, Lacey. Something I thought was dead forever."

He pressed his lips to mine once more before I had a chance to consider his words.

Instead I melted into his kiss. His lips and tongue stayed occupied with my mouth while his hands deftly removed my leather chaps and riding boots. They plopped to the floor next to my jacket. My T-shirt and jeans went next, and soon I stood in only my bra and panties.

Scratch that.

Only my panties.

Rock made quick work of my bra.

He breathed in. "I smell you. Apples and roses. Nothing on earth smells as good as you do when you're ripe." He thrust one hand beneath my panties and through my slick folds. "So wet. So wet for me. Damn."

I moved my hips in a slow rhythm against his fingers, moaning and closing my eyes. My hard nipples poked out, aching and yearning for Rock's lips. As if he'd read my mind, he lowered his head and kissed one and then the other. One finger, and then two, slipped into my wet channel, and I rode him while he nibbled at my hard nipples.

"God, Rock. Oh my—"

A knock on the door startled me.

"Damn it." Rock removed his fingers from my pussy. "Not fucking now!"

"Seems we lost the moment." I attempted a smile. "You might as well see who it is. Meet me in the shower."

49

ROCK

M y fingers were still slick with Lacey's sweet cream. When the shower water whooshed, all I could think about was Lacey's gorgeous wet body...and I had to answer the damned door.

"Yeah, what is—" I opened the door and dropped my mouth open.

My brother Roy stood on the other side of the door. "Hi, Rock."

"What are you doing here, Roy?"

He stood silently for a couple seconds. Then, "May I come in?"

"Oh. Yeah. Sure." I closed the door behind him.

"Sorry to bust up your weekend."

"I'm not here alone, Roy."

"I figured as much. I won't keep you."

"What do you mean you won't keep me? You just flew two thousand miles, Roy. You obviously have something important to say or do here."

"Yeah." He looked down at his feet. "I'm just not sure how to begin."

Yeah. I'd known he was hiding something. So much for that shower with Lacey. "Always best to begin at the beginning. Have a seat." I motioned toward the couch. "Want a drink?"

"No thanks."

"Do *I* need one?"

"I don't know. Maybe."

Okay. Whatever was bothering my brother, I was going to have to pull it out of him with pliers.

Roy and I had never been close. Hell, I wasn't close to any of them, but Roy was by far the most of a stranger. I hadn't had hardly any contact with either him or Riley since I'd left New York in the first place. I wasn't even sure he had my Montana address, but he could have easily gotten it from Reid.

"Who's here with you?" Roy asked.

"None of your damned business." Who was I kidding? Lacey would walk out as soon as she was clean and dressed. I couldn't hide it. "Lacey Ward."

"Dad's lawyer? I'm not surprised, the way you were glaring at her date at the tavern the other night."

"Yeah, well, she's here, and she'll be done showering soon, so you want to get on with it?"

He stood. "You know? This was a mistake."

"For God's sake, Roy. Sit down."

He plopped back down in an almost obedient manner.

"What is it?" I asked again.

"Give me a minute or two, okay?" Roy's face had whitened, and his eyes were sunken and sad.

"What happened?" I said.

"Nothing. Well, not nothing."

"Which is it?" I asked, rapidly losing patience.

"I... I..."

I sighed. My brother and I had exchanged more words in the

last week and a half than we had in our entire lives. A sad state of affairs, one I'd perpetuated myself.

"Roy," I said, "what do you need? I'll help if I can."

"I needed your help a long time ago," he said with indignation, "but you weren't there."

I lifted my brow. "What exactly are you talking about?"

"Nothing." He clammed up again. "Forget it."

"You drop that bomb on me and tell me to forget it? No dice."

"I think I'll take that drink now."

I stood. "I'll do you one better. Lacey and I are going to dinner. Let's all go. After that, you need to relax and unwind a little."

"I won't deny that."

"I know the perfect place. We'll go after dinner."

TAKING A YOUNGER brother to a strip club was something most guys did well before my age. I'd missed out on a lot by leaving my siblings behind when I finally got out of military school. Roy was such an introvert. I honestly didn't know if he'd ever even had sex. He hadn't said much during our dinner with Lacey, and she looked relieved when I dropped her off and gave her a quick peck on the lips.

"Behave yourself," was all she said.

She didn't have to worry. Even if I had an inclination to misbehave, which I didn't, my shy and reclusive brother would have put an end to it. I couldn't abandon him.

I looked around briefly when we arrived. No Hoss yet. Roy and I found a table close to the stage. Two dancers were already in a clench. My brother's eyes went wide.

"Have you never been to a strip club?" I asked.

"No, actually."

"Ever watch girl-on-girl porn?"

"Well...no."

"Regular porn."

"Occasionally."

Damn. I really had neglected him. "What do you do for fun, then?"

"I paint. I read. I have a drink with a few friends every now and then, but not often. I watch movies sometimes. Work out. My building has a great gym."

My brother looked to be in tip-top shape. The Wolfe genes were good, but I could also tell he'd worked at it. "Do you date?"

"On occasion. Not a lot. Women don't seem to dig me."

"I can't believe that."

"It's true. I scare them or something. Every time I get interested in someone, she decides to end it."

"That doesn't make any sense, Roy."

He shrugged. "Something about me, I guess."

"Are you...?"

He chuckled. "Gay? No. I mean, I wouldn't kick Ryan Reynolds out of bed, but I like women."

"Then what's the issue?"

He stayed silent.

"Come on, Roy. You flew across the country to talk to me. So talk to me."

"Not here." He twirled the light brown bourbon in his glass.

"All right. After, then." From the corner of my eye, I spied Hoss entering and taking a seat at the bar. "There's someone I need to talk to."

"You're going to leave me here?"

"For fuck's sake, Roy, enjoy yourself. It's not that difficult. There are naked ladies here, man." I stood and walked over to the bar.

"Rock," Hoss said when I tapped him on his shoulder. "Two times in one day. Good to see you."

"Yeah, you too. Manny around?"

"Nah. He doesn't do too well here. Plus, he sees all the pussy he needs to every day at work."

A little nausea hit me. First, thinking Hoss did "well" at a strip club. But that was nothing compared to the image of Manny salivating at pussy between the stirrups. I'd never be able to unsee that one.

"Just as well." I signaled the bartender. "I need to talk to you alone."

"I figured as much."

"You did?"

"Sure. You need information. You know I have it."

"I'm that obvious?"

"Pretty much. I can see how you'd think I'd be your better bet. I'm sorry, though. Attorney-client privilege is as sacred as doctor-patient privilege."

"I'll make it worth your while. Big time."

Hoss chuckled. "I know you can. Big Wolfe money now."

"Does that sway you any?"

"I'd be lying if I said it didn't, and if my client were some scumbag I'd probably roll over. But we're talking about Manny here. He's not just a client. He's my best friend."

"Look, Hoss. Someone is playing with fire here. Whoever it is wants to frame me for my father's murder, but I have an ironclad alibi. So they're going after Lacey."

"And does she have an ironclad alibi?"

"She has an alibi, but it's hardly ironclad. She was alone in her apartment at the time."

Hoss opened his mouth to reply, but the bartender finally got to us.

"House bourbon on the rocks," I said, "and another for my friend here."

The barkeep nodded and got to work.

"She seems like a nice girl. I've never known you to be so serious about someone."

"What makes you think I'm serious?"

"You brought her out here, didn't you?"

"Good point." I took a drink of the bourbon the bartender had set in front of me.

"So this one means something to you, huh?"

I cleared my throat. "I didn't come over here to talk to you about my love life."

"I'm sure you didn't. Can't blame me for trying to change the subject."

"Guess I can't."

"So just how much money are we talking about, Rock?"

"Friend," I said, "write your own damned tick— Oh, fuck." I set my drink on the bar and walked swiftly back over to Roy.

My brother was red-faced and stiff as a board as a well-endowed stripper nearly suffocated him with her silicone wonders. He squirmed in his seat.

He pleaded at me with his eyes.

I couldn't help a chuckle. Poor Roy couldn't relax and enjoy himself. I tapped the lady on her bare shoulder. "Sweetheart, I think you need to try someone else."

"But he's so hot," she whined. "I never get to lap dance a hot guy like this. Only the slobbering fat ones.

"Did he ask you for a lap dance?"

"No, but he was staring at me."

I pulled a few bills out of my wallet and handed them to her. "He's not up for anything tonight. Go on to the next one."

She sauntered off with a smile. She'd gotten what she wanted. Money.

"Roy, you look like a deer caught in the headlights. Not your type, huh?"

"Her boobs were too big." He laughed. "Well, not too big. Just too fake."

"Yeah, I'm not much for the fake ones either. Could have been an easy lay for you, though."

"A lay? They actually let you fuck these girls?"

"For the right amount of money, you can get just about anything here. You want me to get her back?"

"God, no. Though if I'd known a fuck was in the running, I might have been a little more open to it. The idea of a lap dance kind of disgusts me. I don't want to explode in my jeans like some teenager."

"I hear that one. They don't do much for me either."

"Did you talk to your friend?"

"Shit." I'd forgotten about Hoss. He'd sounded like he was ready to play ball. "You okay here?"

"I don't mind watching. They just need to leave me alone."

"That might be difficult. You're the best looking guy in here. The male Riley Wolfe."

"If I had a nickel for every time I've been compared to my model sister. Being pretty is part of the problem. Women want someone rugged like you and Reid."

"Wait a minute. Is that why you think women don't go for you?"

"What else could it be?"

"Uh...women don't usually have a problem with great looking guys, Roy. The issue is your introversion. You have "hands off" tattooed across your forehead. Anyone can see it."

"That's not true."

"That *is* true. Look around. Pick any woman in here. Loosen up a little and let her know you're interested. I guarantee you'll get lucky."

"The only women in here are strippers, Rock."

"First of all, you're wrong. Most of the servers are women. As for the dancers, a lot of them are nice girls who just want to make a living."

"You just said I could get whatever I wanted for the right price."

"I said *most* of them are nice girls. There are definitely a few who—" I looked toward the bar. "Shit!"

"What?"

"The guy I was talking to is gone." Damn. He'd been ready, too, and instead of paying him off, I'd rescued my brother from a stripper.

"Stay here," I told Roy. "Pick out a pretty girl who's just dancing and getting tips. Make eye contact. Open up a little. You'll see what I mean. I'll be right back."

"Rock..."

I ignored him and sped to the door. Maybe I could catch Hoss.

I saw him, all right. His bike was speeding out of the parking lot.

Damn. I'd been sure he was going to talk. My own fault. I gave him a chance to change his mind.

I walked back into the club, sighing, but then a smile spread on my face. Roy was talking to one of the servers. Good for him. He'd decided against a stripper. The server was tall and thin, blond and blue-eyed. Fair skinned. A perfect contrast to Roy's darkness.

I didn't want to intervene. My brother badly needed to get lucky.

I texted Roy quickly that I was heading home and left him to his night.

50

LACEY

I awoke to the beginnings of an orgasm.

Rock was between my legs, licking and sucking.

"Rock!" I whispered urgently. "Where's your brother?"

"The other bedroom," he said, his chin glistening.

"Stop it. He'll hear us!"

"Do I look like I care?" He winked and then returned to what he was doing.

I closed my eyes and sighed. Might as well enjoy it, though I vowed to remain quiet.

The climax rolled through me swiftly, and I grabbed bunches of the cotton sheets, arching my back and attempting to moan quietly.

In another moment, Rock was on top of me and inside me, pumping, pumping, pumping...until another climax rose within me.

"That's it, baby. I can feel you coming. God, Lacey. God!"

He thrust into me more deeply than ever, and I no longer held back.

"Rock. Oh, Rock!"

We stayed joined together until our orgasms slowed, and

then he rolled off of me. I laughed softly. "So much for me being quiet."

"This is my house, Lace. You can be as loud as you want to be, especially when a guest is uninvited."

"He's your brother."

"He's still uninvited."

"Is he okay?"

He shook his head. "Damned if I know. He's hiding something, something he wants to tell me. He flew across the country to get to me."

"I'm not sure he came here to talk to you about anything."

"You mean you don't think he's hiding something?"

"No. I agree with you there. He's definitely hiding something. But I don't think he came here to talk, Rock. He came here to run away from something."

"He wasn't running away. He knew I'd be here."

"True. But he also knew you'd be back in a couple days. There wasn't any reason for him to fly here just to talk to you."

"That's true." Rock sat up in bed. "Something's eating him for sure. I should check on him. Then I'll make some coffee."

"Sounds good." I leaned forward and kissed the back of his tanned shoulder. "I'll be out in a few."

After Rock left, I went to the bathroom and ran a brush through my disheveled hair. I was about to wash up, when my cellphone buzzed.

A Manhattan number I didn't recognize. "Hello, this is Lacey."

"Lacey, it's Charlie. I'm so sorry to bother you over the weekend, but it's urgent."

"Yeah? What is it, Charlie?"

"A detective came to talk to me at home last night. Late last night, actually. It freaked me out."

"Shit. Are you okay?"

"Yeah. I'm fine. I asked to see his badge and then called the police dispatcher to make sure he was legit. He was."

"Was it that detective who came to the office?"

"No, it was a different guy. A little younger."

"What did he want?"

"He had a lot of questions..." She hedged. "About you."

My stomach dropped. After yesterday morning, this was the last thing I needed to hear. "What did they ask you, Charlie?"

"Mostly about your connections to Derek Wolfe."

I cleared my throat. "And...what did you tell them?"

"Only what I knew. He was a new client of yours that you inherited from Robert Mayes. They poked and prodded, but I didn't know the answers to any of their questions. Lacey...are you in some kind of trouble?"

I paused a few seconds. Then, "I didn't do anything wrong, Charlie."

"I know you didn't, but someone sure thinks you did."

"Listen, don't talk to anyone else until I get back, okay? Especially not late in the evening like that. I smell a rat."

"I do too."

"Good. We're on the same page."

"I shouldn't have let him in, but he checked out."

"You didn't do anything wrong, Charlie. Just lie low until I get back tomorrow, okay?"

"I'll try."

I sighed. That meant she'd lie low, but if someone came to her door asking more questions, she'd cooperate.

I couldn't ask any more of her than that. My nerves jumped as I quickly washed up and pulled on jeans and a light blue tank top. I padded barefoot out to the kitchen where the welcoming scent of coffee greeted me.

Rock and his brother sat at the table. If the Wolfe men weren't the most gorgeous beings in the universe, I didn't know who were. Roy's long hair was pulled back into a ponytail. It was straighter and calmer than Rock's, which was now cut short. They both wore jeans and were bare-chested.

Damn.

If I weren't totally in love with Rock, I'd actually be contemplating a threesome right about now. Not that either of them would ever do it. The Wolfe brothers didn't share. I knew that instinctively.

I swallowed. How could I be thinking of a threesome when I was being investigated for murder?

"Hey, babe," Rock said. "Coffee?"

I motioned for him to stay seated. "I'll get it. Good morning, Roy."

"Morning." Roy sipped his coffee.

"Roy and I have been talking," Rock said. "We think it's best that we go back to New York right away."

"Don't expect me to disagree," I said. "I just got a pretty distressing phone call."

Rock lifted his brow. "Oh? What's going on?"

"Apparently a detective questioned my assistant last night. At her home. At nine p.m."

"Nine p.m.?" Rock lifted his brow further.

"Yeah."

"Doesn't sound right," Roy said.

"I agree," Rock said. "I'm definitely not liking this one bit. You two get packed up. I'll call and get the jet ready to move."

ROCK and I made it back to my apartment by late afternoon with the time change. I plunked down in my recliner.

Now what?

Rock's gun—the same model, though not the same gun, that had killed his father—was missing.

Rock's fingerprints were on the gun that *did* kill his father, despite the fact that Rock had been two thousand miles away when the murder occurred.

An unidentified woman had told her gynecologist that Rock had gone to New York.

Rock's brother Roy was hiding something—something he flew across the country for.

I'd nearly been arrested in Montana, and now a new detective was sniffing around my assistant after hours.

What did it all mean? And why?

The limo driver dropped our bags on the floor.

"Thanks, man." Rock handed him a few bills and then closed the door.

We were alone.

Now that I was back in my own home, reality abruptly sank in. I was being investigated for murder. This was no joke. It was truly happening.

Rock pulled out his cellphone. "Time for some damage control."

"What can you possibly do?"

"Me? Not much. My money? That's another story."

I stood. "No, Rock. Don't go bribing people. Please."

"You were okay with me paying Hoss."

"I wasn't exactly okay with it. Besides, this is totally different. We're talking police detectives here, not a Harley-riding attorney."

"Doesn't matter, babe. I didn't learn much from the asshole prick who fathered me, but I did learn one thing. Everyone eventually has a price."

I didn't doubt his words. But I was an attorney. An officer of the court. I couldn't let this happen.

"Please. Promise me you won't do this."

"This is on me, Lacey. These people are going after you to get to me. I have to put a stop to it. One way or the other, this won't end well unless I nip it in the bud right now."

"We're both innocent. We have to trust the system, Rock."

"The system?" He scoffed. "Do you know how many times my old man gamed the system? And those are just the things I knew about before I left home at fourteen. Even my warped mind can't imagine what he did from that point until his death. And frankly, this shit has Derek Wolfe smeared all over it."

"The man is dead."

"So? He put something into play before he died."

"He was murdered. He had no idea he was about to die, Rock."

"Maybe he did. Maybe he knew he'd been marked, and he decided to fuck me over from the grave."

"I doubt it. You said yourself his money could buy anything. If he knew he was marked, he'd have paid someone off, or taken care of whoever marked him first."

Rock didn't bother denying it. He knew I was right.

"What else could be going on?"

"Hell if I know." He raked his fingers through his hair. "My dad made lots of enemies in his lifetime. I suppose there could be one he never knew about."

"He was cocky," I said. "Maybe he got *too* cocky."

"Meaning?"

"Meaning he overlooked people who might have a grudge against him."

Rock raised one eyebrow. "That's an interesting perspective. You might be on to something."

"You never know. At this point, we can't leave any stone unturned."

Rock heaved a sigh. "That's a lot of stones, baby."

"How many enemies could one man have?"

"Lacey, the man was evil."

"The man built a billion dollar company."

"What? You think you can't have one without the other? Derek Wolfe was not a good man."

"I'm aware he was no saint, but was he really so horrible?"

He sighed again. "You're going to have to take my word for it."

51

ROCK

My head and eyes throbbed.

I'd taken a hell of a beating, but I'd kept the fucking bastards out of my ass.

Military school had turned out to be a playground for psychopaths. My father must have known the kind of place this was. He must have.

I'd always thought he hated me. Now I knew for sure.

Hazing, they called it. Most of the guys let it happen, told me it would be over soon. That we'd be doing it next year.

Never. I'd never participate in hazing.

Fucking never.

The cuts healed and the bruises faded.

School years blended into each other.

Then senior year.

Watching the guys in my class—guys who'd been raped years earlier—fuck the freshmen was a horror I would never unsee.

"Come on, Wolfe," one said. "Take some ass. You've earned it. Do it. Do it."

The words rang in my ears as if chanted by robotic demons.

Do it.

Do it.

Do it.

I grabbed one of them. A bigger one. I was never one to pick on someone smaller than I was. I'd seen my father do enough of that. I was no bully. I was no coward.

Do it.

Do it.

Do it.

I LEAPED out of the daydream. The thoughts had plagued me since my discussion with Reid about his and Roy's experiences at prep school. Had my brothers been raped?

Nausea swept up my throat. God. I'd escaped it. I hadn't forced myself on anyone else, either, despite the masses chanting around me. Oh, I'd given him a good beating for show, but that was where it had ended.

"I need to talk to your assistant," I said to Lacey.

"Yeah, I want to talk to her too."

"You think we could go see her at her place?"

"It's Sunday, and tomorrow's a holiday."

"So? This is important, baby."

She nodded. "I know. Let me give her a quick call."

I waited while Lacey poked numbers into her phone.

"She's not answering," Lacey said. Then she left a short voicemail asking her to return the call. "Now what?"

"We go to bed?" I lifted my brow.

"That doesn't solve anything."

"It does from where I'm standing." I tried to laugh it off. Then, "I'm sorry."

She shook her head. "It's okay. I'm just not really in the mood."

"I understand." I'd been trying to put off the inevitable. If Lacey and I were going to be together, I owed her the truth. Especially since some elusive person was trying to bring her into this. It had been a long day, and it was about to get longer.

"Baby, I need to tell you some stuff."

"Oh?"

"Yeah." I cleared my throat.

"All right." She sat down on the couch this time and patted the spot next to her. "Sit down?"

"I think I need a drink first."

"I don't have much. Some vodka and wine, I think."

A bourbon would have been nice. "Maybe it's better if I just get it out." I sat down next to her. "This is hard."

"You can tell me anything, Rock."

"I'd like to make you promise you won't leave me if I tell you everything, but I can't do that."

"Okay. Now you're scaring me a little."

I put my hand over hers. "I'm sorry. But I can't lie to you. It's some pretty scary stuff."

"Are you in any trouble?"

"No. I don't think so, anyway."

"Have you done anything wrong?"

"Not regarding my father's murder."

"Okay." She bit her lower lip.

"I'm just going to get out with it. All of it."

She drew her hand away from mine. "I think that would be best."

I cleared my throat. "I was sent to military school when I was fourteen."

"I know that. Your brother Reid explained all of that to me."

"You mean my father didn't?"

"No. He just said you'd left the family when you came of age. I asked him for more details but he wasn't forthcoming. All he'd tell me is that he wanted you at the head of Wolfe Enterprises, and if you didn't do it, the company and all of your other assets would be sold and his children would get nothing."

"Nice guy." I rolled my eyes.

"We all know who he was, Rock."

I sighed once more. Lacey only *thought* she knew who he was. She knew a ruthless businessman who made enemies through deals. She didn't know he abused his children, sexually abused his daughter. Sent his sons off to school to be violated. "Lacey, my father used to beat the shit out of me."

She gasped. Was she truly surprised by this revelation?

"I'm so sorry." She put her hand back on mine.

"I'm long over it. I never forgave him, but I got far away as soon as I could, and I never looked back. But that's not what I need to tell you."

"All right..."

"My parents sent me away when I was fourteen because..." Damn. This was hard.

"Because why, Rock?" She squeezed my hand.

Blurred images catapulted through my mind.

My lack of thought, only instinctual actions—had to protect my sister—as I grabbed a chef's knife from the kitchen.

The resistance, like the thick skin of a grapefruit, as the knife sank into my father's flesh.

The panicked treble voice of my sister.

"Don't hurt Daddy, Rock!"

Then my father's strong body overpowering my adolescent one.

Thud to my jaw. Thud to my brow. Thud to my groin.

Lying in a fetal position in Riley's room.

No tears.

No fucking tears.

Bastard would not make me cry.

Days passed in a blur, locked in my room. No brothers. No sister.

Then...

Military school.

The hazing, the beatings, the sodomy I luckily escaped but witnessed perpetrated on weaker students.

The emotional abuse.

Then senior year.

I became the monster.

All because I'd failed in killing an evil bastard.

"Because I tried to kill my father."

52

LACEY

I went numb.

Icy numb.

I wanted to pull my hand away from his, but something stopped me.

The numbness. I couldn't move.

Time seemed to be suspended. Had he said those words a second ago or an hour ago? He was rigid next to me on the sofa.

"Are you going to say something?"

The words sounded off, as if he were speaking underwater.

"Baby?"

Baaaaabbbbbeeeee?

Then he stood, jolting me out of my dreamscape. "I shouldn't have said anything. I shouldn't have told you. I'm out of here."

I gasped, my head finally above the imaginary water. "Wait! Don't leave!"

"Why the fuck not? You're going to dump me now, and I don't blame you."

Dump him? I loved him. More than anything, even though shards of fear knifed through me. Part of me was afraid of part of him. How could I say all this? I opened my mouth, but all that came out was, "Dump you?"

"Yeah. I'm a fucking wreck, Lace. I'm a... I mean, I'm not a... Shit."

"Just tell me. Tell me everything, Rock. Please."

Beatings. Emotional abuse. A broken bone once. Protecting Roy and Reid. And...Riley. Poor Riley.

"I only just found out about the 'princess trips' my father took her on after I left," he was saying. "Roy and Reid were terribly jealous, but I know what he did to her on those trips." He wrung his hands together.

"Your brothers really don't know?"

"They don't seem to."

"And they don't know why you were sent away?"

"No. Not the real reason. No one on earth does. Except my mother."

My skin was still tight and numb around me.

My mother.

I had so many questions—so many that they melded together in my mind into a sea of incoherence. I needed every scintilla of information Rock had, needed to know what he was capable of, whether he'd ever even slightly thought of doing something like...

I couldn't even finish the thought in my mind.

I wasn't sure how much time had passed when Rock said, "Lace, you've got to say something. Please."

"I don't know what to say." True words.

The gun. His prints were on the murder weapon. And his gun had been stolen.

But Rock was innocent. He was in Montana.

Wasn't he?

Was I truly beginning to have doubts?

"...since then. Never."

"What?" I said.

"You're not hearing me, Lace."

"I'm sorry. What?"

"I was arrested once for getting into a fight at a bar. That's it. I've never tried... Never even wanted to..." He rubbed his forehead. "Fuck."

I just stared at him. Big and strong, handsome and magnificent...and Rock Wolfe was reduced to a nervous wreck. I couldn't bear to see him like this. Finally, I reached toward him and took his hand.

"We'll figure this out," I said.

Relief visibly swept over him. "Thank God."

"This doesn't mean I don't have questions. A lot of questions."

"I know. I'm just glad you're talking."

"I need to wrap my head around the whole thing. But I love you. I can't just fall out of love with you."

"Thank God," he said again.

"You thought I could?"

"Baby, I didn't know. This is big. I know how big this is. But I swear to you, I'm not a killer, and I did *not* off my father."

"I can see why you think your mother's involved in framing me. She thinks you'll do anything to save me."

"I will."

"It won't come to that. Not if we figure out what's going on first."

"How? How the hell are my prints on that gun?"

"We know it's not your gun, though. Whoever stole yours and thought they could frame you didn't stop to consider that guns are easily identifiable by serial number and registration."

"So not the brightest bulb."

"Yeah. But the bigger question is how did your prints get on the gun that killed your father?"

He shook his head. "Fuck if I know."

"Does anyone you know have the same model gun?" I asked.

"I have no idea. I go shooting alone most of the time. The only time I'm with others is when I hunt, and we use different firearms for that."

"All right. When did you buy the gun in question?"

"Shit. About six months ago. It's my newest one."

Now we were getting somewhere. "Did you shoot the same model before you bought it?"

"Yeah, I always—" He grabbed me and pulled me into a hug. "You're a genius!"

I pulled away quickly, not quite ready to be close to him yet. I'd be okay, but I needed a little time. "It's a theory right now. But we're going to have to figure out exactly where you shot that model before you decided to purchase."

He tensed a little, blowing air out of his lungs. "There was a gun show in Billings. I was looking at handguns... And then again at a sportsman's shop."

"So you fired that same model twice? Two different guns?"

"Yeah. Then I went back and bought the gun at the shop later that week after I got paid."

"Simple enough, then," I said. "Someone got hold of one of those guns after you fired it. That's the murder weapon."

53

ROCK

"It's still a theory," Lacey said. "But it makes more sense than someone planting prints on a weapon. I'm not sure that can even be done."

"It makes perfect sense. And if you're right, someone's been watching my every move for a while." Prickles ran over my skin. Who the hell would violate my privacy like that?

Someone who hated my old man. Damn. Could be anyone.

"If it's been six months since you handled them," she said, "we know your father's death was being planned at least six months ago and probably for longer. We need to find those guns."

"I'm pretty sure one has already been found—the one used to off my father. We need to figure out how it got there and who fired it."

She nodded. "We will."

"Damn right we will. I'll put the best in the business on it."

"For once, I'm not going to object to you throwing money around," she said, still not smiling, though.

I was the world's biggest jerk. Lacey was scared. Freaked. She'd been cuffed and nearly arrested—would have been if I hadn't pulled a gun on the dirty fucker. So what do I do? I tell her my deepest darkest secret to add to her fear.

"I'm sorry, Lace."

"For what?"

"For...everything. All of this. Dragging you into it."

"You didn't drag me into anything."

She didn't sound convinced.

"I'm sorry anyway."

"Look, I'm a big girl, okay? I could have said no to you. I could have..."

"Could have what?"

Nothing. Silence.

"Could have what, Lacey? Not fallen in love with me? Is that what you're thinking?"

Again, silence.

"Fuck." I rubbed my temple, my head beginning to ache.

"What's done is done," Lacey said.

"I wish I could change who I am," I said. Then, "Fuck that. It's a lie. I don't wish I could change who I am. This is me. Everything in my past has made me what I am today."

She seemed to soften then, as if my words had finally penetrated the hard shell she'd formed around her heart. She took my hand and entwined her fingers around mine.

"You're right," she said. "You are who you are, and I'll never ask you to be anyone else. You're the man I fell in love with. You, Rock."

I pulled her to me, and this time she didn't pull away. We stood together, embracing, our bodies melded together, her warmth seeping into me.

I'd put myself out there for this woman, told her things no one—save my mother—knew about me. She could have run away. Indeed maybe she should have, and for a few tense moments, I'd feared she would.

"I was afraid you'd leave me," I said into her hair.

"No. I won't leave you. I love you, Rock."

"God, I love you too. I love you so fucking much. More than I've ever loved anyone."

How long had it been since I'd allowed myself to fully feel something? Too damned long. Riley. My baby sister. My love for her was what had propelled me to protect her. I'd failed her.

I wouldn't fail a person I loved again. Ever.

Lacey pulled away again, but this time she wasn't rigid. She met my gaze. "Who else knows why you were sent away?"

"Only my mother, as far as I know."

"Okay, then. Damage should be minimal, unless your mother has talked."

"Connie Wolfe? Talk? Not a chance. She'd look less than perfect in the world's eyes if she knew her son had attempted murder at fourteen and her dead husband had molested his only daughter."

"Are you sure Riley is the only one he molested?"

"Yeah. Well, I think so. He never touched me sexually. And Roy and Reid never said anything. The bastard used to kick Reid's ass on a regular basis. He pretty much said he was the new target after I got shipped off."

"And all your siblings have alibis?"

"As far as I know."

"I can see now why you think your mother is behind the deputy trying to arrest me."

"I'm still not convinced otherwise," I said. "But we're not going to leave any stone unturned. We need to solve this, Lace."

"Yeah. Before I get arrested."

"You won't get arrested. Let's go talk to the doorman right now."

∾

"Who?" I demanded. "Who's been asking questions?"

The doorman went pale. "A detective, Hank something."

"Morgan," Lacey said.

"Yeah, that's him. And another guy."

"Who?" I demanded again.

"I...can't. He had a...gun. Said he'd kill me."

"If you don't give me the name, *I'll* fucking ki—"

"Rock"—Lacey grabbed my arm—"that isn't helping." She turned to the doorman. "Bobby, someone is trying to implicate me in a crime. We need to know who it is."

"He didn't tell me his name."

"Of course he didn't," I scoffed.

"Can you describe him at least?"

"He wore a black overcoat."

"Yeah, that's helpful," I said.

"The guy had a gun on me. I wasn't exactly noticing the details."

"It's okay," Lacey said to Bobby. "I know you were on duty that night when I got home. Do you remember?"

"Yeah. I think so."

"You were also on duty the next morning, when I left the building. Remember?"

"Yeah. But I wasn't on during the night."

"I know," Lacey said. "We'll talk to the night guy. I rarely see him. What's his name?"

"There are two. Blaine and Humphrey. I don't remember who relieved me that evening or who was there the next morning."

"That's easy enough to find out," Lacey said. "The main thing is that you remember me coming home and leaving the next morning. Would you be willing to tell the police that?"

"I..."

"Sure, he's willing," I said, staring Bobby down. "Right?"

"Y-Yeah. Sure," Bobby stammered.

"Bobby," Lacey said, as gently as she could, "this is really important."

"I know, Ms. Ward. I know."

"He'll cooperate," I said tersely, "won't you, Bobby?"

Bobby nodded. Not overly adamantly, but at least he nodded.

"Is that a yes?" I asked, again tersely.

"Yeah," Bobby said. "Yes, I'll cooperate."

"Thank you," Lacey said. "It means a lot. See you later, Bobby."

Lacey and I headed back up to her apartment.

"You get it all?" I asked.

She grabbed the phone out of her purse and played back the recording of our conversation with Bobby. "Yeah. Got it all."

"Good."

"You do know that this most likely isn't admissible in court," she said.

"I know. But it's good to have it for corroboration anyway."

"I can't disagree," she said. "Now we just have to talk to whoever was on that night and morning."

"We'll do it, baby." I pulled her to me and kissed her forehead. "We'll get us both out of this mess."

I closed my eyes, inhaling the tropical scent of her hair...and hoping to God I was right.

54

LACEY

I dragged Rock with me to the soup kitchen for volunteer work on Memorial Day, and when I saw him interact with the veteran heroes, I knew I'd fallen in love with a truly good man. Sure, he'd come off as a douchebag at first, but inside his harsh exterior was a warm and good human being. A good human being who'd been through hell.

The man I loved.

The next day, we were both off to the office once more.

A little over an hour after I sat down, my cellphone buzzed. Rock.

"You're going to love me," he said into my ear.

"I already do."

"Yeah? You're going to love me even more. Guess what I just found out?"

"What?"

"I had a very interesting talk with the owner of your building."

"Oh?"

"Yup. Did you know he installed security cameras a couple months ago?"

"No, I didn't. You mean...?"

"You got it. Everyone who has gone in and out of your building is on tape. We need to get the tape of the night my father was killed, and you'll be off the hook."

I let out a big sigh, letting go of tension I didn't even realize I'd been holding. "Did you call Hank Morgan? Does he already know?"

"You only recently became a person of interest. He might not know yet. Let's call him now."

"We can't both call him." I jerked as my door flew open.

Rock grinned as he stood in my doorway. As always, my heart skipped a beat just looking at him. He slipped his phone in his pocket.

"Shouldn't you be at your own office?" I asked.

"I want this put to bed. We have enough on our plates trying to solve this thing. We need to get you off the hook."

"Okay. Go for it. You call. You have more sway. After all, I'm not a Wolfe."

"You're not a Wolfe"—he smiled, his green eyes twinkling —"yet."

My heart raced and tingles skittered along my skin. Was that a proposal? Hardly. Rock was entering numbers into his phone.

"Detective, hi. Rock Wolfe."

Pause.

"I have some good news you might not know about yet. There's a security video for Lacey's apartment the night of my father's murder. It should exonerate her."

Pause.

"What do you mean?"

Pause.

My heart was firing like a freaking cannon. Morgan was clearly talking...about the tape. And that couldn't mean anything good.

"That's fucking ridiculous!"

Forget the cannonballs. My heart was pounding more like a stampede of angry wildebeests. Seconds passed like hours as I waited for Rock to utter something else. Anything else.

Rock's face reddened, his eyes no longer twinkling. Anger oozed out of his pores.

Still he didn't speak.

Didn't speak.

Didn't speak.

Until finally—

"Someone is playing a dangerous game, Detective. You'd better find out who, because if you don't, I will."

Pause.

"Don't even *think* about threatening me."

A chill swept the back of my neck. What was Morgan saying?

"This conversation is over." Rock shoved his phone back in his pocket.

My lips trembled. "I'm afraid to ask," I said meekly.

"Fucking detective."

"Is he dirty?" I asked.

"I don't think so, but someone is sending him on a wild goose chase."

I swallowed the lump in my throat. Or tried to. I was unsuccessful. "The video?" I said.

He shook his head. "Gone."

My whole body turned numb. "G-Gone?"

"You're innocent, baby, and so am I. And so are Roy, Reid, and Riley. Even my mother is innocent, at least in this."

"Roy, Reid...and what?"

"Somehow, every single one of us has been implicated in the bastard's murder. He's got all of our prints at the scene."

My hammering heart fell into my stomach. "But...you're his kids. Of course your prints would be..."

Didn't matter. A detective would know what kind of evidence implicated grown children of a murder victim.

Somehow, every single one of us has been implicated...

"How? Where did he get prints to match the rest of you? Where?"

"I have no fucking clue. We're getting played, Lacey. Played like a fucking violin. And I'd bet the entire Wolfe fortune that my father himself set this up before he had himself offed."

Oh, God. I fell into Rock's arms. Why had I agreed to draft Derek Wolfe's will?

Rock kissed the top of my head. "We'll get through this."

I choked back a sob. Not a great time to be a whining woman —not that there was ever a good time for that.

Rock held me tightly while I attempted to piece the fragments in my brain into some sort of logical sense.

Derek Wolfe.

He was a mogul. A master strategist. A bastard extraordinaire.

But he was too much of an egotist to end his own life.

Rock was wrong. Derek had not been behind this.

Someone else had.

55

ROCK

Of all the people I cared about—and a select few I didn't—I was the only one with an ironclad alibi.

I hadn't been in the state of New York when the murder occurred.

They could steal my Glock, use another with my prints on it and leave it at the scene, and it was still all circumstantial.

I could not have committed a murder if I wasn't in the state.

But Lacey. Roy. Reid. Riley.

My mother.

Fonda, my father's last flavor of the month.

They had all been here.

I didn't know much about Fonda, but my brothers would. I'd bend their ears as soon as possible.

The others? None of them were guilty, especially not Lacey.

I knew it in my gut.

Someone was, though. Someone had killed my father and set us all up to turn on each other.

Who?

Who hated all of us that much?

I was going to find out.

But first—

"We're getting married," I said to Lacey, kissing the top of her head.

She pulled away, her eyes wide. "Huh?"

"We're getting married. Tomorrow."

"You sweet talker you." The words were teasing, but not her tone. It was monotonous. Robotic.

"I love you, Lacey. You love me. We'd probably get married eventually anyway. This way I can protect you better."

She nodded, again robotically. "Yeah. Okay."

I gripped her shoulders. "Look at me."

She met my gaze, her gorgeous blue eyes filled with terror.

"We *will* get through this. I will protect you. I promise you." I kissed her trembling mouth softly.

She relaxed a bit then, and I deepened the kiss.

I'd protect her—and my siblings—with my life if I had to.

She broke the kiss, meeting my gaze. "I love you, Rock. I'd be honored to marry you."

I cupped her cheek, her skin so silky under my calloused fingertips. "I love you so much, Lacey, and I promise you. We *will* have our happily ever after."

EPILOGUE
ROY

The secret had lodged in my gut, always present, sometimes churning, and occasionally clawing its way up my throat as acidic bile, eating through my flesh.

For most of my life I'd ignored it. Not like I hadn't had years to tamp it down, pretend it didn't exist. Days had begun to pass where I didn't think about it. Days turned into weeks, into months, eventually into years.

But always it was there, like a black cancer haunting me from the inside out.

Who to trust?

I was a recluse, never close to anyone, really—certainly not anyone in my family.

Flying to Montana to talk to Rock had been a mistake. I couldn't expose my secret with his girlfriend there—his girlfriend who was a lawyer, for God's sake.

Now I existed in a perpetual cold sweat, trapped in the ultimate mind fuck.

Help me. Please. Help me.

. . .

WOLFES OF MANHATTAN continues with *Recluse*, coming soon!

A NOTE FROM HELEN

Dear Reader,

Thank you for reading *Rebel*. If you want to find out about my current backlist and future releases, please visit my website, like my Facebook page, and join my mailing list. If you're a fan, please join my street team to help spread the word about my books. I regularly do awesome giveaways for my street team members.

If you enjoyed the story, please take the time to leave a review. I welcome all feedback.

I wish you all the best!

Helen

Facebook

Facebook.com/helenhardt

Newsletter

Helenhardt.com/signup

Street Team

Facebook.com/groups/hardtandsoul

ACKNOWLEDGMENTS

Thank you so much to my editor, Celina Summers; my proofreader, Christie Hartman; my beta readers, Martha Frantz, Theresa Finn, Karen Aguilera, Angela Tyler, Linda Pantlin Dunn, and Toni Barone Paul; and my cover artists, Kim Killion and Marci Clark. You all helped *Rebel* shine!

ALSO BY HELEN HARDT

Steel Brothers Saga:

Trilogy One—Talon and Jade

Craving

Obsession

Possession

Trilogy Two—Jonah and Melanie

Melt

Burn

Surrender

Trilogy Three—Ryan and Ruby

Shattered

Twisted

Unraveled

Trilogy Four—Bryce and Marjorie

Breathless

Ravenous

Insatiable

Trilogy Five—Brad and Daphne (coming soon)

Fate

Legacy

Descent

Follow Me Series (coming soon):

Follow Me Darkly

Follow Me Under

Follow Me Always

Blood Bond Saga:

Unchained

Unhinged

Undaunted

Unmasked

Undefeated

Sex and the Season:

Lily and the Duke

Rose in Bloom

Lady Alexandra's Lover

Sophie's Voice

Temptation Saga:

Tempting Dusty

Teasing Annie

Taking Catie

Taming Angelina

Treasuring Amber

Trusting Sydney

Tantalizing Maria

Standalone Novels and Novellas

Reunited

Misadventures:

Misadventures of a Good Wife (with Meredith Wild)

Misadventures with a Rockstar

The Cougar Chronicles:

The Cowboy and the Cougar

Calendar Boy

Daughters of the Prairie:

The Outlaw's Angel

Lessons of the Heart

Song of the Raven

Collections:

Destination Desire

Her Two Lovers

Non-Fiction:

got style?

ABOUT THE AUTHOR

#1 *New York Times*, #1 *USA Today*, and #1 *Wall Street Journal* best-selling author Helen Hardt's passion for the written word began with the books her mother read to her at bedtime. She wrote her first story at age six and hasn't stopped since. In addition to being an award-winning author of romantic fiction, she's a mother, an attorney, a black belt in Taekwondo, a grammar geek, an appreciator of fine red wine, and a lover of Ben and Jerry's ice cream. She writes from her home in Colorado, where she lives with her family. Helen loves to hear from readers.

http://www.helenhardt.com

CPSIA information can be obtained
at www.ICGtesting.com
Printed in the USA
LVHW020317290721
693949LV00005B/388